CONNOR

CONNOR

BILLIE LUSTIG

NRA
Publishing

AUTHOR'S NOTE

Same rules apply: I don't want to ruin the experience, but I also don't want a claim up my ass because you went in unprepared. Even though I don't consider this very dark, I feel obliged to tell you: they fuck, they say 'fuck', they shoot, and there is blood.

If your reaction to those things isn't: yes, fuck yes, yes please, and hell yes?

Then this ain't for you.

Abort the mission, or read at your own risk.

Billie

1

CONNOR

Three years ago

A n angel.

Her light blonde hair was spread out over my pillow, her pink lips parted in anticipation. Her porcelain skin looks flawless against the gray sheets underneath her curves, and the pink lace still covering her intimate parts makes her look sweet as sin.

She looks like an angel, and I'm ready to clip her wings.

Taking off my boxers, I dip my knees into the mattress, crawling my way over her legs as I trail my fingertips along her skin. A whimper escapes her rosy lips when I move closer to her core, escalating into a moan when I press two fingers against the damp fabric between her thighs. Gently, I brush over the lace, teasing her until she bites her lip and gives me a desperate look.

"I don't play nice, babe," I explain.

Placing my head between her legs, I look up at her with an evil smirk. I'm planning to stretch this out until she's begging me to make her come. She closes her eyes, and I latch my mouth against her core, breathing her in as if my life is depending on it. My nose nuzzles her center, taking in every whiff of her arousal before I'm ready to taste it on my tongue.

She hisses when my tongue darts out to tease the seam of her thong while my nose brings pressure to her clit. Grabbing the fabric with my teeth, I pull it back, scraping her skin. My fingers snake under the fabric, softly tugging it down, and she brings her legs up so I can toss it onto the floor. Without giving her a second to adjust, I press my lips against her sweet folds, her wetness coating my mouth as I start exploring every inch of her.

The saltiness on my tongue makes me hungry for more, wanting to ravish her completely like I haven't had a proper meal for days.

And I'm a hungry guy in general.

"Fuuuuuck. Connor, please. It's too much." She squirms beneath me.

I roughly place my arms on her hips, pinning her down as I continue while ignoring her pleas. Going at a more teasing pace, my kisses turn softer, stroking the area around her center in a scorching way but never diving inside. Flattening my tongue, I move up, all the way to her clit, and a frustrated cry sounds through the room.

"Fucking hell," she mutters.

"You like that, babe?" I tease, blowing her folds before wrapping my lips around her clit, giving it a soft suck. She gasps for air, fisting the sheet with her slender hands, and I repeat the move. "You do, don't you? You like being my dinner. But I never skip dessert, you know?"

Her head jerks forward, looking at me with an incredulous and pissed off look on her face.

"You don't like dessert?" I shoot her an innocent smile.

"Make me come, Connor," she growls. The halo I'd envisioned above her head bursts, making my cock twitch. Gone is her sweet, angelic expression as she glares at me, demanding me to make her come.

She's fucking sexy.

I like feeling *'angel'* twisting and turning underneath my palm, but fucking *'devil'* until she begs for mercy sounds even more appealing. She narrows her eyes at me, waiting for me to keep going with a scowl on her face.

"You want this, babe?" I roughly push two fingers inside of her, and she sucks in a sharp breath while her lashes flutter in pleasure.

"Fuck yeah."

"Or this?" Pulling my finger out, I let my tongue circle her clit before I suck the sensitive nub at the same time I plunge my fingers deep inside her.

"Oh my god." She arches her back as she throws her head back. "More. I want more. Give me more," she begs, reaching out to run her hand through my hair.

"Sssh, no more talking."

I keep feeding on her lust while my fingers plunge in and out of her core, until her moans become more desperate, and I curl my fingers inside of her like I'm stirring into a honey pot while my thumb starts to rub around her clit. My lips keep nibbling on her skin while my tongue slowly runs up and down inner folds.

"Oh my god, Connor. I need to come."

Pulling my fingers out, I plunge my tongue inside of her, digging deep as I lick the cream off her walls, determined to feel her come all over my lips. Two fingers pressed against her hood, I start to rub it in a frantic pace, her panting feeding

3

the urge to keep going. She starts to moan more uncontrollably when I feel her tighten under me, pressing her nails into my scalp.

"YES!" she screams when I feel her release rush through her, and I suck up the fluid that starts to coat my tongue. Eager for more, my lips move around her center once more, thrusting my tongue in, desperate to lick up every single drop she can give me.

She shivers, and I keep my mouth in place until I feel her go limp underneath me. Bringing my head up with a smug grin tugging on the corner of my mouth, I lick my lips, then lock my eyes with hers. She's staring back at me with her big blue eyes, looking completely spent with a satisfied look.

"You look so damn hot with your lips shining from my juices," she muses.

My brows shoot up in surprise. I didn't expect anything like that coming from her sweet mouth, but I'm all here for it. Greedy, I crawl over her until my cock softly rubs her soaking pussy, and my face is hovering above hers.

"You know, it tastes even better than it looks?"

Before she can answer, I press my lips against hers, my tongue delving inside of her as our mouths start to dance with each other. She grabs my face while she moans in my mouth, relishing me as if it's the last day on earth. Our tongues grind together, heated and sizzling, while my hands move up to cup her perky tits. They perfectly fit into my hands, making it easy for me to squeeze them as I let them roll under my palm.

"Fuck, you are sexy," I huff out between kisses.

She roughly grabs my chin while her free hand painfully digs into my shoulder and I whimper under her touch. Her eyes have turned to a dark lapis, completely erasing the angel face I met in the bar earlier tonight, and my heart stops at the welcoming realization that she is feistier than I'd expected her to be.

"Connor," she scowls.

"Yeah?"

"Fuck me." Her tone is low and husky, but the command is clearly audible in her voice, something I'm not used to.

I dominate.

In and outside of the bedroom. But there is something about this tiny thing bossing me around that turns me the fuck on. She may look like an angel, but it's clear she's longing to dance with the devil.

"Watch your tongue, babe. Before you can blink, I'll shut you up with my cock in your mouth." I chuckle, aligning my shaft with her center.

"Talking is overrated anyway." She gives me a daring look, and I shove my length inside of her, giving her no time to adjust while I thrust against her walls.

"Oh!" she screeches before I leave a bruising kiss against her filthy mouth.

"If you still have your big girl pants on after I'm done with you, feel free to wrap your lips around my cock any time of day." I start thrusting inside of her. Moving my chest up, I settle on my knees, hoisting her legs up in the air to give me full access to her drowned pussy. Pressing my palm flat against her stomach, I keep her pressed tight against the mattress as I start to pound into her. She pushes her cheek against the pillow in pleasured agony, the skin on her neck flushing as she grabs my upper thighs to hold on to while I ride her into oblivion.

"Fuck, you're tight," I mutter, pressing my fingers into the sides of her belly.

Her blonde hair wiggles beside her head because of the rough movements, and I lean forward, licking the seam of her lip.

"You taste like sin, angel. Luckily, for you, I'm not afraid to go to hell." I crash my mouth into hers with demand, then quickly pull out of her before flipping her on her stomach, pulling up her ass so she's face down.

"I don't think I've seen anything more perfect," I hum, dragging my fingers along her slick folds, glowing with her wetness. Not being able to resist, I dive in once more, burying my nose in her entrance like the hungry motherfucker that I am. My tongue licks her opening while my thumb rotates around her asshole, and she bucks her back deeper into my face, craving for more.

"What the fuck!" she yelps , pushing her face into the pillow. I can hear her let out a tormented scream that makes me chuckle in pleasure.

"Remember how I make you feel, babe."

I move back up, grabbing her hips with force as I push my throbbing cock inside of her and she winces beneath me. I grab her hair and pull her head back, holding onto her blonde strands like they are my personal reins, not giving the faintest fuck if I'm hurting her.

"Oh, fuck, Connor. You feel so good." Pleased at her tolerance for pain, I keep going, repeating my words.

"Remember." Thrust. "How." Thrust. "I." Thrust. "Make." Thrust. "You." Thrust. "Feel."

"Yes! Yes!" she cries, impatiently moving her ass farther up so I have more access to fully take her. A feral growl escapes my lips, seeing how responsive she is, and I bite my lip to make sure I don't shoot my load prematurely.

"Spank me, Connor," she rasps, and for a second I halt, thinking I didn't hear her correctly.

"Spank me!" she yells, this time with more authority. "Spank me like you own me!"

I connect my palm with her ass, her fair skin immediately turning rosy in the shape of my palm. I take a moment to admire my work before I do it again.

"This what you want, you little devil?" I keep spanking her as I continue to push inside of her.

"God, yes!"

"You want me to hurt you?" I pull her head back some more, leaning in to press my cheek against her ear. "You want me to mark you? Make sure you'll never forget who made you feel like this?"

She nods as she feels how I completely fill her up. I open my mouth, leaning in to bite her earlobe, then move down to sink my teeth in the delicate area on her neck. My teeth leave visible indentations on her skin, though I don't bite deep enough to draw blood. She doesn't respond other than giving me an appreciative moan.

"You want my teeth marking your skin like a permanent reminder, babe? I can do that. I can brand you like I own you." I latch onto her shoulder, biting hard enough to graze her soft flesh.

"Fuck," she whimpers.

Satisfied with my work, I move back up, reddening the skin on the swell of her ass once more when I slap my flat palm on it.

"Argh!" she yelps, but she never protests, getting wetter by the second.

"Bring your hand to your clit," I command.

She does so without objection, placing her hand over her

sensitive nub, starting to tease herself, her hips longingly up in the air.

"I'm going to spank you three more times," I announce, tugging onto her hair a little more. Without waiting for her reaction, I slam my hand against her body.

"One."

I softly stroke a finger over the redness I created, then do it again.

"Two."

She cries out, still not telling me to stop, instead working her clit like a maniac. I slowly pull out my cock, teasing her entrance before I slam back into her at the same time I spank her one final time.

"Motherfucker!" she shouts before a burst of moans leave her lips, and I can feel her walls tighten around me. I keep thrusting inside of her, completely losing myself between her sweet pussy covering me and her tortured grunts, which evoke a wild feeling inside of me. Completely caught up in the moment, I feel lightheaded with every surge I make as I chase us both off the cliff towards our own nirvanas.

"Keep going, Connor. Don't stop," she wheezes, motivating me to pick up the pace.

Finally, I feel that she's pushed over the point of no return, her pussy milking my cock as she shatters in my hands with a wail echoing through the room. The muscles in my face tighten as I feel how I'm getting closer with every second. Digging my fingers deep into her sides, I hold on for dear life until finally, I feel my balls contract and shoot my load deep inside of her, and a gratified roar pushes out of my throat. I moan a few more times in blissful anguish, pumping out every last drop of my cum in her tight pussy before I crash on top of her, completely worn out.

"That was…" She tries to catch her breath, and I move my body next to her, my nose in her hair to breathe in the sweet combination of her exotic scent mixed with sweat.

A combination I'd call *devilishly good* if I could bottle it up.

"That was…" she gasps, lost for words.

"That was devilishly good," I smirk.

"If that was devilishly good, I'll pick hell over heaven any day of the week." I can hear the smile in her words.

"If it's hell you choose, you may see me again sometime, babe."

2

Beacon Hill.

Charlestown.

Maybe even Chelsea. That was the goal. That's where I imagined coming home after a long day at the courthouse. I'd imagine my husband cooking for me while the kids would be watching TV after a long day of school.

Where I always wanted to raise my children. Have a family.

When my dad got arrested for grand theft and smuggling five kilos of coke across the Canadian border, *the fucking tool*, I knew my dream would have to wait a bit longer since I was now the one who had to take care of my little brother. But I still thought the dream was within my grasp. Sure, the plan got delayed, but the plan was still there.

I didn't get accepted to Harvard Law School on a scholarship for no reason. I was smart. I was determined. I made it this far, I was going to get there in the end.

So I kept going. Kept working on the plan, albeit a bit different now.

Work my ass off until Damien goes to college, then go back to school, get my degree, and become a lawyer like I always wanted. That has been the new plan for the last few years, and I'm so damn close to succeeding.

Damien turns eighteen next month, ready to go to Northeastern on a full scholarship, giving me the time and money to finish law school at night while keeping my decent pay as a legal assistant. It will be hard, but you gotta work hard to play hard, right?

Or something like that.

I've done good with Damien. Things have been tight for the last five years, but he stayed out of trouble, was at the top of his class, and we developed a routine together. I found a cheap house in Roxbury, because we couldn't afford our old house with my dad being locked up, and we had food on the table every night. It's not the best neighborhood or anything more than microwave meals that we end up eating on our laps in front of the TV, but we aren't complaining. And we are definitely comfortable enough for me to keep faith in the dream I'd envisioned.

We managed.

I managed.

But then I woke up on what I thought would be a typical day, and life decided to fuck me sideways.

Two pink lines.

That was all it took to fuck it all up and roughly burst my bubble.

For a lot of people, those pink lines mean everything. Thousands of women wait for those pink lines every single day. Many women will never see those pink lines in their life.

I have just been staring at them for the last ten minutes, hoping that maybe, just maybe, if I stare long enough, they will disappear. They will turn into one pink line ... that this is just a glitch.

I just happened to pick up three tests from the drugstore that are broken.

That's possible, right?

It happens?

Staring at my reflection in the mirror, I swallow my fear away, giving myself a faint smile to try and comfort myself. My chest is slowly moving up and down as I do my best to keep my breathing at a steady pace. It feels as if the oxygen is slowly leaving my tiny bathroom, suffocating me until I feel like I may pass out. My manicured hands grip the cold surface of the stone sink, letting my head hang as I close my eyes.

Maybe it really is just a mistake?

A sarcastic chuckle escapes my lips, and I shake my head before raising it back up, looking into my deep blue eyes.

Who am I kidding?

Three pregnancy tests, all with two pink lines, don't tell me all is *well* in the world, as if nothing has changed, and I can go on with my life.

No, stupid. It tells exactly what it's supposed to.

I'm pregnant, and I'm fucked.

How the hell am I going to raise a child in our tiny, two-bedroom apartment? Not to mention the extra mouth to feed. Damien going off to college would solve that, but then how the hell am I going to work during the day with a baby? I don't earn nearly enough to afford daycare.

My eyes are getting wetter by the second, and I keep staring at my reflection, looking a total mess. My pale cheeks are stained with red skin, now glimmering from the tears that slowly run down, all the way to my neck.

"For fuck's sake, Lily. You're in some wicked shit now," I grumble with a trembling lip.

My heart pounds against my chest with loud thuds, making me feel like it echoes through the room, even though it's as silent as the dead.

I sigh.

Not wanting to look at myself any longer, I turn around, placing my back against the sink, my hands covering my face as the last ten minutes of complete denial seem to catch up with me.

Despair enters my body in waves, and my tears seem to now come in bucket loads, making me sob against my palms. For someone who stays out of trouble most of the time, I sure as fuck dragged a deep pile of shit to my doorstep.

That night was one of the most incredible nights of my life, and I've enjoyed reliving it in my head every single day since with my hands between my thighs. I wanted to see him again. I wanted him to touch me one more time and give me that high that had me walking on sunshine for a week. But I knew who he was. I knew it was a bad idea to get involved with any of the gangs in Boston. Hanging with those guys would be asking for trouble.

So I didn't.

But even though I didn't ask, trouble seemed to have found me, nonetheless.

My sobs continue uncontrollably when I hear the front door slam closed.

I suck in a sharp breath, spinning on the spot, glancing up at my stained cheeks. My hand reaches for the faucet to muffle my cries with the running water while I wet my hands to wash my face.

"Lily? I'm home," Damien shouts through the door.

"Okay, I'll be right out." I take a washcloth, running it under the cold water before dabbing it against my skin to get rid of the flushed look on my skin.

"Are you all right?" he asks suspiciously.

I take a deep breath while my lips are still trembling, doing my best to push out a steady voice as I stare at my reflection in the mirror.

"I'm fine. I just got my period. Having some wicked bad cramps. I'll be out in a minute. Can you start supper?"

"Yeah, 'course." I hold my ear close to the door, listening to his footsteps slowly fading until I hear the sound of a pan being pulled out of the kitchen cabinet.

My eyes shut, resting my head against the door, doing my best to pull myself together.

What the fuck am I going to do now?

3

Present day

A satisfied smile escapes my lips when I look at my baby boy. Having the night off, there is nothing I enjoy more than putting my boy to bed like a normal mom.

Tucking him in, reading him a book, giving him a good-night kiss... On the two nights I'm off every week, I can't help myself, checking on him every single hour. Not because I'm one of those obsessed moms who freak out every time they fall, but just because I like to stare at my perfect creation. There is nothing more beautiful than your own child.

Ask any mom.

Okay, maybe I'm a little obsessed.

"Sweet dreams, baby." The back of my fingers brush his chubby face, and he stirs a little at the touch, though it doesn't wake him up. I lean in to press a kiss on his forehead, a smile curling the corner of my mouth when I give him one last rub over his head.

Tiptoeing, I close the doors of what used to be my twenty square feet walk-in closet before walking back to the parlor. The tiny room is crowded but looks even more cluttered because of the toys that seem to have found residence all over the place. Combined with the smell of the cream pie I made this afternoon still lingering in the air, it's home. Fatigue sits deep in my muscles after only three hours of sleep, but knowing I won't be able to relax in this mess, I start picking up Colin's toys, throwing them one by one into the toy chest. When I'm done, I move on to the kitchen and do the dishes, cleaning the rest of the kitchen until I finally drop onto the worn out couch with a big sigh.

When I found out I was pregnant, I stayed on as a legal assistant for as long as I could. But after Colin was born, I took a job as a cocktail waitress downtown so that Damien could go to school, and he could stay home with Colin at night. It wasn't ideal, but it meant I could spend time with my baby boy and pay the bills. Not to mention the tips are wicked high.

I reach for the clicker on the coffee table and start zipping through the channels with my entire body spread out over the piece of furniture, feeling the relaxation sink into my muscles. Settling for a rerun of *Friends*, I throw the device back on the table and settle my head into one of the cushions.

After an hour, my eyes start to feel heavier. I must have fallen asleep because I startle awake when the front door closes with a loud thud.

I sit up with a fuzzy head, glancing at the clock in the kitchen when Damien walks in.

"It's three in the morning, Dame." I rub a hand over my face, trying to wake myself up a bit more as I look at my not so little brother.

Last year, the *little* was replaced by *big*.

He started working out, and quickly, his athletic teenage body was replaced by a bulkier physique. However, his face can't hide the fact that he just turned twenty-one.

He brushes his hand through his blond hair that sits messily on his head. His gray Boston Bruins hoodie is smeared with dirt and bloodstains, and I blink with a flash of shock when I notice the cut on his chin.

"What happened?" I bark, my tone sharp as a blade.

He lets out a sigh, making me jump up and take two steps to get into his face like the big sister I am. I peer up at him, now that he's taller than I am, my eyes narrowing.

"Where have you been?"

"Look, I'm fine, okay?" he says adamantly, bringing up his arms in a placating way before he walks into the kitchen. I know inside he wants to tell me to fuck off, but he respects me too much to do that.

"Fine? You're covered in blood, Damien. You're *fine*? Is the other person also *fine*?" I snort with a crude chuckle, though there is nothing funny about this. "I told you to stay away from Emerson Jones. That man is bad news!"

Damien has always been a good boy, staying out of trouble, helping me around the house. But my efforts to keep him shielded from the dark sides of Boston seem futile now that he started taking jobs for one of the big guys in this town.

And by big guys, I mean dangerous, merciless criminals who run our city.

Emerson Jones is not as big as the Wolfes, but word on the street is he's worse.

A sadistic asshole who doesn't mind terrorizing or torturing anyone who gets in his way, including the people around him.

"Hey, it helps with the bills, doesn't it?" He grabs a carton of milk out of the fridge, eyeing me with a daring look on his face.

Damien dropped out after the first year of college, telling me he was *'going to work and pitch in.'* I thought it meant he was going to get a decent job, help me with the bills. But when he threw a stack of twenties on the kitchen table with a wide grin on his face at eight in the morning... Well, I realized he had different plans. That day, after he'd watched me struggle for years, I knew it was only a matter of time before Damien would be wrapped up in the daily business of one of the many criminals who run the city of Boston. I guess that time was now.

"I'd rather not pay the bills if it could mean it's going to get you killed," I scowl.

"It's not going to get me killed, Lily. I'm twenty-one. I can take care of myself." He wipes his milk mustache with the back of his hand, a smile on his face that I'm assuming should be comforting.

It's not.

All I see is a little boy in a man's body, *thinking* he's grown up enough to run with the big boys. But after seeing our father hang with the wrong crowd and all the shit it brought to our doorstep, I know better. My little brother doesn't stand a chance against the real criminals in this city. He feels like a big shot now, throwing cash in my face, making him feel like he's providing for Colin and me. But in reality, he's nothing more than a foot soldier.

Disposable.

Replaceable.

He puts the carton back in the fridge, dipping his head in.

"Ooh, you made cream pie?" He turns his head towards me, his eyes sparkling.

"Don't change the subject."

"Look, we're more like a brotherhood." He straightens his back, giving me a cavalier smile, like a wise guy. "We take care of each other. It's wicked pissah. Trust me. Soon I'll be moved to the bigger jobs, then we can finally move out to a bigger place, give Colin an actual bedroom." Pride lights his eyes, and my heart falls a little, realizing he actually believes that. Thinks he's actually helping us towards a better life.

"You don't know who you're messing with, Damien. That Jones guy has no morals. He'll throw you in front of a bus without a second thought if it's ever you or him. He will push your limits until one day you don't remember who you are." I suck in a deep breath, the fresh smell of the lemon sanitizer I used in the kitchen earlier entering my nose.

I know my brother means well. I know he does everything out of the pure kindness of his heart, wanting to provide for his nephew, but sometimes I wonder if I protected him too much. If my shielding him from all the bad things after our mother died made him naïve and gullible. Damien never knew the kind of life our father lived because I was there to cover it up. And when he went to prison, I did my best to keep Damien off the streets as much as I could, hoping I could help him start a better future.

But then I had a baby out of wedlock, and shit hit the fan.

For fuck's sake.

"I don't want you hanging around with those guys. It's dangerous."

"It's solid money, Lily. We need money."

He makes it sound so easy, but I know that's not how this works. You don't just work for the gangs in Boston. Once you're in their circle … they own you. They control you, and if you piss them off, they *will* kill you.

"I know we need money. I pay the bills every single fucking month because I work my ass off at night!"

"You pay the bills and then we barely have food to eat. Colin is wearing new clothes because of the money I earn!" he exclaims.

"Colin can do with hand-me-downs." I mutter, my scowl still in place when I cross my arms in front of my body. "But he can't do without his *uncle*."

"Ah, are you silently telling me you love me?" he jokes.

"No. I'm silently telling you your nephew loves you." I frown, irritated by the fact that I can't seem to control my little brother anymore. What am I going to do? Tie him up to a chair? The guy is twenty-one, stronger than me, and at least a foot taller than I am.

"Nothing is going to happen to me, *sis*." A smug grin washes over his face when he plants his hands on my shoulders, pressing a kiss to my forehead.

"You don't know that," I mumble against his chest, refusing to wrap my arms around him like a stubborn sibling.

"Trust me. Soon we'll have more than enough money to afford daycare, and you can quit your night job. I will even be able to buy you a first edition of Peter and Wendy." He smiles.

"Not if you're dead."

A sigh fans my face as I look up at him.

"I'll make it happen. I'm going to bed. Night, sis." His lips push a kiss on top of my head before he turns around and walks towards his bedroom.

"I'll make it happen." I repeat his words with a mocking tone when he's out of sight. "Yeah, that's exactly what I'm afraid of."

4

CONNOR

It's Killian's birthday.

And even though he couldn't care less if we throw him a party or not, it's the best way to mingle with the important people in the city.

Or at least that's what Franklin, my oldest brother, always says. I wouldn't know shit about it because I'm not the one who *mingles*.

My brothers are.

Franklin and Killian are the chameleons, the ones who can sift through any social layer, being equally charming as menacing, depending on what the situation requires.

And Reign, my youngest brother, is a copy of Prince Charming, making anyone's wife want to drop their panties on the spot. But as for me? I'm the one you call when hell breaks loose. Or if you *want* hell to break loose. I'm the one people fear the most, knowing I have no tolerance for bullshit and that I'd rather break your jaw first before listening to any pleas.

They call me the beast, and the beast doesn't mingle.

In fact, the only reason I've been at this damn party for the last hour is because Franklin decided to throw it in the massive dining room of our family mansion right outside of the city.

I watch how Killian is eyeing Kendall sitting at the bar with Reign across the room.

"Just give her a chance, man," I whisper into Killian's ear, trying to make sure Franklin doesn't catch my words from where he's standing on the other side of Killian. "Franklin has a good feeling about her. He wouldn't risk everything for a girl."

"I am trying."

"Right," I scoff, bringing my bottle of Sam Adams to my lips.

"I am. I swear. I'm trying, okay?" Killian argues, glancing at me from the corner of his eyes.

"All right," I mumble, dropping the subject.

I get why Killian is hesitant. Living the lives we do, you have to be really careful who you let in to your circle, but Franky has never taken an interest in a woman like he has now, and I'm enjoying the more frequent smiles on his face. Besides, he pursued Kendall, not the other way around.

My eye catches someone walking through the door, and I turn my head to see who it is.

With widened eyes, my fingers tighten around the beer in my hand, and my jaw tics when I realize who it is. Instantly, voices fade, and our men draw their weapons, pointing them at the idiot who dared to crash a Wolfe party. He enters the room followed by a dozen of his men, his Glock hanging loosely in his hand while he struts through the room with a taunting smile across his face. I glance at Reign, who steps in front of Kendall in a protective way, a flash of fear lightening her eyes.

"Oh, a buffet!" Emerson Jones exclaims through the room before turning to Franklin, challenging him with a single glare. My brother holds his gaze, his mouth a firm line, refusing to give our biggest enemy any kind of reaction while my blood starts to boil inside of me.

"Do you mind?" Without waiting for any response, Emerson walks to the buffet while his men spread out through the room, like they are going to the packie for some cigarettes. Then he takes a shrimp off the table before popping it into his mouth. "Oh, these are good! Who's your caterer?"

"You've got some nerve, Jones," I growl, straightening my body some more as I ball my hand into a fist, reading to charge if I get the chance. "Walking into our family home like this."

"I thought I'd already shown you that I've got some nerve?" Emerson smiles before he saunters through the room again. "I mean, was it not enough? Do I have to be more specific? Do you want more visuals? More blood maybe? I can do that."

Emerson's eyes find Reign's before I see the panic on Kendall's face when he turns his attention to her with that same malicious smile.

"Reign!" he cheers, cocking his head a little. "New girl-friend?" Emerson smirks.

Kendall starts to blink rapidly, distress written all over her face as she locks eyes with Franklin in what looks like a cry for help.

"Or is she yours, *Franky*?" He turns his face back to Franklin.

Franklin's shoulders are now tense, his jaw tight, and he's breathing through his nose to try to mask the fact that his lethal side wants to take over. Killian throws his hand in front of his chest, holding him back, making sure he doesn't make any hasty decisions, I'm sure.

"Oh, she *is* yours!" Emerson chuckles, stepping closer towards her. "She's pretty."

To the outside world, my oldest brother is always calm, the one in control of his emotions. He just chooses to hide it from the outside world. However, I know my brother, and right now?

He wants to kill Emerson Jones for threatening our family by walking into our home.

And he wants to torture him for silently threatening his girl.

"What do you want, Emerson?" Reign grunts at Emerson, whose focus is solely set on Kendall, staring her down like she's his next prey.

"Simple. More money. More power," he answers with his arms wide, then continues to wander through the room.

"Don't we all?" Killian huffs sarcastically, rolling his eyes.

Adrenaline rushes through my body, putting me on edge while I watch him walk through our dining room. Doing my best to hold in the explosion that's forming inside of me, I plant my feet wide apart, crossing my arms in front of my chest as I raise my chin, following his every move with a scowl.

"Sure." Emerson shrugs, then points his gun at Lydia Bates, one of the banker's wives.

She lets out a screech, her lip trembling before her eyes start to well up, and her body starts to shake. Her husband reaches out his hand to drag her away with fear washing his face, but before he can get to her, one of Emerson's guys points his gun at him, making him stand statue-still. I let out a growl through my gritted teeth, torn over whether I should just charge and rip his head off, or stay put and avoid creating a war zone.

Emerson snaps his head back to Kendall, now covering her mouth in anguish, looking like she's about to faint.

"You, get over here, or I'll shoot her."

"No," Reign roars as Franklin groans next to me. Quickly, Emerson cocks his gun, his gaze fixated on Kendall.

"It's okay," she whispers to Reign, gently pushing his arm away and stepping in front of him while she briefly glances at Franklin.

"Tut tut, a little faster, sweetheart." Emerson's finger moves closer to the trigger, holding the gun a little closer to Lydia's forehead, her face now as white as snow.

"No, no! L-let her go. I'm coming. I'm here," Kendall cries out.

Emerson holds out his hand, grabbing Kendall's before he twirls her around so that her back is pressed against his chest, his gun against her temple. The terrified look on her face makes it hard for me to not intervene, every bone in my body ready to tear Emerson Jones apart.

"What do you want, Jones?" Killian asks again, sounding unimpressed.

"It's time for a new king," Emerson explains while he walks them backward to the open door he came in through. "*Bow.* Bow, agree to a tax fee, and this will work just fine. You may think you're the top dogs, but you won't be for long. Be smart and bow down now, or I'll be forced to start a war," he says with a relaxed look on his face. The laid back tone of his request makes it sound like he's asking if we can bring him anything from Dunks, pissing me off even more.

Franklin steps forward, clearly having enough of this tool spewing bullshit.

"Let go of her. Now."

"Sure, no worries. You can keep your whore." Emerson pushes her into Franklin's arms, and she sucks in a sharp breath when her body collides with his. Not willing to tolerate him in our house any longer, I start moving, followed by Killian and the rest of our men, as we draft Emerson and his men towards the exit.

"But I'm serious, Franklin," Emerson says, unaffected by all our glaring faces, a mocking grin still tugging on the corner of his mouth. "Tick tock, tick tock. I want an answer within two weeks. If not? I'll take that sweet little cunt of yours and make her my own."

He turns to walk out, then halts one more time, right in front of Nigel, who is pressed against the wall. His eyes widen with worry, tension spreading across his face when Emerson looks him straight in the eye.

"Sorry, man. I need to show them I'm serious," he says, then nudges his chin to one of his boys, who looks like he's barely out of his teens. "Kill him."

My chest tightens, my adrenaline shooting through the roof as the realization of his words hit me in the face, and Nigel's face turns stone, fear coating his eyes as Emerson walks away. Before anyone can act, the boy takes the last step so that he's now in front of Nigel, pulling the trigger without hesitation. Several bullets run through Nigel's body, and before I know it, his body is leaking blood in several places while Emerson and his crew rapidly disappear from our sight. Screams echo through the room as I look at Nigel, who's giving me one last glance, shocked, until life leaves his eyes, and his body collapses onto the floor.

I stand, frozen in place, my nostrils flaring as the raging feeling inside of me explodes, and I let out a feral roar.

He's gone.

5

CONNOR

My hands tremble as I stare at his lifeless body in front of me. A mental fog showers my mind, and I feel time passing by while the people around me erupt in screams. The tightness forming inside my chest holds me frozen to the spot as the blood starts to seep out of his now torn veins.

Reign and Killian rush over to Nigel, assessing the damage, but I already know.

I saw it in his eyes, that last second. There is no use. He's gone. Murdered by order of Emerson Jones.

A body crashes against mine, trying to escape the sight of the horror on the floor, snapping me out of my daze.

"Connor, are you okay?" Reign asks with concern in his eyes.

I can feel my heartbeat in my throat when I lift my lip up in a malicious grin.

"I will be." My feet are finally finding movement again, strutting to the front door with big strides.

"Connor! NO! Get back!" Reign calls out to my back. "Shit!"

But my mind doesn't want to listen anymore. I'm done listening.

Emerson Jones needs to die. *Right now.* My body is tensing while I crack my knuckles, walking outside. I watch Emerson get into the SUV waiting for him with a smirk on his face. He salutes me, then the car takes off with squealing tires. Driven by anger, I start to run, determined to pull his sorry ass out of the car and beat him until he's nothing but pulp. With my teeth tightly pressed together, I speed up as fast as I can, feeling my body temperature rising when my heart starts to race in my chest, pushing my stamina. Before the end of the driveway, I reach the back of the SUV for a brief moment until they turn onto the road, hitting the throttle even more, escaping my grasp. I push myself for another fifty yards or so until I slow down my pace, watching them disappear into the darkness.

A feral roar leaves my chest, reverberating into the air. I look at the side of the road, picking up the first stone I can see to throw through their window, but as expected, it doesn't even come close.

"FUCK!"

"Connor?"

"What?!" I bark, turning around, looking into my little brother's worried eyes.

"I need you to breathe," Reign says, taking a step closer. He holds his hands up placatingly as he slowly approaches me like I'm a dog with rabies.

Close.

"They killed him, Reign!" I roar, feeling manic as fuck.

"I know."

"He's just a kid!" I say, pulling my hair, wanting to feel the scorching pain on my scalp. Anything to prevent me from letting in the pain that is dying to enter my chest.

I don't want it. I don't want to feel this. It's the same feeling I had when my brothers and I got separated, when we were put into the system after Franklin got arrested.

The feeling of inadequacy.

The feeling of losing control.

At least when Dad was around, I could still protect my brothers from his raging fist, but I couldn't protect them from anything when they were in a different city. On the outside, I appeared to be in control. But I tore myself up inside for the whole three months I was with my foster family because I couldn't do anything. I couldn't help my brothers.

This feels just like that, and I don't want it.

My chest is heaving as my eyes remain locked with Reign's.

"It's okay."

"It's not okay!" I seethe.

It's not okay. None of this is okay. We should've killed Emerson when we got the chance. He's been fucking with us for too long.

"We are going to make him suffer, Connor," Reign says. "I promise. I will find him, and he will wish he never set foot in Boston."

Reign's face is filled with the same determination I feel, a glint of grief in his eyes. A piece of grief he's probably pushing aside to make sure I don't do anything stupid.

I want to do something stupid. I want to get into my truck and walk into Emerson's bar with an M5, ready to shoot every living being who dared to step foot inside our home tonight.

Casualties be damned.

"We gotta be smart, Connor," Reign adds.

I clear my throat, my hands balled into fists.

I know he's right. We need to be smart about this before we unchain a war in Boston that will affect the rest of the city. But every single molecule inside me wants to find Emerson Jones right now and torture him until he's begging me for mercy.

"I will find him." Reign gives me another reassuring look while I keep staring at him.

My chest moves as I try to take deep breaths, breathing in through my nose while exhaling through my mouth. I'm still on edge, but my impulsive nature is starting to simmer down just a little.

Finally, I give him a menacing grin, still feeling the need to punch something.

"Oh, I know. And it's going to be epic," I reply when I start to walk back to the house.

6

I t's almost three a.m. when I walk through the front door after a long night at the bar. I'm grateful for my job, and for the most part it's fun. The customers are nice, apart from the occasional chucklehead who wants to hit on me, and the tips are a major blessing. But my legs are always killing me by the time it's time to close down.

Pulling my boots from my feet, I stumble to the parlor, finding Damien draped on the couch with his eyes closed. A rerun of *Jersey Shore* is on, and I grab the clicker to turn down the volume, poking my brother in the side.

His eyes slowly open, but he shuts them when he notices the menacing glare on my face.

"Hi, Lily," he mumbles, snuggling into the cushions a little bit more.

"Wake up!" I poke him once more, repeating the move until he smacks my hand away with a look that matches my glare.

"Stoppp!"

"Get up," I bark, planting my ass on the coffee table in front of him, physically showing him I'm not letting him off the hook this time. Not after all the things I just heard.

He sits his body up with a growl, rubbing his face before dropping his hand with a loud thud on his thigh.

"What, Lily?" he says, obviously aggravated.

"I heard some news from those banker wives at the bar today. "

"Oh, yeah. What now? Anything special from the cougars of Boston?" His tone is dull and uninterested, pissing me off even more.

"Really special," I muse. "You see, they were telling me how Killian Wolfe's birthday was last night."

Damien sucks in a breath, faking shock.

"Oh, no. Call The Boston Globe."

"Funny." I smile. My anger rises, and all I want to do is smack my brother over the head. He knows damn well where this conversation is headed, and he has no right to give me an attitude. "They also told me Emerson Jones and his crew crashed the party." I watch as a frown creases his forehead, waiting for him to give any response, but he stays quiet.

"A pretty bold move, if you ask me. Pissing off the uncrowned king of the city is one thing, but doing it at his home? Pssh. Emerson Jones must have a death wish."

I carefully watch how Damien's eyes darken by the second, his mouth pursing in annoyance. I'm ready for him to snap at any moment now, telling me it's all bullshit. Or at least that he wasn't there, but the nagging feeling in my gut already knows what the deal is.

He holds my gaze, pressing his tongue against his cheek, then he rolls his eyes.

"What do you want me to say?" he blurts when the

tension of my eyes piercing through him becomes too much. His *tough guy* stance from a minute ago shrivels away, my little brother taking its place.

There he is.

He can act like he's all grown up, rolling with the big boys now. But I know my little brother. It's nothing more than an act.

"At first, I was relieved you walked out of it alive, thinking it was nothing more than a power play between two gang leaders, and *thank fuck*, my baby brother walked out of that unharmed. But there was more, and by the time they were on their third round, they became wicked chatty." I let out a sarcastic chuckle, joyfully slapping my brother's knee before resting my elbows on my thighs, my face hardening. "You see, they were chatting about how not only Emerson crashed the birthday party to show off his power, but how he took one of the banker wives hostage, scaring the shit out of her. Now, I know my sweet little brother would never do shit like that, so at this point I was just listening with interest, clinging on like it was some fantastical story."

"Right," he mutters, deflecting his gaze.

"No. No. Wait." I squeeze his knee to force him to look at me. "This is the best part. They told me how Emerson first took hostage of the banker's wife, then switched her with some other girl who supposedly is Franklin Wolfe's new girlfriend."

My hands now grip both his knees, hovering above his face.

"But the real kicker was the fact that he ordered some *foot soldier* to kill one of Wolfe's guys to prove a point," I grate out, watching him closely.

I notice his Adam's apple bob as he swallows hard, his

face turning as white as a ghost, while his forehead glimmers with sweat. His eyes start to well up, and he finally locks his eyes with mine as a tear runs down his cheek.

"I'm sorry," he sniffs.

"Goddammit!" I jump up, anger rushing through my veins as I ball my hands into fists and start walking back and forth between the kitchen and the parlor. It's only three steps, but I need to keep moving to make sure I don't punch my shithead of a brother in the fucking face.

Do a run or two for Emerson Jones? Sure.

Sell some drugs for Emerson Jones? Okay.

Protect Emerson Jones for cash? Fine.

But taking people hostage and watching as he randomly starts killing people? That's a whole other story.

"I told you to stay away from them!" I growl with a hushed tone, not wanting to wake up Colin who's sleeping in my bedroom.

"I know!" Damien presses his fingers deep into his sockets to stop the tears. "We were going to scare them. That's all."

"They killed a guy, *Damien!*"

"I didn't know that, Lily! I swear. I didn't know that was the plan."

I shake my head.

"You should've known that running with that crew is trouble. He killed a guy to make a statement. You need out, Damien. Get a decent job, go back to school, we will make it work."

He wipes his tears away with the back of his hand, then gives me an incredulous look.

"We both know that isn't happening. I'm in now. There is no way out." Emotion seems to leave his eyes while I carefully watch him, until there's nothing left but a hollow shell.

He reminds me of the thirteenth-year-old version I once had to tell his dad wasn't coming home. He'd cried until he looked completely defeated. For weeks, I had no clue what to do with him other than give him the time to adjust to the new situation. To grieve the loss of not just one parent but both. Four weeks later, he started to smile more, and we grew into a routine.

But seeing him here, like this, I know it's naïve for me to think this could be the same. There is no settling into this situation. He's already in too deep, has seen things that can't handle the daylight. This is a crossroad he took and can't come back from. Not unless we pack our bags and leave the city. I don't even know what else my brother has already seen, and at this point? I don't think I want to know.

"We have to, Damien."

"We can't, Lily. I crossed a line."

"Maybe we can! It's not like you killed that guy. You were just a witness. Maybe we can still pull you out."

He closes his eyes, a sad smile forming on his lips before he opens his eyes, turning his head my way.

"It's too late. I'm in." The cracking of his voice makes my heart break a little, wanting to wrap him in my arms and fix it, just like when he was little. He gets up, stopping in front of me, rubbing his hands over my shoulders. "Don't worry. I'll always protect you and Colin, Lily. I'm going to fix it. I'll keep you safe."

I blink, doing my best to keep my tears at bay while I look at the puddle of a human in front of me, despair washing his face as he tries to keep up a strong front.

It's nothing more than a façade.

"I'm the older one. I'm supposed to protect *you*, silly."

"And you did a great job," he sighs. "But I'm twenty-one.

It's my turn to protect you now. And Colin." His hand wraps around my neck, tucking me against his chest as he presses a kiss to my forehead.

"I don't like this, Damien," I mutter against the fabric of his hoodie.

"It will be fine."

His words come out in one firm line, but I can hear the uncertainty etched in his voice.

There is not a hair on my head that believes a word he's saying, but to be honest, I don't think he does either. He used to be this innocent boy, getting good grades, helping out his sister whenever he could. But in the last six months, the streets of Boston stripped him of his innocence, even though he clearly wasn't ready to let it go just yet.

"Damien, these men are not fucking around. If you piss them off, it won't take long before they end up at our doorstep."

"They don't know where I live. I'll never tell them where we live."

"What about the Wolfes? If they know you're part of Emerson Jones's crew, you're a target, and if you are a target, so are we."

"The Wolfes don't know me," he explains, tugging me deeper into his chest. "I'll be careful, I swear." I listen to the beating of his heart as the words leave him.

He wants to do right by me, and I love him even more for it.

Maybe he is right.

Fuck, I hope he is.

I don't care that he's doing shit on the other side of the law. I'm not a saint, and I'll never pretend to be one, but it's the part where I know you don't mean shit as a foot soldier that scares the crap out of me. The part where you have to sell your soul and corrupt your mind to move up the criminal ladder. I don't think my little brother is strong enough to come back from that. Damien has more empathy in his little pinky than most men, and I don't think he can just ignore that and do whatever Emerson Jones might ask him to do next. Not unless he changes his entire being to the point of no return.

"I hope you're right, Damien," I answer with worry. I hope he's right, and it will all work out, but something is telling me trouble might come bursting through that door sooner than later.

7

CONNOR

Reign frowns, turning in his desk chair to face me as I walk into his condo. We own a family mansion just outside of Boston where I live permanently. But all three of my brothers also have places in the city where they stay half the time. We all have keys to each other's apartments, but I rarely use them.

His desk is placed next to one of the floor to ceiling windows, covered with six screens and a lot of wires.

Don't ask me about tech shit.

I know how to work my phone, and that's all I need.

But Reign can hack into almost anything at any time, including whatever government shit there is to hack, which is a convenience in our line of work.

Walking past his white leather sofa, I give him a faint smile, stopping in front of the window. I glance outside, looking over the Seaport District, my hands in the pockets of my dark jeans.

"Hey, man. You okay?" I can see Reign from the corner

of my eye, slouching in his chair with a worried look on his face.

I'm furious.

I'd expected my anger to have died down after some sleep, but I only woke up with a thundercloud taking residence above my head. I'm known for having a scowl on my face ninety percent of the time, walking around like the Hulk while grunting and growling, but after last night, it's like my grimace is made out of stone.

"Connor?"

"I'm fine," I grumble.

I look fine, but really it feels like my anger is eating me whole from the inside, doing its best to crawl out of my skin. I want to destroy someone, to release the tension. Punch anyone to pulp.

Something.

Anything.

Nigel was just some punk kid I picked up from the streets a few years back, looking for trouble with some other townies, and he threw a good punch. Told him to come work for us. He was seventeen at the time, nothing more than a kid searching for a way to kill time. But I kept him close, and soon, he started to feel like family.

"Right," Reign says after a few silent moments. "As much as I don't mind you staring out of my window all day, you wanna tell me why you're here? Do you need me? Or can I just keep on working while you just stand there?"

I turn to him and glare.

"Hey, it's up to you, man. I'm cool with whatever." He offers me his famous boyish grin, then turns serious again.

"Really, Connor. What do you need?"

"An address."

"Cryptic, okay. Can I pick any address I like?"

I look at him with a straight face, not in the mood for his theatrics.

"Fine, an address," he calls out when I don't respond. "Who's address?"

"The boy who shot Nigel."

He suddenly stills, his brows raising up. I can almost see the cogs turning in his head as he eyes me with a wary look.

"I don't know who that is."

Like that's an issue for him. He needs an internet connection and his fingers to work the keyboard. Nothing more than that.

"So find him."

"Connor, no."

"Ya-huh."

"*No-suh.*"

"Reign, for fuck's sake!" I shout.

"Franklin is going to kill you."

I throw my arm in the air, waving his comment away.

"Like you give a shit? You love pissing him off." Sure, Franklin is going to be pissed. He will probably yell some, maybe even throw me a punch or two, but I don't motherfucking care. He'll get over it. And if not, well, whatever.

An eye for an eye.

I'm not settling for any less. I need to fire off the raging ball that's burning inside of me, and finding the guy who killed Nigel is the way to do it. Right before I make Emerson Jones wish he never messed with us Wolfes in the first place.

"You know Franklin won't let this one slide, right? He *will* avenge him."

"Yeah, like next month," I argue. "I want it *now*." Slamming my fist on his desk, I look at my little brother. He's looking at me with the green eyes all four of us inherited from our mother, giving me a sad look. His eyes tell me he's unimpressed by my aggression but knows I'm not going to leave without an address.

I know he will cave because I know he understands my pain.

He feels for me. Which pisses me off even more, but I'm willing to let that one slide if he gives me what I want.

Reign is the brother with the biggest heart. The one who likes to see the good in people, even though eighty percent of the world is rotten. How he manages to keep his heart in check like that after his four years in foster care beats the hell out of me. I was only in for three months, and it was hell.

It changed me. And not for the better.

"Just give me the damn address, Reign."

"Connor, come on," he coaxes.

"I'm not fucking with you, Reign."

He scratches his head with a pleading look.

"Don't kill him."

"I can't promise you that."

My instinct is to tell him I'll keep him alive if he gives me what I want, but at this time, I just want to use him as a punching bag until he's wishing for me to finish him off. Then I want to patch him back up and do it all over again. He might die in the process, he might not.

Who knows?

Who cares?

Reign lets out a big sigh, then shakes his head before turning his focus to the screens in front of him and starts typing.

"Look, I know you're hurt. I am too. But he only obeyed

an order. It's Emerson Jones we need to end," he says as he gets to work.

"I know. That's why he's next."

"Please tell me you're not going on a killing spree through town to kill Emerson and his crew?" He gives me a quick glance while his fingers never stop moving.

Sounds tempting, not gonna lie.

"I'm angry. Not stupid."

"Could've fooled me," he mumbles.

"Shut up, Reign."

I walk to the kitchen. Knowing this may take a while, I open up the fridge.

"You want anything?" I yell.

"A Coke."

I grab a can of Coke off the shelf and grab a bottle of beer for myself when I notice the box of Dunks. Setting the drinks on the counter, I open the box, grabbing two glazed ones with one hand. Letting my teeth sink into one of them, I enjoy the sweet taste of the fluffy dough while picking up the drinks with my other hand and walking back to the parlor. I place the can of Coke next to Reign before settling myself on the edge of his desk.

"It's noon, Connor," he scolds when his eye catches the beer in my hand.

I place the beer cap between my teeth to open the bottle, then spit it across the room. Reign follows the cap that lands on the floor in front of his couch with a glare.

"You gonna pick that up, asshole?"

"You gonna give me that address, *tool?*" Provokingly, I take a huge bite out of my donut.

"You're unbelievable," he mutters, moving his attention back to the screens.

Ignoring him, I take a pull from my beer. It tastes more bitter than usual, and I wonder if it's because of my gloomy state of mind. Nonetheless, I appreciate the cold drink surging down my throat.

"You're not going to give me one?" Reign nudges his chin towards the two donuts in my hand.

My forehead creases.

"No."

I don't share food. With anyone. It's what happens when you know how it feels to not eat for days. I love my brothers, and I'll share just about anything with them. But not anything that is edible.

"Can you find anything?" I ask when I've devoured both donuts. I brush my hands against each other to get rid of some excess dough, then wipe the glaze on the tips of my fingers against my jeans.

"Not in five minutes, no." Reign glares at me. "Have a seat, dickhead. This is going to take a while."

Not appreciating his attitude, I ruffle his hair to annoy him some more before I throw myself on his couch, grabbing the clicker and settling into the pillows. I scan through the channels until I find a rerun of a Bruins game.

I wanted to be a hockey player. A Boston Bruin. Once upon a time.

I actually was pretty good until I was thirteen or something. That's when shit went bad. Well, actually, it's always been shit, but we never knew better. Let's just say that's when we couldn't even pretend shit was fine anymore. My dad was a serious alcoholic, and like many of those liquor loving assholes, his hands were his greatest weapons. He used to beat my mom up on a daily basis and us kids at least once a week or so. He seemed to really have it out for Franklin and me, us being the older ones. But to be honest, we wouldn't have had it any other way.

Franklin and I always made sure Killian and Reign were protected or hidden whenever he would run through the house like an intoxicated hurricane. But right after Franklin's fourteenth birthday, he had a growth spurt in height and weight. Within three months, he was as big as Daddy Wolfe and was no longer willing to let us all get beaten up by him. At least not when he was around.

It also meant that I was the next best thing when it came to his abuse whenever Franklin wasn't around. Playing hockey was not only a welcoming outlet, it was also a great way to excuse the bruises that were inflicted by Daddy Dearest. But before I even turned fourteen, I had already broken my arm three times and came to practice with a black eye more than once. The suspicious look in my coach's eyes told me he knew those injuries didn't come from pushing and pulling on the ice, so before he called social services on my ass, I quit the team.

The love for the sport didn't die, though. I have season passes and never miss a game.

"Okay." Reign spins his desk chair to face me, and I take a pull of my beer while looking at him. "His name is Damien Johnson."

"Sounds like a tool."

"He killed one of us. He's not only a tool but a pretty stupid one as well," he deadpans before he continues. "He's twenty-one and living with his sister in some crappy ass apartment in Roxbury." He holds out a piece of paper, and I lean in to grab it out of his hand.

Before I can reach it, he pulls back, holding it up in the air.

"You can't kill him, Connor." His green eyes flash with a warning that does fuck all.

"Suck me, Reign."

"I mean it. Beat him to a pulp, lock him up in the garage. Have your fun, let it all out, but whatever you do... *Don't* kill him. He's just a kid. We need to be smart about this."

"Nigel was just a *kid*." I quickly lift my body to grab Reign's knee and drag him towards me, but the fucker rapidly pushes his desk chair a few feet back. Before I can jump up to force the piece out of his hand, he grabs a lighter from the desk and holds it near the edge of the paper.

I glare at him, not saying a word, grinding my teeth in annoyance.

I'm not agreeing to anything. I'm not an idiot. I'm not going to blow a bullet through the kid's brain, but if he happens to die because I gave him a punch too much?

Let me think... Yeah, no fucks are given.

"Connor, *swear*," Reign grates out, narrowing his eyes on me.

I'm about to dive at my little brother when I hear the front door open behind us, and I quickly turn my head. Kilian walks through the door with a scowl on his face as if he's accompanied by the same thundercloud I am.

Who knows, maybe it was a two for one deal.

"I thought we'd meet at the bar?" Reign asks, confused.

"The fuck are you doing here?" Killian calls out to me, ignoring Reign while he makes way to us.

"Give it, Reign," I hiss, doing my best to make sure Killian doesn't hear us. I'm sure he wouldn't disagree with my current mission, but I know him well enough to know he's going to call Franklin the second I walk out that door if he knows what I'm up to.

"*Swear*, Connor," Reign repeats, refusing to give in.

"*I swear*," I bark. I can barely get the words out of my throat, and when a pleased grin appears on his pretty face, I can't help feeling the urge to slam my fist against his cheek. Throwing him another glare, I yank the piece of paper out of his grasp right before Killian reaches my side, and I swiftly push it in the back pocket of my jeans.

"What are you two up to?" Killian frowns, his brows pinched together with wariness sparking his eyes. I gaze at him impassively, ignoring his question as I turn around to make my way towards the door.

"You're welcome, *asshole*," Reign bellows to my back.

"Where are you going?" Killian calls out.

I keep walking while flipping them off, not feeling like answering my brothers. I've got shit to do, people to beat up. When I hear the door close behind me, I pull the piece of paper out of my pocket.

2058 Stanton Hollow Road.

8

I walk through the parlor, scooping up Colin from the floor.

"Time for bed, little buddy."

He rapidly starts to shake his head with a defiant look.

"No, Mommy. No bed."

The slight scowl on his sweet face makes me chuckle.

"Yes, bed, little monster," I say while I tickle him on his sides. The squeals of laughter pouring from him warm my heart. I bring him to the small bathroom, putting him on the counter next to the sink before reaching up to the cabinet to get his toothbrush and toothpaste. His focus is on my hands, watching every move closely, as if I'm performing a magic trick of some sort.

"Okay, Mommy first and then Colin," I tell him, putting toothpaste on his toothbrush.

"Yes," he claps.

"All right, open up."

He opens up his mouth with a loud 'aaaah', and I get to

work. I switch sides every few seconds with a different transportation sound to keep him entertained. He enjoys them all, but it's the race car that really makes it hard for him to not laugh. When I'm done, I give him a sip of water and clean his face with a washcloth.

"Show me your teeth." I show him mine as an example, and he shows me his with a big smile. "Yeah, all clean and shiny!" I pick him up, popping him on my hip, then walk us both to my bedroom to put his pajamas on. When he's all ready and spread out on my queen-size bed, I take the chance to give him a few more tickles, making him squirm under my touch. His giggles switch back and forth between screeching and laughing before I close it off with a big blow on his chubby belly.

"More, Mommy!"

"No, no more. Time for bed." I pluck him from the bed, turning around to put him down in the small crib in my closet. There is enough room for a crib with a changing table on the other side, but I watch him grow every single day, and I wonder how long this is going to fit. Within a year, there is a big chance he will need a bigger bed, and that just isn't going to fit in here.

I tuck him in, giving him a goodnight kiss and a brush through his light blond hair.

"Goodnight, my baby."

"Night, mommy." He smiles.

I flip the nightlight on, then press play on his music box before softly closing the door behind me.

When I reach the kitchen, I pour myself a glass of wine and grab a bag of chips, then I walk back to the parlor. I drop myself onto the worn out couch, grabbing my book from the side table before settling in with my wine in hand and my chips on my lap.

I flip through the pages to the chapter where I left off, taking a sip of my wine.

Perfect.

I'm halfway through the chapter when a loud bang echoes across the apartment. The sound is loud enough to make me think there is a small explosion outside the front door. Shocked, I feel my heart almost jump out of my chest, my wine spilling all over my hoodie. My head turns with wide eyes as my heart starts to race. Before I can get up to check out what's going on, a large man walks into the parlor with an intimidating scowl on his face. I shriek in horror, angst seeping through my veins until he silences me with his hand on my neck. My glass drops on the floor with a thud, and my hands cover his to try to escape his grasp.

"Where is he?!" he shouts, hovering above my face.

It feels like my eyes are going to pop out of my head, making me shake my head with a pleading look while I try to catch some air.

"C-can't breathe," I push out, my voice cracking.

He loosens his grip just enough for me to breathe, but his grip remains tight enough to keep me from being able to move.

"Where is he?" he repeats as I suck in a deep breath, his roaring tone making my eyes flutter shut. When I open them again, I blink a few times when I recognize the scar on his lip combined with the short, but ruffled, blond hair.

"Connor?"

A frown forms on his face, a brief questioning in his eyes before his face returns to the hateful scowl he entered with.

"Don't make me ask again!" he shouts. "Where is he?!"

"Who?!"

"Damien! Where?!"

"I don't know!" I yell back desperately, knowing he means business. I may know who he is right now, but he clearly doesn't give a shit who I am.

I always knew one day I'd see him again. Living in the same city, there is no hiding forever. But I wasn't expecting it so soon, and definitely not because of my dumbass brother.

I knew that fool was going to bring trouble to my doorstep.

Connor narrows his eyes, examining my face as I hold his gaze fiercely, panting like I'm about to faint like a little girl, but doing my best not to back down, nonetheless.

Not sure how long I'm going to keep that up.

"I know you," he growls, a little less hostile now.

I nod in agreement, hoping he will take it easy on me when he realizes we have a history. Hoping maybe that will prevent him from really hurting me.

"I'm Lily. We slept to—"

"We fucked," he interrupts, blunt as hell.

"Yeah." I want to make a move, fight, do anything to get out of this terrifying situation, being held down against my couch by one of the biggest criminals in Boston. But my legs are paralyzed, frozen by fear of what he might do if he finds out I'm not alone. My heart is still beating like a drum in my chest, and at this point, I'm trying to stay as quiet as possible, hoping Colin doesn't wake up.

It's a blessing the kid sleeps like a log.

"Doesn't mean shit. Tell me where your brother is," he snarls, the scar on his lip making him look even more brutal.

I remember this man as rugged, rough, and a bit scary, always wearing a scowl on his face. I remember how his energy always made people step to the side when he entered a room. All Wolfe men have a presence over them you have to acknowledge, you have to obey. But Connor Wolfe is the one who sparks straight up fear in most people. Yet he made me feel worshipped when he seduced me into his bed. He made me feel things that had me craving for more, trying things I'd never dared. It was only one night, but I would've been willing to let him explore my body for weeks.

But right now, I want to grab my baby and run for the hills. I was just a piece of ass for him back then, and I'm just a girl standing in his way to my brother right now.

My mouth starts to feel dry as sandpaper. I swallow a few times, then clear my throat.

"I don't know. I swear. He went out. He probably won't be back until morning."

He lets out a growl, staring me down with his piercing green eyes as if he's trying to detect my lie. They are dark green on the outside and a light green on the inside with specks of amber surrounding the pupils that lure you in. The tension rises between us as our eyes engage in a silent fight for power, my body relaxing a little under his heavy touch. My senses are still sharp, but I'm slowly believing he's not going to hurt me any more than he has so far.

"I don't know where he is," I plead with a whisper.

His jaw tics at my words, then he roughly pushes me harder against the furniture before straightening his back and letting me go.

"I'll find him." A sinister look washes over his face, making my heart stop for a second as panic hits me. He turns around, not giving me another glance as a shiver trickles down my spine.

"Are you going to kill him?" My voice breaks, and my eyes

turn moist. He stops in his tracks, waiting a moment before he faces me, a dark glimmer in his eyes.

"Eventually, yes."

I frantically start to shake my head, my hand covering my mouth.

"Please, no. He's all I got. Don't kill him," I beg.

Damien is a stupid kid, messing around with the wrong people, but he doesn't deserve this. He's no Emerson Jones. He's no Wolfe. He's just a kid, trying to get by. I'm not going to lose him.

I can't lose him.

Determined to convince him, I jump off the couch, throwing myself in front of his feet, my hands wrapped together in a praying gesture.

"Please, please. He's just a kid."

Fear grips my chest, while my head starts to spin because of my futile attempt.

"No excuse," he grunts.

"We'll move. We'll move out of Boston, start a life somewhere new. You'll never hear from us again. He just hangs with the wrong crowd. He's been a good kid up until now. I swear. I made sure of that."

"Nigel doesn't get all that. He's getting a funeral instead." He moves his body, ready to leave, but I pull his jeans in a desperate plea while tears start to run down my face.

"He made mistakes. Have mercy."

"I never have mercy."

"Please! I beg you. Don't hurt him. Take me. Take me instead. Please."

The words leave my lips before I really realize what I'm saying, hoping he will have mercy on me because we have a history. But I understand my mistake when the corner of his mouth curls in a diabolical smile.

"Okay," he says as a gasp leaves my mouth. Colin's plump face flashes in front of my eyes, and terror enters my face. But before I can get another word out, my world turns black.

9

CONNOR

T hirty minutes later, I'm carrying an unconscious Lily from my truck and walking into the mansion.

Franklin is going to throw a fit.

When I realized why she looked familiar, I almost lost my concentration, thinking back to that night. I still remember her perky ass sitting on my face before she wrapped her lips around my cock.

Not a bad memory.

Not bad at all.

Not gonna lie, that's definitely part of why I took her up on her offer so fast. There's a slight chance she'll suck my cock like a lollipop again, but in the meantime, she's nice to look at.

I walk up the stairs, her body limp in my arms while I debate which room to put her in. All our rooms have locks while the guest rooms don't—since Franklin is a notorious control freak—so that's not an option. But I sure as fuck ain't putting her in my room, and the thing is, my brothers still come home like once a week. When I reach the top of the stairs, I look at Franklin's bedroom door at the end of the hall. Shrugging my shoulders, I decide to put her in his room, thinking he's gonna be with Kendall at the penthouse anyway, like he has been for the last few weeks. I walk through the massive oak door, my nose greeted by Franklin's musky cologne lurking in the room, before I place her on the bed. Straightening her body a little to make sure she's comfortable, I let my eyes roam over her once again.

Her hoodie covers up the curves of her upper body, but her tight skinny jeans bring out the toned arcs of her legs and ass.

My tongue darts out, and I lick my lips, resisting my impulse to feel them under my palm before sucking in an irked breath and turning around to leave the room. Closing the door behind me, I lock the door with an evil smirk on my face.

This will be entertaining until I have her damn brother in my hands.

I walk down the stairs at the same time Franklin walks through the door.

"What's doin', man?" I grin. "You've got a smile on your face."

"Shut up." He rolls his eyes, shutting the door behind him, following me while I walk to the kitchen.

"I thought you were taking Kendall to the shooting range?"

"I did."

"Then why are you acting like you just got some?" I ask, pushing the door open to enter the kitchen before I take a seat at the breakfast bar. Franklin moves to the fridge, grabbing two bottles of beer and sets them on the bar. I reach out for one, placing the cap between my teeth to tear it off, then hand the bottle back to Franklin who is giving me a cocky look.

"You need me to answer that question?"

"You dirty bastard, you fucked her at the shooting range?" A hint of pride is audible in my voice while I repeat the move to open my own beer.

"Shut up, Connor."

"What?" My big brother having sex in public, taking this girl everywhere? Yeah, he's got it bad, and I'm enjoying this way too much. "You're not the adventurous type, but she pushes you out of your comfort zone. I like it."

He shakes his head a little, ignoring my remark before his eyes give me a sympathetic look.

"How are you holding up?"

The humor on my face completely gone, I take a pull from my beer, looking at him from above the bottle.

"Shit happens." There is no better answer to it. It's as simple as that. Nigel is dead, and I'm determined to take my revenge. I will feel better once I do. The girl locked up upstairs being the first step.

"You're allowed to be sad, you know. Just because you're a fucking asshole doesn't mean you're not allowed to have feelings. I know you loved that kid."

"I did," I admit, looking at Franklin's stern face. "And I will avenge him, but there's nothing I can do to bring him back. So we move on." I shrug, pushing the anguish that runs through my body to the side.

"You called me out here because you found something?"

I nod, taking another sip of my beer.

"Yeah, Reign found out where that kid lives."

"What kid?"

"The one who shot Nigel. His name is Damien Johnson," I explain smugly. Franklin is not going to like what I'm about to say next, but who fucking cares?

"Okay," he drawls, a scowl on his face. "What did you do?"

"Busted through his door."

"Then what happened?"

"He wasn't there."

He lets out a sigh, then his face softens, probably relieved I didn't get the chance to kill anyone.

"So I took his sister."

Franklin freezes, blinking.

"Are you shitting me?" He darts forward, glaring as he presses his hands on the breakfast bar. He looks at me, shocked, disbelief sparking in his green eyes. "You didn't."

"I did," I reply, taking another pull from my beer.

He rubs his face, aggravation clear in the sharp features of his face.

"You took *her*? You kidnapped a girl?"

"Yeah, I actually know her." I shrug.

"You know…? What the…?" Franklin screeches.

"Yeah, I slept with her a while back."

He keeps staring at me as if he's wondering if I lost my mind.

"You took the girl you once slept with."

"Like years ago, and technically," the corner of my mouth rises, "she offered herself up."

"What the fuck are you talking about? She offered to be *taken*?"

"Well, no. But she was begging me not to hurt her little

59

shit of a brother. Offered herself instead. I took her up on the offer."

"Connor!" he shouts. "That's a fucking felony. We don't go around kidnapping women!"

"Well, she didn't want to tell me where her brother was, so I figured we could trade her for her brother. If he loves his sister, he'll take the trade without a second thought. It's a win-win." I know my relaxed attitude about this pisses him off even more, and maybe it wasn't the smartest move. But I was pissed off, and I needed to do *something*.

"A win-win?"

"Okay, maybe not a win-win, but you know what, I don't care. That little shithead killed Nigel. An eye for an eye, Franky. I want him to pay. If I have to do that by taking his sister, so be it." The aggravation is growing in my voice, and I can see Franklin's stance soften a little. "You would've done the same thing if that had been any of us."

"You are my little brother," he counters.

"And Nigel was a little brother to me," I yell, slamming my fist on the surface.

"Okay," he concedes, rubbing the back of his neck. "I get it. But now we'll need to find a way to shut her up once she's free to go."

"I think killing her little brother will shut her up."

"Yeah, that'll probably do the trick," he agrees sarcastically. "Where is she now?"

I turn my head away, knowing he'll want to punch me when I answer that question.

"Connor?"

"Your bedroom."

"Goddamm … you're a fucking bigger shit than Reign is right now!" he yells, his face turning a slight shade of red.

"Well, you've been at the penthouse with Kendall. Figured you weren't coming home soon."

"You're an asshole."

"Yeah, well, that makes two of us." With a cocky smile, I bring my bottle up to cheer. "Don't worry about it, she's cool."

"She's cool?" he repeats, confusion creasing his face.

"Yeah. Her name is Lily."

"For now, I'm gonna pretend that I don't know about this girl. We already have enough shit on our plates as it is. Don't tell Reign and Kill about her either. We're keeping this between you and me. I don't need any more people knowing you're keeping some girl you fucked hostage upstairs. Don't want to give Killian any more reason to not trust my judgment."

"Cool." I shrug, ready to change the subject. "He's still giving you a hard time about Kendall?"

"Yeah, says she's running around with Emerson."

"And is she?" I ask.

"She is, but nothing I don't know about."

"You're serious about this girl, aren't you?" I take another pull from my beer with a questioning look on my face. "I mean, you can't deny it because you even quit smoking for her. Something you said you'd never do."

My smug grin is returned with a glare, and a silent chuckle escapes my lips.

"Just admit it, Franky. You're stuck on her."

He sucks in a deep breath, as if he's done fighting it.

"Are you cool with that?"

My gaze locks with his as I look at the hard features of my big brother. I know Killian has his reservations about Kendall, and we never take his judgment lightly. But to be honest, I kinda like her. She's different from Franklin's regular hook ups.

"Yeah, I'm cool with that. She seems like a good girl. But you better be right about Kendall, Franklin." I point my bottle at him with a slight scowl.

"Yeah, I know," he replies.

10

Slightly opening my eyes, I let them roam around the room, feeling a pain in the back of my neck. Rubbing my back muscles, I take in my surroundings. Everything is dark gray with gold elements, and the room is spacious but dark with only a small lamp in the corner of the room.

Fuck, where am I?

I jerk up, sucking in a sharp, shocked breath as I place my hand in front of my mouth. My heart starts to race, goosebumps trickling down my body, while the panic in my body feels like it's about to suffocate me.

Fuck, I'm not home.

Where's Colin?

Oh my god.

I jump up, alarm rushing through my body, screaming at the top of my lungs for the person I saw last.

"Connor!" I shout, while reaching for the door handle.

I'm not surprised it's locked, so I frantically start pounding against the door.

"Connor!" I yell as loud as I can, the fear imprinted in my voice.

"Oh god. My baby. Where is my baby? Connor!! Open the damn door!" My fist hurts more with each hit to the wooden surface, but I don't stop, shouting Connor's name until finally I hear a key turning in the door. I'm ready to bolt through the door, but I run into a hard chest before I look up, my eyes wide as saucers. His big hands enclose around my upper arms while he dips his chin, looking down at me with a vicious scowl on his face.

"What?!" he barks, walking us back into the room and closing the door with his foot, his eyes never leaving mine.

For a second I'm frozen, intimidated by his piercing green eyes, my hands situated against his broad shoulders.

"Where am I?! You have to let me go!"

"Not a chance," he chuckles evilly.

"You don't understand!" My eyes start to well, and the desperation is audible in the cracking of my voice. "My baby. Where is my baby?! Is he safe?"

"Baby? What baby?"

"Connor, please. I'll give you anything. Just let me see my baby!"

"The fuck you blabbering about, girl?!" he growls, more impatient this time. When I realize he has no clue, the terror almost gives me a heart attack, my knees buckling under me as I start to cry. I don't live in a friendly neighborhood, but there is a chance someone heard my screams when Connor threw himself through my front door. The last thing I need is social services up my ass because I left my toddler unattended. Intentionally or not.

"What are you talking about, Lily? What baby?" he presses, trying to hold me up as my body goes soft in his arms.

I shake my head.

"I wasn't alone, Connor. I have a son. He was sleeping in the bedroom. He's all alone."

His brows move up in surprise as I look at him, tears streaming down my face.

"Are you fucking with me?! Is this some kind of trick?" he roars in my face while his hands squeeze my biceps in an aggressive way.

"It's not, Connor. I swear. My boy, he's still there."

"There was no one in the apartment. I checked."

"He sleeps in my closet," I explain, sobbing.

"For fuck's sake." One of his hands lets go to rub a hand over his face before his eyes land back on me. He lifts me off the floor, placing me back on the bed.

"You stay. I'll get the boy," he mutters and turns to walk away. Suddenly, he spins on the spot, grabbing my chin in a painful way.

"If you turn out to be fucking me over, I will tear you up, limb for limb. Do you get me?"

I nod, bile creeping up my throat.

"I'm not, I swear. I just want my boy. Please, I just want to know he's safe."

He lets out another grunt before roughly pushing my chin back and walking out the door.

"Stay here, and behave," he snarls, then he slams the door shut behind him, and I hear the door being locked with a key again.

I push out a breath, dropping my face in my hands, my tears streaming down like a waterfall.

How the fuck did this happen?

When Damien started hanging with Emerson Jones and his crew, I knew life was going to change, that he'd be in danger more. I didn't for a second think that Colin and I would be paying the price for it. The thought of Colin alone in his crib right now holds a tight grip around my heart, slowly suffocating me.

"Please, please, let him be okay," I whisper, my hands folded together even though I'm anything but religious. Throwing my body to the side, I rest my head against the pillow, settling in the bed as I know I can't do anything right now.

All I can do is hope, pray, and hold on. Hold on to the hope that Connor is a Wolfe. The Wolfes are more influential in this city than any other person. If Colin is not at home anymore, Connor can find him. I just need to pray my feelings didn't fool me the first time I met him. I just need to pray he's really not as bad as he seems.

11

CONNOR

Pulling my phone out of my pocket, I stomp down the stairs as I dial Reign's number.

"What's up, bro?" Reign's voice sounds tired, as if he's already in bed.

Makes sense since it's the middle of the night.

"You didn't tell me she had a kid." I storm through the front door.

"Didn't think it was relevant."

"It wasn't. Until I burst through her front door and took her."

"You what?!" he yelps.

"Yah-huh."

"You took a girl? Like kidnapped? Holding her hostage? Your own little prisoner?" I can hear the smile on his face, pissing me off a little more.

"Whatever." I click my key fob, opening my truck before climbing in.

"No-suh!" He chuckles when I deflect the question. "Franklin is going to freak."

"He already knows."

"Ha! I guess I'm no longer number one on his shitlist."

I roll my eyes at his comment, knowing that's bullshit.

"He's on yours. You're never on his, Reign." Franklin and Reign used to be the closest out of all of us four, but while Franklin is prepared to forsake his morals to keep his family safe, Reign has just too much empathy for people. Always wanting to see the good in people. When Reign found out Franklin has done more shit that can never see the light of day than Reign realized ... he freaked. Reign is loyal to a fault, but it was the day he lost respect for his big brother, and Franklin never bothered to tell him the truth about half of the shit he did. He still doesn't. Some bullshit about him wanting Reign to realize it himself.

It's a battle Killian and I are commanded to stay out of, and we have.

Most of the time.

But fuck me, it's annoying as shit.

"Whatever." I hear Reign mutter before the phone call comes through the speakers of my truck.

"Where are you going?" he asks, clearly hearing the difference in sound. "It's two a.m."

"To pick you up, dickhead. You call Killian," I order as I drive on to the road.

"What? Why? Where the fuck we going?"

"To pick up the kid."

Silence envelops us for a while, then a deep sigh echoes through the truck.

"You took the girl, but you didn't take the kid?" he asks.

"No, *you tool*. I didn't *know* there was a kid because my shithead of a brother failed to share that important part."

"The fuck, Connor? You wanted the address of her brother! I didn't think you'd take his fucking sister!"

"Well, I did," I deadpan.

"Clearly."

"Just get dressed. I'll be there in five minutes."

"Why do I have to come?"

"Because it could be a trap," I pause, "and I don't know shit about kids."

Before he can reply, I hang up, grinding my teeth together, discomfort settling inside of me. Gripping the wheel a bit tighter, I softly shake my head.

That kid better be safe and sound in his bed. I don't want to explain to any kind of authorities why he was alone in his bed with a front door busted out of its frame.

Or explain where his mother is right now.

Great move, Connor.

12

CONNOR

Killian walks out of the building with a glare on his face.

"Why the fuck are you calling me out of bed at two in the fucking morning?"

He's not really a night owl. Killian prefers his days structured and planned, meaning he wants to be in bed by eleven if he has the night off.

He takes the seat in the middle of the cab, staring at the backs of our heads.

Ignoring him, I put my truck in drive and head out to go back to Lily's apartment.

"Because Connor kidnapped a girl but wasn't aware she had a kid. Now we need to pick up the kid," Reign replies from the passenger seat with a smirk on his pretty face.

A pretty face I'd love to punch right now.

I look at Killian through the rearview mirror, his eyes wide as he slowly blinks, moving his head back and forth between the two of us, appearing astounded as he looks me straight in the eye.

I expect him to throw a small fit, but instead, he shakes his head, running a hand through his chocolate brown hair, letting out a big sigh.

"Where is she now?" Killian asks.

"At the mansion."

A frown forms on his forehead as he thinks about that answer, then he gives me a warning look, cocking his head a little.

"She better not be in my room."

"No, she's in Franklin's." Reign grins while tapping on his phone. His hoodie is covering his hair, and he's leaning against the door like a slouchy teenager, enjoying this entire situation a little too much to my taste.

"No-suh!" Killian bellows.

"Yah-huh." Reign chimes in.

"Shut up, both of you," I bark, not needing any of these tools telling me I screwed up.

I'm not a pussy. In fact, I can be a sadistic son of a bitch. I have no problem admitting that torturing Lily's little brother is going to be something I'll enjoy to the fullest. Like I've enjoyed torturing many people before him, but I draw the line with kids. I'd never hurt a kid, having seen the sick shit people do to kids. And I never would've burst through that door if I'd known her kid was in the house. I came for her little brother, and she seemed like the next best thing.

It was impulsive.

Maybe even a little bit stupid.

Not that I'd actually admit that to anyone.

But either way, I don't need them to tell me shit about it. I just need to get back to that shitty apartment and see the kid with my own eyes, to make sure he's all right.

We arrive in Roxbury a few minutes later, and I park my truck on the sidewalk in front of her building.

"There's a parking lot, right there." Reign points to a free spot in the resident parking lot.

"So?" I scowl, exiting the car while both my brothers follow me. We walk inside, stomping up the stairs, and I take a closer look at the peeled layers of paint on the wall. When I walked these stairs earlier tonight, I was pissed as a raging bull, ready to charge whatever, not giving a flying fuck who was coming in my way. But now I look at it a bit differently. The wooden stairs make a cracking sound under my feet, and I seriously wonder if this is a good place to live with a toddler.

"What a shithole," I mutter.

"Do we have a plan?" Killian softly asks, walking behind me.

"Get the kid and get the fuck out."

"Okay, Captain Obvious. What if the kid is not there?" Reign asks cynically.

"Then you go and fetch your laptop, and find out where he is so we can get him."

"Sure, let Reign fix it," he replies with a whiny voice like a ten-year-old.

I don't want to think about the possibilities of the kid not being there. It's only been two hours, and he's a kid. They sleep through everything, right? I wasn't that loud, was I?

"Jesus fuck, Connor," Killian mutters when we reach the top floor and turn to the right to get to Lily's apartment.

Okay, maybe I was loud.

I look at the front door, hanging crooked in its frame, splinters all over the floor.

"How did you get her out the door without any neighbors calling the cops on your ass?" Killian grabs the door to try and hang it a bit straighter so he can fully push it open.

"Look around. I don't think anyone in this building really cares. They probably hear gunshots or men beating up their wives on a daily basis."

"A screaming woman didn't make any heads pop out of their front doors?" Killian glances over his shoulder as we walk into the parlor while Reign stays in the hallway to keep an eye out.

"Who says she was screaming?" I keep a straight face.

"She didn't scream?"

"It was more of a screech," I shrug.

He rolls his eyes at me.

"Whatever, let's grab the kid."

"Yeah, she said he was in the bedroom closet."

We make our way to the tiny bedroom and open up the dark closet. The space is completely converted into the smallest nursery I've ever seen, with a changing table on the left and his crib on the right. I look for a light switch before flipping it, then stretch my neck to anxiously look for the little boy.

I let out a sigh of relief when I see a toddler, sound asleep in his dinosaur pajamas, holding a teddy bear against his chest. His blanket is tucked over his waist, and the relaxed muscles in his face tell me he didn't hear a thing from my loud entrance earlier tonight.

Thank fuck.

"Now what?" Killian hisses, trying to not wake up the kid.

"I don't know," I whisper shout back at him. "Do I look like I know what to do with a kid?"

As if he can feel our presence, he stirs in his bed, slowly opening his eyes. He blinks a few times, waking up, before a frightened look appears on his face.

"Shit," I mutter right before he starts to cry as loud as a damn siren.

"Good job, Connor." Killian glares.

"The fuck did I do?" I give him an incredulous look before lowering myself as I squat down, trying to put him at ease by leveling with him. "Hey, buddy. Sssh. It's okay. We're not going to hurt you."

"Mamaaaaa!" he shouts even harder, his cheeks turning bright red.

"If he's going to keep screaming like that, people are going to wake up. What's his name?"

"Uh, I don't know," I admit, not sure what to do here.

"Come on, Connor!"

"Okay, okay, let me think!" I grunt, getting back up while pinching the bridge of my nose to ignore the deafening sound of the toddler.

Who the fuck knew these tiny fuckers could scream this damn loud?

"What the fuck are you two doing? He's going to wake up the entire neighborhood," Reign scolds, walking into the bedroom, pushing Killian to the side, and placing himself in front of the crib.

"Colin!" I bellow, remembering what Lily called him when she begged me to go get him. "Lily mentioned his name was Colin."

Colin's frantic cry tones down to a quiet sob when he

hears his name, while Reign gives me a mocking look, cocking his eyebrow.

"She's 'Lily' now?"

"What? I know the girl."

"Wait? What?" Killian pulls my shoulder back so he can look me in the eye, a judgmental look written all over his face. "You know the girl?"

"Slept with her a few years back." I shrug.

Reign chuckles, then lowers himself next to Colin, offering him his famous smile.

"Hey, little man. Are you Colin?"

Colin still weeps a little, sniffing his tears away while his eyes remain focused on Reign.

"Really, you're really Colin? *The* Colin?"

Colin nods.

"Wowww, I've heard so much about you! Your mommy told us you are a super kid. Is that true?" A beaming smile appears on Colin's tear-stained face, and the corner of my mouth curls up a bit, amazed at how good my brother is at this.

"Supa kid!" Colin says, pointing his little finger at his chest.

Reign lets out a relieved sigh, excitement dripping off his face as he grips his heart.

"Wowww, I'm so happy to meet you! I'm Reign." He offers his hand, and Colin grabs it before Reign softly shakes it.

"Colin, your mommy had to go to our house because we need her help, and she asked us to bring you to her."

"Mommy you house?" he asks.

"Yes, Mommy is at our house. You see, she had to help us with something in our castle."

"Castle?" Colin's eyebrows shoot up in amazement, and I hear Killian snicker behind me.

"Yeah! These are my big brothers, and we all live in a castle outside of the city." He points his thumb at us, and Colin looks at us with a wary look. "I know they are a bit scary, but I'm not scary, right?"

Colin shakes his head as his body seems to relax a bit more, though his hands are still tightly clasped around his teddy bear.

"That's what I thought. So what do you say, little man? You're gonna come with me and check out my castle? Go and see your mommy?"

Colin nods his head, glancing at Killian and me, this time no longer with a cautious look in his eyes.

"Who's that?" Reign points at the gray teddy bear in his hand.

"Boot," he answers, cuddling the bear even tighter, with a pleased look on his face.

"He's going to come with us?"

"Yah-huh!" A slight frown creases his little forehead as he shoots Reign a look that basically says 'duh.'

Killian and I chuckle, appreciating the little man's attitude.

"All right, Boots can come," Reign says before holding out his arms. "Come here, superkid. Let's go."

Colin stands up in his crib, lifting his arms so Reign can pick him up, placing him on his waist like he's been doing this his entire life.

I blink at him, a little impressed by his skills with the toddler.

"What?" His eyes find mine, giving me a bored look.

"Where did you learn that?"

He huffs, a smile on his face that doesn't completely match his eyes.

"Foster care. Where else? Shall we go?" He doesn't wait for my reply, walking past us, and I press my lips to small slits, hating that answer.

"I should've known," I mutter before I follow my little brother out of the bedroom.

13

My desperate tears dried up after about thirty minutes, and I've been staring at the ceiling for the last hour, my mind going a hundred miles a minute.

Before you become a mom, a lot of mothers tell you how your life will change the second you hold that tiny bundle of new life in your arms. That you'll become a different person, and from that day on, your mind will be wired differently.

I'm no exception.

When I found out I was pregnant, I was scared as fuck. I'd been taking care of my little brother since his early teens, but taking care of a baby was a whole different game. Damien had been pretty self-sufficient as long as I made sure there was food on the table every day. I had a good job, so that hadn't been an issue. Luckily, he never gave me a lot of trouble, being the good kid that he was. But taking care of a newborn frightened me something fierce. At the time, I would've rather thrown myself into a snake pit.

But the moment Colin landed on my chest, that fear vanished into thin air, and all that was left was love. So much love, it's ridiculous. I didn't even know I was capable of loving someone that much, and in the first few weeks, it was overwhelming. There were times I burst into tears simply because the love I felt for that tiny human was all-consuming.

And soon, a different fear crept up on me.

The fear of losing him.

The fear of him getting hurt.

Today my worst fear became reality, and the uncertainty is making it wicked hard for my heart to keep beating while I wait for any news from Connor. I try to comfort myself with the knowledge that the Wolfes rule the city. If the authorities have found him, I'm pretty sure the Wolfes will be able to get him back, but the thought of Colin being alone in our apartment tears me up inside.

Not to mention the fact that I have no clue if the Wolfes are against harming children to get what they want. I like to believe they don't. But I slept with Connor *once*. It's not exactly enough criteria to claim to really know a person.

Finally, I hear the key being placed in the lock, and I jump up, bolting towards the door.

"Is he okay?" I ask, my voice laced with panic.

Before Connor can answer, someone I recognize as one of his brothers walks in with Colin on his hip, a glowing smile on Colin's face, when he sees me.

"Oh, my baby!" I cry, pulling him into my arms. My hand presses his little head against my body while my arm holds him in a tight grip, cradling him as I start to sob once more.

Closing my eyes, I breathe him in as I dip my nose into his soft blond hair.

"Thank God, you are all right, baby," I whisper in his ear when my heart finally starts to settle down, relief calming my nerves.

Planting a kiss on his hair, I try to wipe away the tears before he brings his head up, gripping my cheeks with his small hands.

"Mommy sad?"

"Yes." I smile. "Mommy was missing you."

"Colin here!" he cheers, throwing his hands in the air.

I hear chuckles behind us, and I turn around, looking at the three men staring at us.

Connor stands in the middle, his hands in his pockets, his broad shoulders looking huge in his white t-shirt. The look on his face is straight as ever when our eyes lock. Any amusement he may have expressed because of Colin completely gone.

"We brought him some stuff. And you." The one with a black leather jacket on holds up my duffle bag.

"Thank you." I push the words past my lips, a little annoyed.

Now that I have my child safely in my arms, the anger is taking over and a glare forms on my face.

"Is this how you usually treat people? Knock them over the head and kidnap them?"

Connor licks his lips, folding his arms in front of his body.

"You offered, babe."

"Don't *babe* me," I snarl, rocking Colin in my arms, his head now resting on my shoulder. "I asked you to not hurt my brother. Nobody said anything about kidnapping me and leaving my child alone in the middle of the night, you asshole."

Connor tilts his head a little towards the man on his right. His hair is a lighter brown, a little longer than the man on Connor's left. He's wearing a hoodie and has a kind smile on his face. He's really handsome, looking like a little Casanova.

I'm assuming he's the youngest brother.

"Reign, can you please take care of Colin for another minute? Lily and I are going to need a little talk."

I quickly take a step back.

"Hell no. You're not taking my child away again."

"As you can see, my brother knows how to handle kids. I think he will be fine." A sarcastic tone is audible in his voice, pissing me off even more.

"I will cut you up piece by piece if you come any closer." I might not stand a chance, but I'll protect my own even if it kills me, and there is no chance in hell Colin is leaving this room without me.

"You and what army?" Connor smirks.

"Look, everyone is on edge. Let's just calm down. I know you don't know us. I'm Reign," Casanova introduces himself, offering me a smile with his hands up in a placating way, clearly trying to put me at ease. "That's Killian," He points at the other guy who offers me a little nod in acknowledgment. "You've met Connor."

"I really wish I hadn't," I counter while rolling my eyes.

"Yeah, I get that. He's a bit of a caveman. I actually call him the ruffian," Reign snickers, putting a small smile on my face.

"Seems wicked fitting," I say, glancing at Connor, who's now glaring at me with a feral look in his eyes.

I remember how he intimidated me the first time I met him, staring me down with that savage gaze he has. My heart starts racing when he puts his focus on me, but I've never really been scared of him. Not like the rest of the city is. The ferocious, simple way he communicated, bluntly telling me what he wanted, turned me on more than anything. I loved the fact that he just went straight for the bullseye, not wasting any time seducing me.

"How about I just go into the bathroom with Colin?" Reign suggests, pointing at the door behind me. "I'll freshen up Colin. Killian can go and find a toothbrush and something we can put on one side of the bed so he won't fall out, and when the two of you are done, we can all go to bed. What do you say?"

I look at Reign, thinking about his request, eyeing the bathroom door before turning my head back to Connor.

"You better not pull anything."

"The fuck? He's suggesting it, so why are you looking at me?"

"Because you're the one who hit me over the head."

Killian and Reign both press their lips together to suppress their smiles before Killian waves and leaves the room without saying a word. Reign approaches me, holding out his arms to take Colin while he gives me a charming wink.

"I'll keep him safe, don't worry. We are not going anywhere."

I press another kiss on Colin's head as I let Reign pull him out of my arms.

Watching them go into the bathroom, I fold my arms in front of my chest before turning towards Connor, popping a hip in a defiant stance.

"You didn't have this much spunk the first time I met you," he mutters. "At least not *with* your clothes on."

He closes the door behind him before pressing his back

against the wood, a smug look on his face as he mimics my stance.

"You didn't take me by force the first time I met you."

"Shame, sounds like fun."

"Are you flirting with me?"

"Maybe?"

"You are unbelievable." I give him an incredulous look.

"*That's* what you said the last time I saw you."

"Will you shut up? This is not funny. You took me against my will."

He cocks his head a little.

"Not really. You *did* actually offer yourself up."

"I thought you were going to hurt my brother!" I hiss, taking a step forward in frustration. "Besides, if I was here of my own free will, I would've walked out of my apartment myself. But you knocked me out like I'm a fucking coconut."

"A coconut?" An amused grin appears on his face as he takes a few steps closer, closing the distance between us until he's right in front of me. He's peering down at me like the feral animal that he is, that hypnotizing glint in his eyes I remember oh so well. His masculine scent enters my nose when he gets into my personal space, making me gulp at the potent mix of a sweet and citrusy cologne.

Looking up at him, my heart starts to race, but not out of fear. Memories of that one night start to rush into my head as flashbacks, making it hard for me to concentrate on holding my own against this wall of a man. My hands are desperate to reach out, to feel his shoulders under my palms, and automatically, my eyes dart to his lips.

When he notices, he casually licks his lips, then places two fingers under my chin, forcing me to look into his eyes.

"I can crack you open like a coconut. *Easy.*"

I gasp for air, my mind having a hard time keeping it together as I push him off me to create some distance.

"Stop! You sound like a psychopath."

He rapidly grabs my arm and yanks me back into his hard chest.

"Didn't stop you the first time. Do you still remember? Because I do." I can feel his breath fanning my face, and my eyes grow wide as his free hand lands on my shoulder, his fingers slowly moving up towards my neck in a scorching way. "I still remember how you looked like an angel in your tight jeans and white top. And I remember how your wings came off the second you landed on the bed." He moves his face closer, our noses only an inch apart as he cups the front of my neck. "How you looked like a little devil beneath my fingers when I wrapped them around your slender neck." His eyes slowly turn a dark green, and a longing feeling develops between my thighs.

I stay quiet, torn between wanting to slap him for his arrogance and wanting to kiss him.

"I hate you," I finally mutter after a few moments of silence as we stare into each other's eyes.

The corner of his mouth curls.

"You mean you're horny."

"I'm as dry as the Sahara desert."

"I can feel your pulse. It's talking to me. Wanna know what it says?" he whispers.

He doesn't wait for my reply as he brings his mouth flush with my ear.

"It says you're as wet as Niagara Falls."

He roughly lets go of me, slightly pushing me back before he struts over to the bathroom.

"You can come out now, Reign," Connor says, knocking on the door.

A little flustered about his last move, I hold his gaze, my eyes shooting daggers at him while I wait for Reign to walk out with Colin.

"That's what you wanted? To fuck with my head?"

"No. That was just for fun. But you better tone it down a notch before I make you a lot less comfortable than you are right now." The features on his face harden, the hungry look in his eyes fading as he glares at me.

Realizing the situation I'm in, I grab Colin from Reign's arms before turning my focus back on Connor with a pleading look.

"Are you going to hurt my brother?"

"Yes," he says without hesitation.

"Please don't, Connor."

He clenches his jaw, the rage that's now washing his face making me brace myself for whatever is coming. He glances at Colin, acknowledging his proximity before he opens his mouth.

"Don't act like you know me. You don't," he growls intimidatingly, even though his volume never rises. "Your brother fucked up. He's going to get what's coming to him."

He storms out of the room, leaving me alone with Reign just as Killian walks back in with a steel gate in his hands.

"The fuck did you find that?" Reign asks his brother.

"The garage."

"Damien is just a kid." I shake my head, my eyes catching Reign's, shooting me another smile before he and Killian set up the gate against the right side of the bed. It looks a lot like prison bars, and I wonder what the fuck it originally was.

"Just get some sleep." Reign lays a comforting hand on the small of my back. "Bye, little man. I'll see you in the morning, okay? Fist bump." He holds his fist up for Colin, and Colin places his fist against his with a big grin on his face.

"Good night," Reign says to me before both of them walk out, and I hear the door being locked again.

"Well, I guess we are going to stay here for a while, little buddy."

"Castle, Mommy!" He opens his arms to show me how big it is.

"It's a castle? We're sleeping in a castle?" My mouth forms an 'O' as he nods his head in excitement. "Well, then you must be a prince!"

"Colin, prince. Mommy princess." He wraps his little arms around my neck, giving me a tight hug.

"Oh, that's wicked sweet. But now it's time for bed, little prince."

"Sleep with Mommy?" His eyes hold a spark, and I let out a chuckle, thinking about how we need to be kidnapped before I will finally let him sleep in my own bed, telling him no since the day he was born.

"Yes, it's your lucky night. You're a prince, sleeping in a castle, and you get to sleep next to Mommy."

He claps his hands while I walk us over to the bed, settling us in.

It's his lucky night.

Not sure if it's mine, though.

14

CONNOR

I walk up the stairs after a long day, holding a tray in my hands with supper on it for Lily and Colin. I had to work all day, making all the rounds, so Reign offered to keep an eye on them during the day. We don't take a lot of people against their will, but when we do, I normally don't give a shit. I just want to punch until I get what I want, and let's be honest, it's way more effective.

But Lily and her little boy are a bit different. Even though I stand by my decision, I kinda feel bad for keeping a mother with her child against their will. If I knew Colin had been home, I would've staked out the place first and waited for Damien to get home.

Giving a knock first, I put the key in the lock before I open the door, being met by a set of blue eyes and a beaming smile that falls when she looks up at me from the bed.

"Oh, it's you."

"Sorry, Prince Charming couldn't make it," I mock.

"So he sent the *beast?*"

"It was good enough once." I place the tray on the dresser, then plant my ass against it to face her, crossing my arms in front of my body.

Colin is playing with some blocks on the bed with Lily sitting next to him, a book in her lap.

"Where did you get that?" I nudge my chin to the book.

"Reign gave it to me." She eyes me with a glare, probably hoping looks can kill, and I will drop dead any second now.

Tough luck, babe. Many have tried, many have failed.

With a sigh leaving her lips, she gets up, her small hips swaying as she heads towards me, stopping in front of me to look at the tray.

"You made this?"

I glance at the two plates. One with some vegetables, potatoes, and a piece of steak. The other is a plate of spaghetti Bolognese.

"I don't cook, babe." I lean in, my voice husky and deep. "I only *eat* out."

I notice her chest heaving at my suggestive words as she continues staring at me. The look on her face reminds me of the night I tempted her into my bed, a compelling mix of fear and intrigue, as if she was scared to trust me with her body, yet she was too captivated to make me stop.

"I just wanted to go to Dunks, but Reign insisted that isn't a meal for a toddler." I pull my head back, trying to put her a bit more at ease.

"Reign is right," she says, grabbing a piece of potato and popping it into her mouth, her eyes never leaving mine. Slowly, her tongue darts out to lick her upper lip, making my balls tighten in my jeans. Seconds seem to tick by, neither of us averting our attention as tension builds between us. I loudly breathe through my nose, doing my best to not press my lips against hers, knowing she's thinking about the same thing as I am.

When her eyes move down to my lips, I part mine, waiting for her to close the distance between us, my cock growing as the moment stretches. Instead, she takes another piece of potato from the plate, placing it in her mouth, then turns around to walk away from me.

"When is Reign coming back?" she casually asks, defiantly glancing over her shoulder.

Stunned, I swiftly grab her upper arm, yanking her back with a vicious scowl on my face.

"You got a thing for my brother now?" My jaw clenches in aggravation.

Her face matches my rage as she eyes my hand on her arm.

"At least *he* treats me right."

"I brought you supper, didn't I?"

"That's just human decency. Besides, you can't trade me for my brother if I'm dead because you didn't feed me. You don't get points for that."

"Who says I'm trying to earn points?"

"You're trying to do something," she states.

"Don't get ahead of yourself, babe. As soon as your brother surrenders himself, you and your kid will be free to go. Until then, I'm not doing shit."

"Whatever. Can you let me go now?"

I let go of her arm, and she walks back to Colin.

"Colin, are you hungry?"

"No, Mommy," he responds.

He's adorable, with his puffy cheeks and blond hair clearly inherited from his mother. His innocent face reminds me of Reign when he was little, trying to keep up with

Franklin and me. I protected my little brothers with every-thing I had, and the moments when Kilian and Reign played without a care in the world are the most vivid memories in my head.

Colin stares at the blocks in concentration, the tip of his tongue stuck between his lips as he tries to build a house or something. The determined look on his face makes me believe he's going to be a fearless troublemaker and notorious playboy when he's older, a thought that brings a smile to my face.

When he catches me watching him, he gives me a cautious look from the corner of his eyes, and a bummed feeling showers my body.

I'm not like Reign.

I'm not good with people, let alone kids. When I was younger, I learned to survive by being the strongest, not by charming people. I took care of my brothers by keeping them safe in the most primal form there is, making sure I got all the punches so they wouldn't. That's my skill. If you need strength, I'm your guy.

"It's not you," Lily explains when she sees the disappoint-ment on my face.

"It's okay."

Her face softens a little.

"He's wary of all new men, not just you." She ruffles his hair with a loving look. "How long are you going to keep us here?"

Feeling accommodating, I reply, "Not long. I need to find your brother and get Emerson Jones out of the picture."

She stays quiet, looking at Colin before she gets up and motions me to the balcony to keep us out of hearing range of Colin.

"Are you going to kill him?" She leans over the railing, staring into the trees surrounding the estate, and I notice her eyes start to shine with tears.

"Which one?"

"My brother. I don't give a shit about Emerson Jones," she snaps, giving me an incredulous look.

"Yes," I admit.

"Why, Connor?" She cries out with a desperate tone in her voice. "He's just a kid who got caught up with the wrong people. He's just running with them. Nothing more than a soldier, you know that."

"I don't know how much you know, but he's not just a soldier."

"Yes, he is! He's only doing it to give Colin and me a better life. He's only doing it for the money, going on runs and all that bullshit."

I crowd her space, growling.

"Is that what you think?" I ask, grabbing her chin in a tight grip. "That he's just a soldier? Going on some drug runs? That may be how it started once upon a time, but your brother crossed that line a while ago. Have you heard about the boy who died this weekend? His name was Nigel. I plucked him from the streets a few years ago. He trusted me. His *mother* trusted me. Trusted me to keep him safe. And I did. I kept him out of the most dangerous situations, making sure he could come home to his mother every single night. And then he died on my brother's *birthday*. In our home. His blood spilled all over our dining room downstairs," I grunt, pointing to the floor.

"My brother was just there." A tear stains her cheek, and my forehead creases in confusion.

"Your brother killed him, Lily."

Her eyes widen in shock.

Her head frantically starts to shake, forcing me to let go of her, and she takes a step back with her hands in front of her mouth.

"No," she gasps.

"Yeah."

"No. No. No. Not my brother. He wouldn't do that. He wouldn't kill someone."

"He would if he's ordered to kill." I watch how she grabs the railing, her legs buckling underneath her as she drops onto the cold concrete floor. Her eyes look as though she's in a trance as she keeps shaking her head, staring at the floor. A minute passes, and a heavy feeling forms in my gut the longer I watch her sob on the floor.

"Get up, Lily," I order, not sure what to do right now. Moving towards her, I crouch down.

"Hey, come on. Get up. Colin is inside." The name of her little boy seems to snap her out of it, and I help her up, holding her steady on her upper arms as I examine her face.

"Did he really do that?" she sniffs.

Seeing her like this does more to me than I expected, making me feel like a shithead for making her cry.

"I'm sorry," I tell her, even though I'm not sure what I'm sorry for.

She keeps crying, and I want to make it stop. I want to put her at ease before I leave her alone again; the thought of her crying her heart out with Colin next to her makes me restless.

"Look, don't worry about it, okay? Nothing is happening anytime soon. Just play with Colin, and get some rest."

Swallowing her tears away, she looks up at me, and I wipe one away with my thumb.

"Promise me I will get to see him before you hurt him?" The fierce look she once showed me sparkles in her eyes, sending a pang to my heart.

There she is.

I know I can't make these promises, but I don't want to upset her more, knowing she probably needs a minute to wrap her head around what I just told her.

"I promise," I lie, instantly annoyed with myself.

15

Four days.

  That's how long I've been stuck in this room. Reign spends breakfast and lunch with us, and it's the highlight of our days, while at night, Connor is the one who brings us our food. He always stays for a few minutes before he leaves us again, but every night he seems a little less grouchy.

Progress, I guess?

Even Colin seems to be opening up to him, greeting him when he arrives, showing him the things he made during the day. Reign gave him some coloring books, Legos, and dinosaurs to play with so we don't have to watch TV all day. And yesterday, he made a drawing for Connor with one of those weird stick people kids love to draw. It's clear Connor doesn't easily melt, but I could've sworn I saw the corner of his lip curl up a bit.

Reign left after breakfast, and it's nine in the morning when I decide I want a shower.

Walking towards the door, I start slamming the wood to grab Reign's attention, knowing he's walking around the house somewhere.

"Reign!" I call out a few times, listening for any movement every couple of seconds. "Reign! Can you come up, please?"

I open my mouth to call him once more when I hear the key slide into the lock, and the door opens.

"Morning," Connor grunts as his eyes shamelessly move up and down my body. I'm wearing some gray sweats and a crop top I found in the duffle bag they brought me, and suddenly, I'm completely aware of the fact that I'm not wearing a bra. My nipples turn as hard as rocks when he keeps staring at me with an appreciative smile while heat is running up my neck, making me blush like a damn tomato. Embarrassment hits me before I suck in a breath to pull myself together, putting up an act of indifference.

I snap my fingers in front of his face.

"My eyes are up here. Where is Reign?" I wrap my arms around my body, trying to cover up my now aching breasts.

Damn you, Connor.

"He needed to head back to his apartment for the rest of the day. Do you need anything?"

"Yeah, a shower."

"Okay?" He gives me a confused look. "So go shower. Or do you need me to help you?" A suggestive look appears on his face, hitting me right in between my legs.

I roll my eyes at his comment, keeping up my stance, though I can't deny the amused feeling inside of me.

"No, you tool. I need you to watch Colin."

The lustful look in his eyes is quickly replaced with a fuzzy glimmer.

"What do you mean? He's playing. He'll be fine."

"He's two," I deadpan.

"So?"

"So you can't leave a two-year-old by themselves."

"Why not?" he asks, confused.

"Because he's *two*."

Giving him a knowing look, I turn around.

"Colin, Mommy is going to shower. Connor is going to stay with you, okay?"

He hums in agreement, and I look at a stunned Connor.

"I don't know how to handle a kid. What do I do with him?"

"Make sure he doesn't get hurt." I shrug, chuckling when I look at the panic in his eyes.

The man throws punches every chance he gets on a daily basis and is nicknamed *the beast*, but he's scared of a two-year-old.

"I'll be right there." I point at the bathroom door. "I'll be back in twenty minutes."

"What if he needs to poop? Or throw up?"

"He's two, not born last week."

"So? I don't know shit about kids."

"Well, don't say *chips* for one. Just play with him. Or at least make sure he doesn't hurt himself. I'll be right back." Before he can say anything else, I strut into the bathroom, locking the door behind me.

I take my clothes off and get into the shower, the warm water relaxing the muscles in my back as I think about the man outside the door, while a huge grin forms on my face. Maybe it's mean to throw him to the sharks like that. I could've waited until Reign was back since he's a natural with kids. But this seems like the perfect opportunity to soften up the growling beast. He's not as scary and hateful as he was when he crashed through my front door, doing his best to not scare Colin with his permanent scowl. Which for some fucked-up reason makes me think of all the faces he made while he was thrusting into me. There were a lot of them, and every single one of them still turns me on when they cross my mind. Now that he's stormed his way into my days for the last week, I've been having vivid dreams about that night. The way his fingers would explore my entire body. The way he spanked my ass cheeks until they burned, leaving his palm as an imprint on my fair skin. The way his kisses on my neck turned me into jelly. He was dominant and rough in the most delicious way, and I enjoyed every second of it. My thoughts stir a longing between my legs, and without hesitation, I bring my hand down, then softly start to rub the skin around my sensitive nub.

Closing my eyes, I rest my forehead against the tiles while the water keeps running down my body. A soft moan leaves my lips every single time I rub my clit between my index and middle finger, forming a perfect V that gives the right amount of friction with every move. I bring my fingers up to my mouth, wetting them some more with my slick saliva before dipping them back down. The tips of my fingers slip over me like the softness of a tongue, and instantly, I imagine a set of green eyes looking up at me while he's settled between my legs. His lips are wrapped over my clit, and the hunger in his eyes makes me bite my lip as I keep applying pressure around the bundle of nerves, softly stroking my flesh. A deep flutter forms in my stomach when I envision Connor's hands digging into my ass as he presses me closer to his mouth, eating me whole like I'm breakfast. I spread my legs some more, giving myself more access when I plunge two fingers inside of me, pretending it's Connor who's licking my aching folds. My nipples are as hard as rocks, and I pinch one with my other hand, a whimper leaving my lips because of the burning sting. My fingers start to move more rapidly as I chase my climax as if my life depends on it, and I start panting uncontrollably. I can feel the muscles tighten in my ass, my legs starting to spasm when I try to suppress the wail that's in the back of my throat as my orgasm rushes through me without mercy. My toes curl when the high of my pleasure erupts inside of me, struggling to stay on my feet while I ride it out.

Closing my eyes, I try to catch my breath with my hands pressed against the wall until the muscles in my body relax again, the water rejuvenating me.

Damn, I should start the day like this more often.

A smile tugs on the corner of my mouth, and with a ray of sunshine planted above my head, I wash my hair, then brush my teeth before moving on to the rest of my body. My good mood is audible in the song I'm humming as I put on some fresh clothes. I wrap my towel over my wet hair before I walk out of the bathroom, my feet freezing on the spot when I look at the sight in front of me.

"Vroom vroooooooom. EEEP. Truck crashing. Truck crashing. EEEP. Boom!" Connor is holding Colin between his hands in a horizontal position before pushing him against the pillows on the bed while Colin laughs enthusiastically. When Connor's eyes catch me, he stops, though the smile on his face stays in place, warming my heart. I bite my lip, enjoying the image in front of me when Connor spins Colin in his hands, then places him on the bed with a small thud.

"There's Mommy. I'll see you later, all right big guy?" He ruffles his hair, and Colin gives him a beaming smile.

"Conno play vroom vroom?"

"Yes, big guy. I'll play some more with you later today. I have to get some work done now. You be nice to your mom, okay?"

"Kay," Colin replies with a grin then grabs his dinosaur.

I fold my arms in front of my body with a smug grin on my face.

When I left Colin with him, I expected my boy to pull down Connor's walls a little, hoping I'd see a bit more of the man I suspect he is underneath that brick layer, because let's be honest, who can resist a wicked cute two-year-old? But this exceeds all my expectations.

Connor turns his body towards me, sauntering my way with a hungry look in his eyes, his playful stance gone.

"You enjoyed your shower?" he asks, closing the distance between us. I stand my ground, nodding while I feel my heart pound loudly against my chest, still pressing my teeth into my lower lip. When he gets into my personal space, he pushes his fingers against my belly, slowly backing me up against the wall. His hand cups my chin as he starts to drag my lower lip out of my teeth, making me part my lips when he comes closer.

"You know," he begins, the sound of his baritone voice vibrating against my lashes. "I still remember the look on your face after I made you come."

His index finger creeps along my jaw, slowly moving down my neck. I swallow thickly, the ache between my legs starting to burn once more.

"How your cheeks flush with a perfect pink shade. That

hazy glimmer covering your beautiful blue eyes. Your plump lips swollen from biting so hard."

The tension rises between us when he keeps staring into my eyes with that hungry gaze, waiting for me to say anything while he slowly moves his finger to my collarbone, brushing the soft skin at a blistering pace.

"Were you thinking about me?" he questions in a whisper without shame. "Were you imagining my lips sucking on your clit like a lollipop? Were you pretending it was my fingers diving into your pussy?"

"Connor!" I finally hiss, glancing over my shoulder to look at Colin, hoping he needs my attention, but he's still occupied with his dinosaur.

"Don't look at him." He nudges my chin to turn my focus back on him. "Look at me." His hand digs into my hips, and he squeezes demandingly as he leans in, his lips flush with my ear. I can feel his breath fanning the sensitive skin on my neck, and I close my eyes to keep it together. "It's okay. I thought of you last night when I jerked myself off. Imagining it was your lips wrapped around my cock. You still make me wonder how that would feel, you know. But next time you make yourself come in my shower, you better invite me. I like my breakfast wet." He gently scrapes his teeth over my earlobe, making me gasp for air before he pushes off of me, taking a step back with a smug grin on his face.

Automatically, my hands reach to my ear, feeling the place his mouth was last while I give him an incredulous look. My mind wants me to smack him over the head, asking him where he gets the nerve to talk to me like that. But my heart and my pussy are wondering why I'm not begging him for more. Begging him to finish what I started in the shower.

"You're louder than you think, babe." He winks before he

turns around, walking towards the door. "I'll see you later, Colin!"

"Bye, Conno!" Colin waves as we both watch Connor walk out the door, leaving me pressed against the wall, completely stunned.

What the fuck?

16

CONNOR

I look at the clouded sky, breathing in the fresh air,
wondering if it's going to rain soon.

I've been dreading this day.

I doubt anyone is really 'good' at funerals, but I suck at
them. I have the empathy of a doorknob, and even though
I'm the one who's desperate to avenge Nigel's death, I also
know that crying won't get me anywhere. When all four of us
went to visit Nigel's mother and siblings to offer our condo-
lences, I let the woman cry in my arms.

Like what else was I going to do? I didn't mind, the
woman just lost her kid for crying out loud, but did it make
me feel awkward as fuck? Of course it did.

I'm Connor Wolfe.

I'm the Wolfe who doesn't offer comfort nor show empathy. I'm the one who takes action. The one who doesn't bat
an eye if someone needs to be tortured, killed, and vanished.

And most of the time, I prefer all of that. It's Franklin
who holds empathy. And it's Reign who will give it to you in

bucket-loads. Killian will give you a pat on the shoulder unless he's convinced you deserve more, but at least that part feels natural to him.

Whenever someone is crying, I just want to find the guy who caused it.

Today being no exception.

"You ready for this?" Killian asks as we walk into the cemetery.

I roll my eyes.

"I'm not some fragile doll."

"No shit, tool," he mocks. "Just checking."

We line up around the casket hanging above the open grave, standing across from the family seated next to it. All three of my brothers are wearing black suits, dressed for the occasion, while I changed my regular casual wear for a black dress shirt and some black jeans, covered by my black leather jacket.

What can I say? I don't do suits.

I can feel eyes staring at us as we all clasp our hands together in front of our bodies, holding our heads high with straight faces.

"Reign, did you find Damien Johnson?" Franklin asks in a hushed tone, only audible to us four.

"He's either dead, left the city, vanished into thin air, or buried inside of a whore in a cellar or something," he replies, resulting in a snicker from Killian.

"What are the chances he's dead?" I ask.

Killian clears his throat.

"You want a truthful answer?"

"Yes," Franklin chimes in.

"Ninety-nine percent." A grunt leaves my lips before he continues to explain why. "He wasn't part of Emerson's crew for long. Rumor on the street is he freaked out after that command, telling Emerson he wanted out. My guess? Emerson gave him a permanent one."

My mind goes to Lily's bright blue eyes and the fact that she's still thinking her brother will come home eventually. I've been thinking he's dead since the first time Reign told me he couldn't find him, but I'm not telling Lily until I've found his body.

"Find him, Reign. Dead or alive."

"Still working on it, but I need someone from Emerson's crew to give me a direction to look in. We haven't found anyone who fits the right description other than those errand boys who make his rounds every night," Reign explains, a hint of disgust in his voice.

"Just give me someone. I'll get all the information they have."

"Well, that's the issue," Killian chides. "We haven't figured out who's worth pulling from the streets yet. If we pull the wrong guy and he goes missing, the rest will be warned, and they will start operating differently, making it impossible to find someone else."

"Fine," Franklin says before I can sputter in protest. "Keep eyes on all their routes. I want to know where Emerson Jones is at all times. Kendall still needs to deal with this motherfucker, and I don't want her to be ambushed by one of his crew when we're not looking."

"We doubled our crew. The Carrillos sent us two dozen of their team to guard the mansion. Kendall will be safe. We just need the right time to end this," Killian retorts, sucking in a deep breath then tilting his head a bit to look at me. "We *will* end this, Connor."

The music starts to play, and Nigel's mom starts to sob

uncontrollably in her hands. Her twelve-year-old daughter throws a comforting arm around her. The sight creates a lump in my stomach, making me let out a deep sigh. Frustration flushes my neck with heat, and I gnash my teeth together in aggravation.

No mother should bury her own child.

"I know," I mutter.

Just not fucking soon enough for my liking.

17

My hands dig into Colin's side, tickling him as his tiny body squirms in delight.

"Did you just say no to Mommy kisses? Are you sure about that?" I growl jokingly.

He tries to escape my grasp, squirming away from me, and I let him until he's far enough for me to grab him by his ankles, only to drag him back to do it all over again. It's his favorite game right before bed, and even though we've been cooped up in this room for almost a week now, I try my best to keep him happy and maintain a routine. It helps that Reign gives me a second to breathe at least once a day, entertaining Colin while I take an extra-long shower or relax in a hot bath. But today I've been more worried about Damien than the days before.

I'd expected us to be traded for my brother after a day or two, but five days have passed, and I have heard nothing about a trade or where my brother is, for that matter. When Connor took me, he also took my phone, giving me no way to contact my brother. I know Connor hasn't got him, he would've told me.

He's been different the last three days.

He checks on us every single night, wishing Colin a good night and asking how our day was. I mostly glare at him in response, because let's be honest, we are nothing more than birds in a cage right now. A pretty and luxurious cage, yes, but a cage, nonetheless. But it only results in a chuckle from him, even though I swear I can see a hint of regret in his eyes.

It makes me wonder if he regrets whatever he's going to do in the next few days or the fact that he took us in the first place. We banter, and I do my best to give him a hard time, but since he started flirting with me, it's hard to stay mad at him when all I really want to do is kiss him.

To wrap my legs around his neck.

As if he can hear my thoughts, a knock grabs my attention, and I look up when the door opens. The man who occupies my dirty mind is standing in the doorframe, his shoulder pressed against the wood with his arms folded in front of his body. I part my lips, appreciating how his body is snuggled tightly by his t-shirt. He gives me a smirk when he sees me ogling him and licks his lip, the tip of his tongue dragging slowly over the scar on it.

Damn, he's sexy.

"Hey," I offer with a coy smile.

"Hey."

Confused by his visit, I look at the time on my wrist.

"It's four o'clock."

"I know."

"You usually come in around seven."

He nods in acknowledgment before he rubs his face.

"Are you okay?" I ask.

"Rough day."

I eye him for a few beats, trying to decipher his frame of mind. I should enjoy whatever agony he's feeling and tell him to fuck off, but my curiosity gets the best of me.

"You wanna talk about it?"

He tilts his head back, pursing his lips as if he's thinking about my offer, and I wait in anticipation. Finally, he saunters through the room, pointing his head towards the balcony.

"Mommy will be right back." I give Colin a kiss on his hair, then get up to follow Connor outside.

He's leaning over the railing, his elbows resting on the black metal while he's staring on to the huge garden. I mimic his stance, waiting until he opens his mouth.

"Nigel's funeral was today," he explains, his voice dim and gloomy.

I suck in a deep breath.

Shit, I forgot.

Reign told me about it, after he explained to me how close Connor was with Nigel. It made me realize the big beast actually has a heart, and that even though he has a permanent scowl on his face, he's not as bad as he likes to portray.

At least not to everyone.

And definitely not how I remember him.

"I'm sorry, Connor. That must've been hard."

"I didn't expect it to be. My mother died, and I didn't shed a tear. I don't really get emotional over anything, but watching Nigel's casket being lowered into the ground ... it did something to me."

I'm surprised that he's opening up to me since he usually either barks shit at me or flirts with me, which gives me a fuzzy feeling, making me want to wrap him in my arms.

Despite the guilt inside of me, I keep my arms in check, knowing I'm not the right person to comfort him right now. Not like that, anyway.

I turn my body towards him, and his head spins my way.

"I'm sorry, Connor. I mean that. I'm sorry my brother killed him. I know I can't bring him back, and it doesn't change shit. But I *am* sorry."

He straightens his spine before his hand moves to the small of my back, and he pulls me flush against his chest. His eyes darken as he examines my face, and I just hold his gaze while my heart starts to beat a little faster. I'm doing everything I can to keep this man at arm's length, to keep my distance and guard my heart. But I can't keep denying he does something to me.

He bites his lip while a hand lands on my neck.

"You look like an angel, you know?"

"I'm not."

"Oh, I know," he smirks,

We both fall silent, staring into each other's eyes. His eyes are a dark green, hypnotizing me like the ripples of a clear-water lake. While his thumb softly brushes my skin, I unintentionally close my eyes for a few seconds, enjoying his touch. The silence between us is thick, creating a bubble around us. It feels like silent bonding.

"Can I ask you something?" I ask when I open my eyes again.

He hums in agreement, narrowing his eyes a little.

"Why haven't you traded me for Damien yet?"

"Because I don't know where he is," he clarifies flatly.

"What? He's missing?"

"Not sure. Reign pulled some other soldier from the street

yesterday, asking him what he knew. He said they haven't seen Damien since Sunday."

My eyes widen in shock.

"You don't think…"

"That he's dead? I don't know. Emerson doesn't care much about life in general. Wouldn't surprise me if he thought he was a loose end." The words leave his lips as if he's giving me a recap of the Bruins' last game, not a fucking care in the world, but goosebumps trickle down my body as stress rushes through my veins.

I start to shake my head, feeling a little light-headed.

"No. No. No," I whisper, a tightness forming in my throat. A feeling of panic surges through me, and it feels like the world starts to spin around me. He's all I've got. I've been taking care of him like he's my own since I had to step up, but he's also my best friend. He's the one constant I've always had in my life. He gives me more stress than a sibling should, but he's also part of my happiest memories.

I need him by my side.

"Hey? I don't know if that's the case. He could be hiding somewhere for all we know." He lowers his head a little, grabbing my chin to look me in the eye. His green eyes peer down at me with sympathy, but all it does is replace my angst with frustration.

"Doesn't really matter, does it? Because even if he is, the second you find him, that's exactly what you're going to do," I snarl, pushing him off me.

"Babe," he sighs right before his scowl returns in its full glory, turning him into the beast everyone is taught to fear.

"What? It's true, right?" I push.

"I never said I'm going to kill him."

"Yeah, you did."

"Okay, I did," he confesses. "But I'm not. Not anymore."

"No, you're just going to beat him up while I pray he survives."

He swiftly cups the front of my neck, dominantly yanking me towards him before he stares down at me, our faces so close I can feel his breath on my skin.

"Your brother made a choice." His grip is controlling but not hurtful, forcing me to stay calm in his hands. "A poor one."

"Did he shoot Nigel because he wanted to or because he was commanded?"

He doesn't reply.

"We both know the answer to that question, don't we? So, did he really have a choice?" I snicker sarcastically. A desperate feeling envelops me, failure hitting me in the face. I've tried so hard to avoid these kinds of situations, but here I am, my back against the wall, knowing I have no other option than to oblige with whatever life throws at me right now. My life dictated by the criminals who control this city. "Do *I* have a choice? While you are here, running the city with an iron fist, there are people out there who just get caught in the crossfire. My brother was only part of that gang because *I* needed money. Because *I* needed to be able to pay for daycare so I could get a better job. Knowing I couldn't keep working at the bar forever."

"I thought you were a legal assistant?" He frowns.

"I was. Until I found out I was pregnant. It's impossible to be a legal assistant and work sixty hours a week when you have a kid. Not when you don't make enough to put him in daycare." I guess I knew I was kinda fucked the moment I got pregnant with Colin. It's hard, if not impossible, to be a mom and have a prosperous career. Looking into Colin's eyes, I'll never regret having him, but I will always wonder what I could've accomplished if the plan had stayed the same. If I could've kept Damien off the street.

"After Colin was born, I started working at Twenty-One Spirits. The money was good, and Damien could stay with Colin during the night. I was making enough bank when it was just the two of us, but it wasn't enough for three. The fact that Damien is running around with Emerson Jones is because of me. If you want to blame anyone, blame *me*."

My eyes water as I hold his gaze with my chin held high and my shoulders back.

He stays silent, his eyes moving back and forth between mine. I swear I can see the cogs turning in his head, but I wait in anticipation until he's ready to say anything.

"What do you want me to do?" he breathes, letting go of my neck.

I look for sarcasm, waiting for a snicker, but nothing comes. He just looks at me as if my opinion matters. As if he thinks I matter. It throws me off a little, but knowing I should take advantage of his sympathy while I can, I don't waste another minute.

"Punish him. Give him a hard time. Scare the shit out of him. Make him suffer. Pretend you'll kill him. But promise me you won't actually do it."

I expect him to snap and roar all kinds of shit in my face, but instead, I can see a slight curl in his lips as he tries to keep them firmly pressed together with a straight face, his eyes turning soft..

"Okay."

"Okay?" I ask, slightly confused.

"Yeah. *Okay*."

"Are you serious?"

"Yes, Lily. I'm serious," he snaps, then rolls his eyes at me. "Why?"

He pushes out a troubled breath, gritting his teeth in annoyance.

"Just say *thank you*."

"Thank you!" The fear lifts from my shoulders while a deep breath of relief is sucked into my lungs. Without thinking, I throw my arms around his neck, giving him a tight hug. I feel him freeze when our bodies connect. Keeping my arms in place, I squeeze him tight, feeling the relief shower me in a comforting way.

"Thank you so much, Connor."

He doesn't reply but wraps his arms around my body, dipping his chin to the crook of my neck, breathing me in, returning the sexual tension in its full glory. I can feel a flutter in my stomach as I slowly let go of him and avert my gaze.

He grabs my chin.

"It's too late to be shy, babe."

"I appreciate what you're doing. I know that's hard for you," I say, ignoring his comment.

"Blame your son. He's making me soft."

I can feel my heart twitch at his words.

"Yeah, he's got special powers," I chuckle.

"Really?" he mocks in amusement.

"Hmm, he can turn the biggest, baddest roaring beast into a soft cuddly teddy bear."

"Pff, please."

"It's true, and you know it," I beam up at him.

A hunger flashes in his eyes, and he pushes me back against the railing, placing his hands on either side of me.

"Don't push it if you don't want me to show you exactly what kind of beast I am."

"Don't you remember?" I purr daringly, feeling completely comfortable with him now that I'm seeing his soft side. "I already know."

I can see his jaw flex as the features in his face turn to steel, clearly conflicted about what he should do. His verdant eyes darken with lust as he stares me down, like a hungry lion. Slowly, he moves his face closer, and I part my lips in anticipation. When his eyes move down to my mouth, I slowly close my eyes, eagerly waiting for what's coming, his lips only an inch away from mine.

I still remember his lips on mine, crushing me in a dominating way. His kisses were full of hunger and desire, the content of many of my daydreams as I sat behind my desk still working as a legal assistant.

"Mommy!" Colin shouts through the closed door, slamming the window to grab my attention. I suck in a sharp breath, startled as he snaps us out of our whirlwind of desire. Connor leaves his head hanging in defeat, a growl escaping his lips.

"I'm coming, baby." I smile, pretending nothing happened, and everything is fine.

Everything is not fine. I want this man, and the burning feeling inside of me seems to magnify by the day. It doesn't help that I haven't had a real man between my legs since forever, my Magic Wand being my best friend.

Fuck me, I'm horny.

I step aside, trying to make my way back inside, pushing away my need to feel his dick between my legs when he holds me back by tugging my arm.

"I'm sorry I dragged you in to this. And Colin. I can't let you go until I know where your brother is, because I don't know what Emerson's next move is. For all I know, he might be looking for you to find your brother. You're safer with me than with Emerson Jones. You're still on lockdown, but you and Colin are free to walk around the house, okay?"

"Really?" I blurt, a bit shocked and excited at the same time.

This man continues to surprise me and my head is starting to wonder if I made the right choice all those years ago. If I should've hunted him down after that amazing night.

He nods, and a huge smile covers my face.

"Everywhere?"

"Well, no. This is your bedroom, and I don't want to see you in any of my brothers' bedrooms." He scowls with a possessive glint in his eyes.

He's still a grade-A asshole who took me and my child, but I like his possessive mode. I like how he makes me feel protected, even though he was the one I needed protection from.

"Can we go outside?"

"Yeah, but don't get any ideas in your head. Since Emerson breached the gates, we've doubled our security. Don't try to escape. I need him dead first."

"I won't. Scout's honor." I place three fingers in the air, straightening my back, then raising my chin.

"Were you a Girl Scout?" he cocks an eyebrow.

"No. But I can bake some great cookies."

"You can?"

"Oh, yeah. I bake for Colin all the time."

He eyes me with a faint grin, mumbling something that I can't figure out before he walks back in. He ruffles Colin's blond hair then takes big steps to leave.

"Connor?" He turns around. "Why? Why now? What changed?"

His attention goes from me to Colin until his gaze lands back on me.

"He's a good kid. He shouldn't be cooped up in this room all day." He shrugs.

The look in his eyes turns affectionate for just a second, then he abruptly turns around and walks out, leaving the door open. I know he's trying to hide it, doing his very best to stay his ruthless self, but I can see it. I can see it in his eyes, in everything he does, every time he walks through that door and rubs his hand through Colin's hair. Connor Wolfe is not the stone cold beast that he claims to be. Or that the city thinks he is.

18

CONNOR

We walk out of Reign's apartment, where we just prepared for the upcoming confrontation with Emerson Jones. I have a gun tucked into the back of my jeans, even though I don't intend on using it.

I prefer my fists.

"I call shotgun," Killian calls out as we walk towards the car.

"Of course you do," Reign comments.

We get into my truck before we take off, followed by a dozen of our men in the SUVs behind us.

"So what's the plan again?" Reign asks from the back.

"Ambush the motherfuckers, and kill as many as we can," I reply with a straight face.

"Sounds good to me." I look into the rearview mirror, watching Reign settle into the car, resting his head against the window. "You and Lily seem to get along pretty good, don't you?" he asks when our eyes briefly meet in the mirror.

"Yeah, we're all right."

The corner of my mouth curls, thinking about the blonde angel strolling around my house with her kid. The other day, she was swaying her luscious hips through the kitchen while Colin was playing outside. She looked like a dream, reminding me of the time she was squirming beneath me.

"That was…" she says, lost for words.

"That was devilishly good," I smirk.

"If that was devilishly good. I'll pick hell over heaven any day of the week." I can hear the smile in her words.

"If it's hell you choose, you may see me again sometime, babe."

She pushes at my side, rolling me over on the bed before she twists her body to face me, her head resting in her hand with a propped up elbow.

"Thank you," she whispers, while I look up at the ceiling.

"What for?"

"For not treating me like a porcelain doll."

I snap my head towards her, feeling my dick twitch at her words.

"Every single guy I ever sleep with treats me like I'm fragile, just because I'm small and tiny. When really … when really…"

"When really you want to be fucked into oblivion while getting spanked until your ass is burning red?" I cock an eyebrow, my chest moving up and down in desire as I wait for her response.

"Yeah, basically," she admits, averting her gaze.

I wrap my arm around her, pulling her body flush against mine.

"You like it rough and rowdy, don't you, angel?" My lips brush against hers as I dig my fingers deep into her red ass, making her wince before her eyes fill with lust once more.

"I'm not as innocent as I look," she shrugs. "People just always want to throw me in the sweet-and-kind-box. And that's easy, that's comfortable. But sometimes I don't want to be comfortable."

My heart jumps for joy hearing those words, loving how she's basically begging me to taint her even more and blur the lines.

"You like to explore your boundaries, babe? You want a guy who pushes you further than you can imagine?"

She nods her head, her blue eyes darkening with excitement, almost turning a deep purple shade. I groan, feeling like I just hit the goddamn jackpot.

"Let me be that guy for you."

"Connor?" Killian's voice snaps me out of my daydream.

"What?"

"Did you tell her the truth about Damien?"

"Yeah, I did. Last week. It's when she loosened up to me. She gets it, she just asked me to not kill him."

"How did you reply?" Reign questions, while Killian keeps his attention focused on me.

I push out a breath, ignoring the amused looks on their faces. I don't even have to look to know they are there. I can just feel them beaming at me.

"You told her you wouldn't, didn't you?" Reign chuckles then pops his head between Killian and me. "You told her you'd beat him, but you wouldn't kill him."

I grind my teeth together, annoyed with how well my brothers know me.

"Last night, she asked me if I knew where he was. *Again.* Did you manage to find anything else?"

"No, but I put our private investigator on it. See if he can give me anything to work with online. You didn't answer the question, though."

"What question?" I sigh, playing dumb.

"Are you going to kill Lily's little brother? Colin's *uncle?*"

"Why do you have to be such a pain?"

"I'm the youngest. It's my fucking job. I can't help it you were born first."

"Yeah, well, maybe I should've punched you more when you were younger," I retort with a glare.

"Oh, please, you love me too much to mess with my pretty face."

"Sometimes I wonder why."

"Because we are your younger brothers, you are destined to love us." Killian smiles, entertained. "Besides, let's be honest. Life became so much more interesting when Reign and I were born."

"You mean more stress?" I laugh.

"But it's a good stress," Reign responds. "Is that a *yes*? Did you tell her you won't kill her baby brother?"

"I did," I give in, rolling my eyes.

"Aaah, told you, Kill. Our big ruffian brother is actually a wicked softie." Reign squeezes my cheek, and I slap his hand away with a scowl, making Killian chuckle at both of us.

"Stop touching me, tool."

"We are here." Killian points at the restaurant. We park the truck behind the building, the rest of our men still trailing behind us.

We all exit our vehicles before Killian gives everyone some final instructions and gets into place. Walking into the back of the building, into the kitchen, we hear the sound of a woman's voice talking in a menacing tone. The rest of the kitchen staff are frozen to their spots when they notice how heavily armed we are. I snap my fingers towards the door, silently telling them to fuck off.

"That's Kendall's roommate, isn't it?" I hiss to Killian, referring to the woman's voice.

"Yeah, Josie. I knew she was in cahoots with Emerson, lying whore."

With quiet steps, we move deeper into the building until

we reach the main area of the restaurant where Kendall has a gun pointed at Emerson while Josie in turn has one pointed at Kendall. Franklin is still sitting at one of the tables behind them, observing the situation in front of him.

"I told you she was a cunning little bitch." Killian's voice sounds through the room while our men spread out around the restaurant, blocking every exit to make sure no one gets out.

"Never said I didn't agree with you," Franklin replies while Reign and I trail behind Killian.

Franklin's eyes catch mine, holding his tumbler in his hand as if he doesn't have a care in the world, but I see the small spark of distress in his gaze. Franklin seems like the most sophisticated of us all, the calm, cunning leader, but he has one weakness: his family. His fears are driven by the thought of losing the people he cares about. He's the complete opposite of Emerson, who showed us how little he thinks about human life by killing Nigel. Franklin knows that my brothers and I can take care of ourselves, but it's his girl facing his enemy that will have his adrenaline pumping through his veins.

He loves Kendall. I know it, even if he isn't ready to admit it.

Emerson's army of sheep turns around, guns pointed at us before all their faces turn sour when they realize we walked in with double the amount of manpower.

"You okay, darling?" Reign asks Kendall.

Her face looks pale, and she's slowly taking breaths to keep it all together.

I feel for her. She's not naturally a tough cookie, but she tries to hold her own in a world that is filled with demons. Although it's clearly not in her nature, she can be brave as fuck. But knowing your best friend fucked you over must suck even more.

"I'm not sure," she admits.

"Put the gun down, girl." Killian's legs are wide, hands on his hips.

"You put your guns down, or I'll shoot her through the head." I can't suppress the growl that leaves the back of my throat when I look at the cunning little bitch. Her black hair reminds me of Cleopatra, and from what I've heard, she's just as psycho. She's an insecure little whore, dying to get her best friend's ex-boyfriend. As far as I'm concerned, they both get a one-way ticket to hell.

Kendall turns her head towards Josie with a wondrous look, I'm guessing still flabbergasted at the foul play of her bestie. My instinct is to stride forward, blow a bullet through Emerson's head, hit Josie in the nose, and get Kendall out of here. But there is a reason why I'm not the one making decisions. I'm impulsive, I'm brutal, I'm straightforward. I don't control my anger issues, I let them out. Not the best way most of the time, but fuck me sideways, it sure as fuck is satisfying.

"No, you won't," Killian rebukes. I can hear the amusement in his voice. My little brother is the spitting image of Franklin in these kinds of situations.

Demanding and in control.

Not to mention they possess the same evil grin that could make the devil cower.

Worry paints Josie's face, panic entering her eyes. The change in her stance is noticed by Kendall, who releases a full belly laugh.

Amused, she holds the gun between her fingers, losing her focus on Emerson. The son of a bitch quickly jumps up, slamming her arm to the side and knocking it into Josie's face.

Unconscious, Josie falls to the floor, and we all jump for cover, knowing this will be the start of fucking chaos erupting. Gunfire echoes through the restaurant, and I duck before plowing my body against the nearest guy who isn't part of our team. I knock him against the floor before I punch him out with my fist against his nose. Blood splashes on the floor, and he passes out before I jump back up to go for the next guy within range.

From the corner of my eye, I notice Cary, Emerson's right hand, fighting off one of our men. I move towards them as they wrestle, ready to rip Cary's head off. Before I reach them, a loud roar pierces my ear, and someone jumps on my back, making me buckle down under the unexpected weight. My adrenaline reaching a peak, I arch my back, throwing the bastard off my body before rolling on top of him and giving him an elbow to the throat. Gasping for air, panic distorts his face when I start to punch him in the face repeatedly.

"Wrong person to jump, you motherfucking coward!" I roar as my fist keeps going. My blood is pumping through my veins at a high speed, fueling my rage more and more.

I see red, and when I do, there is no knowing when I'll snap out of it.

When a gunshot rings closer to my ear than expected, followed by a body falling to the floor behind me, I turn around. Cary looks in front of him with wide eyes, and I follow his gaze. Kendall is standing there, gun pointed at Cary with a blazing look in her eyes. Not wasting another second, Cary jolts up, stumbling and running to the exit before he dashes out to the street. My focus goes back to Kendall, looking fierce as fuck. A proud feeling hits me, putting a smile on my face.

"Shit," I see her lips mutter before she catches my eye,

making the corner of her mouth curl. My face falls when I notice Emerson getting up behind her. She turns around, and her brows shoot up in surprise when they are met by the barrel of Emerson's gun pointed at her head. Franklin is doing his best to get up from the floor, panic marring his face as he looks at the sight in front of him.

Meanwhile, Josie is also getting back on her feet, right behind Kendall, still dazed from the punch to the head she received.

"Goodbye, sweetheart," Emerson smiles, then pulls the trigger.

Bang!

Franklin lets out a ferocious roar, jumping up, smacking Kendall off her feet right before the bullet reaches her. The bullet continues, striking the first thing it can hit, and my eyes widen when Josie falls to the floor like a ragdoll, the bullet piercing through her head in a perfect round. At the same time, Franklin and Kendall fall to the floor, Kendall hitting her head on one of the tables.

Knowing they are outnumbered, the rest of Emerson's guys flee as fast as they can, leaving the dead or unconscious bodies behind. Emerson is looking at Josie's limp body with shock in his eyes. Seeing the perfect opportunity to catch him off guard, I charge.

Fuming, I launch for Emerson, howling like I'm ready to bite his head off before I roughly push him to the floor then headbutt him as I show my teeth in anger.

He passes out, and not waiting for him to wake up, I hold his head between my hands to bring it up before I roughly smash it back to the floor.

"Argh!" I rumble, slamming another punch into his unconscious face. I keep going, needing to unleash the raw feelings I've had about this man for the last few weeks without anything holding me back.

Completely disappearing into my fog of anger, I hear someone calling my name, but only vaguely, like I'm underwater until the voice gets closer to my ear.

"Connor!" Killian yells, snapping me out of my bubble of rage.

"What?" I snarl, my fist covered in blood.

"We still need answers."

"Right," I mutter.

I take a deep breath, staring at a passed out Emerson, his face completely covered in blood. My fists are itching to keep going, and I flex them before making another fist to give him one last punch.

"Connor! Leave him!" Killian hollers while my fist is midair.

Rolling my eyes, I shoot him a glare, then reluctantly stand up.

"Detain him. Bring him to the garage," I order a few of our men.

My attention goes to Franklin, desperately holding Kendall in his arms, begging her to wake up. Reign quickly moves to his knees beside her while Killian yells to call 911 to no one in particular.

"No, wait," Reign starts. He places two fingers against her neck, checking her pulse. "She's got a strong pulse. Call the doc, let him know we're bringing someone in with possible head trauma in ten minutes." Reign locks his eyes with Franklin, waiting for confirmation of his decision.

"I can't lose her, Reign." Franklin shakes his head.

"You won't." Reign gives him a pleading look, knowing Franklin will regret sending her to the hospital unless it's completely necessary. Hospital staff ask questions, resulting in police officers poking around, which will lead to a lot of people to pay off.

Not something we need right now.

If we can avoid any kind of authorities, we always will.

"Do it," Franklin nods to Killian then looks back at Reign. "Are you sure?"

"I'm pretty sure. But we need to get her to the doc asap."

Relief flashes over Franklin's face before he looks for me.

"He dies!" He points at Emerson, and all I can do is nod in agreement. There isn't a bone in my body that doesn't agree with that statement.

I walk towards my brothers and Kendall, crouching down to scoop Kendall in my arms before I get up, her arms and legs completely limp.

"He will suffer," I vow, peering into Franklin's eyes. "Now let's get your girl safe."

19

CONNOR

Reign, Killian, and I walk out of the red brick townhouse in Back Bay around midnight, leaving Franklin at the doc's house to stay with Kendall.

We've known the doc for about ten years now. He's one of the best surgeons in the country and works at Massachusetts General Hospital. He probably has the highest salary in the state, but like most people, he's always eager for more. And good 'ol Doc doesn't mind calling in sick if it means Franklin will give him a big bag of money. After a few years, he now has his own surgery room on his top floor, always ready to patch any of our men up with some nurses he trusts to keep their mouths shut after receiving, once more, a big bag of money of their own.

He checked Kendall thoroughly and said he'd like to keep her overnight to keep an eye on her, but that she'll probably be fine once she wakes up.

"Glad she'll be okay," Killian says as we all pile into my truck.

"You?" Reign settles into the back with a mocking grin on his face. "You're glad she'll be okay?"

"What? I am!"

"Just weird hearing it out of your mouth since three days ago you were convincing me to help you torture her." Reign shrugs with a chuckle.

"I wasn't completely wrong about her."

"You were a bit drastic, though," I pitch in, maneuvering my truck onto the road to start the ten minute drive back to the mansion.

"Says the one who kidnapped a girl and her baby," Killian scowls.

I turn my head towards him with a straight face, not feeling the need to respond to that, even though he does have a point.

It's weird because I don't see it like that.

Okay, so there is no denying that I took Lily against her will, but the way she's strolling around the mansion, Colin's laughter ringing through the house, or how she's loosening up around me... It makes me feel like she's just a guest in our home. I know I'll probably never see her again after this, and the thought makes my heart pang in an uncomfortable way.

"Speaking of Colin," Reign begins.

"Yeah?" Killian tilts his head a little, showing Reign he's listening to him.

"Are we gonna keep ignoring the fact that he's basically a mini version of Connor?"

My neck stretches to look at Reign in the rearview mirror.

Seeing the knowing grin on his face, I turn my head to Killian, who's giving me a troubled look.

"The fuck are you talking about?" I bellow through the

car, a weird feeling settling in my gut while my mind instantly goes into overdrive.

I hear Reign chuckle in the back while Killian stays suspiciously quiet, avoiding my eyes.

"Kill?!" I shout incredulously.

Reign likes to joke around, knowing exactly what will set me off, and right now I can't take him seriously. Or maybe I don't want to, I don't know.

Finally, he rolls his eyes before slowly turning his head my way.

"You really don't see it?"

"You agree with this chucklehead?" I ask, shocked. "That's ridiculous."

"Think about it, Connor. Colin has just turned two. You met Lily three years ago. There is no father listed on his birth certificate. She hasn't dated anyone in the last three years. He's blond, *like you*."

"So is his mother," I counter.

"He has green eyes, *like you*."

"A lot of people have green eyes."

"Only 2 percent of the world's population has green eyes," Killian refutes.

"Not to mention the fact that the kid has the same scowl when he's angry," Reign adds.

"Shut up," I mutter.

"I'm just saying." Reign raises his hands.

I never wanted kids.

Like, ever.

Even though I'm the one who 'only' spent three months in foster care, compared to the two years Killian was in there and the four years Reign spent with those psychopaths, I saw enough to make me realize I never want to bring any kids into this rotten world. Not to mention the constant fight to survive daily life when both my parents were still in the picture.

Yeah, I'll fucking pass. Never wanna put any child in that position.

I know it's what Franklin wants for the three of us, but I've known my entire life that children aren't in the cards for me. I'm a fucking criminal. There's not a hair on my head wants to raise a family.

I'm not gonna lie, the little toddler has gotten under my skin a bit with his chunky cheeks and his baby chuckles, but no more than Nigel did.

"Come on, Connor. You know there is a big chance the kid is yours," Killian utters after a minute of silence.

"She would've told me." The words roll off my tongue, followed by a bitter taste of disbelief.

Would she have told me?

She and I were nothing more than a one-night stand. One hell of a fucking amazing one-night stand, let me tell you that, but that's all it was. She didn't give me her number, and even though I'd expected her to walk into the sports bar the weeks after we hooked up, I never went to look for her when she didn't. I brushed it off, because even though that was one of the best nights of my life, it's not like I was expecting or wanting it to become anything more than that.

A great fuck.

Was I surprised to find her on that couch with her neck underneath my palm? Of course I was, but it was nothing more than a pleasant surprise when I realized she was the blonde who still stirred my dick to life just thinking back to that sole night. Although it was just that one encounter which ended with no expectations, we did have a connection. One I know she felt as well because it's been there for the last two weeks, ever since I kidnapped her back into my life.

"You're a Wolfe. What makes you believe she would've told you?" Killian asks, keeping a straight yet sympathetic look on his face as I think about his words.

She looks like an angel, but I know she isn't one.

She's feisty and tough underneath her good girl exterior.

I raise my chin, locking my eyes with my youngest brother once more.

"Did you check in to this?"

He shrugs his shoulders with a coy smile.

"Would I be joking about it if I hadn't?"

I let out a deep sigh before shaking my head in anger.

That cunning little bitch.

I grip the steering wheel tight as fuck, so tight my knuckles ache, then I slam the center console a few times.

"Goddammit! Argh!" I roar.

"Calm down, Con," Killian tries to calm me as I drive on to the driveway of the mansion.

"Calm down? Calm down? If this is true, that little boy is *my* boy, and she kept him from me! That's my family! That's *our* family! That's a motherfucking Wolfe!" I get louder with every sentence that leaves my lips. "I'm going to kill her," I seethe.

My jaws hurts from how hard I'm clenching it, practically fuming like an angry bull. I'm about to lose it, feeling like a damn hurricane, ready to take everything down that stands in its way.

"Well, I wouldn't do that," Killian replies with a straight face.

"Yeah, not the way to win her over, Con," Reign chimes in.

"I don't give a flying fuck!" I park the car in front of the house, quickly exiting before storming off towards the door.

"Shit. Great timing, Reign," I hear Killian mutter behind me.

"Don't worry about it, Kill. He likes the girl. He's not gonna hurt her."

"Shut up, *tool*," I bark, stalking up the stairs.

20

My eyes fly over the copy of *The Great Gatsby* I found in the library downstairs. When I first entered the room, I was shocked for two reasons. One, I didn't expect any of the Wolfe brothers to read, let alone feel the need to have a library. Two, I didn't expect it to be filled with first editions of all the classics. *Wuthering Heights, Catcher in the Rye, Moby Dick* and even *Jane Eyre*. It makes me wonder which of these playboys is secretly a nerd. My bet goes to Reign. He may look like a prince, charming his way through life, but I bet deep down he's a big nerd.

Hearing the front door, I turn my head to the open door of the bedroom, wondering which one of the brothers just came home. I close the book, glancing at Colin who's still sound asleep before I get up to have a look. Softly, I walk towards the door, not wanting to wake up my little boy. But when I'm almost there, Connor comes storming through the door, and automatically, I take a step back. He's fuming, his typical scowl replaced by a gaze filled completely with rage.

"Is he mine?" he roars.

I wince, then stand statue still, his words sinking in with shock. My heart falls to the floor while I'm standing there, blinking. Letting his words sink in.

"Is he mine?" he repeats in the same extreme volume.

"Shut the fuck up!" I hiss, pointing at Colin still sleeping. My forehead creases with a frown when Reign enters the room, shooting me an apologetic smile.

"I'll just..." Reign points at Colin, not finishing his sentence, just walking over to my son to pull him out of bed while Killian trails behind him. Confused, I look between him and Connor standing in front of me, broad as a wall.

"Is he mine?" he seethes again.

His volume has gone down, but the anger still vibrates off his tongue in waves.

"Hold up," I say, shaking my head when I watch Reign gently step towards the door, cradling a sleeping Colin in his arms. "Where are you taking him?" I ask, panic surging through my veins.

I take a step forward, ready to do anything to stop him from taking my boy.

"It's okay, Lily," Reign whispers, trying to comfort me. "I got him. I'm just going to move him to my room so the two of you can talk. I'll keep him safe. He'll be right down the hall."

Hesitantly, I look at him, my heart racing against my chest. I want to open my mouth and tell him to put him back, but he moves a step forward, looking into my eyes.

"I promise. I'm not taking him away from you." I stare at

his handsome face laced with kindness, believing every word he says.

I finally swallow hard before I give him a short nod. I want to follow him out of the room, not feeling overly excited about dealing with the ranting beast in front of me.

Or Wolfe. However you want to put it.

Folding my arms, I watch as Reign exits the room, followed by Killian, who carries the improvised safety gate for Colin. When my eyes lock with Connor's again, he's breathing loudly through his nose. His hands are balled into fists along his body, his shoulders straight and imposing. All he needs is to turn green, and he'll look like the damn Hulk.

"Is. He. Mine?" he repeats through gritted teeth.

His green eyes are narrowed, looking at me with nothing but contempt.

My eyes fly to the floor while I rub the back of my neck.

"Answer me, Lily!" he shouts at me, making me wince once more.

Pressing my lips together into a firm stripe, I softly shake my head.

This was not how I planned to have this conversation, but to be honest, I'm not sure if I ever was planning to have this conversation. If the bastard hadn't kidnapped me, I probably wouldn't have ever seen him again. I was cautious about it, you know? I avoided the places the Wolfes were known to go, never went to the bars they visited, and I never even went to watch a Bruins game at the sports bar ever again, afraid I might run into him. I needed to protect my family no matter what, and truth to be told, I also had to protect myself. I hadn't trusted myself around Connor Wolfe. I hadn't trusted myself to be able to walk away if Connor promised me another night like the one we'd already shared, and sleeping with him again would come with the risk of getting exposed. The risk of him finding out the truth.

"ANSWER ME!" He takes a step forward, his loud voice rattling me to the point that it feels like my lashes flutter like you see in cartoons.

"YES!" I yelp, feeling my heart almost pound out of my chest when the words leave my lips. My eyes start to well as a heaviness forms in my stomach, and a weight lifts off my shoulders. Never has speaking the truth felt liberating and eviscerating at the same time. I hold my hand against my forehead, scared to look him in the eye while he looks at me in shock.

"What the...? He's mine?" He rakes a hand through his hair, flustered. "He's fucking mine? *Colin* is mine?"

"Yes," I admit, putting my chin in the air to face him.

He stares back at me with a cold look, then takes two long strides to close the distance between us, grabbing me by the throat in a threatening way. Before I can react, he throws me against the nearest wall, pinning me down while I look up at him with regret overwhelming me.

"Colin is *my* boy, yet you didn't care to tell me? How dare you?!" My eyes close when the last sentence is roared against my face.

"I'm sorry." Of course I'm sorry. This is not how I imagined my family would be when I grew up. But he's a *Wolfe*. He's not the fireman dad you take to school on occupation day. He's not the soccer dad you practice your shots with on Saturdays. He's Connor *fucking* Wolfe. Half of the city fears him, the other half wants him dead.

"You're sorry?" he snarls. "You're sorry?" He jams my head against the wall.

"Yes! I'm sorry!" I cry desperately.

"How dare you? How dare you keep my son away from me? Does he know?"

"No."

"So what, he's been your dirty little secret all these years?"

Something snaps in my chest, unchaining my own frustration when I hear him talk about Colin like that.

"Don't you ever call my son a dirty little secret, you asshole!"

"*Our* son, Lily. Our son." He pronounces my name like venom stains his tongue.

"Fine, *our* son." My anger quickly starts to match his. I understand his anger. He has every right to be angry. I'm a bitch for keeping his son away from him, but it's not like I did it because I was ashamed of Colin being a Wolfe.

I did it to protect Colin.

Everything I did in the last three years was to protect Colin.

His eyes darken, his breath fanning my face while I wait for whatever's coming next.

"When we first met, I thought you were an angel. With your angelic hair, your blue eyes, and your bright smile." His grip on my throat tightens, and I do my best to stay calm. "Now I realize you've been the devil all along."

A muscle in my jaw jolts.

"If you want to make me the devil in your story, so be it, Connor. Send me to hell. I'll see you when you get there."

"Why didn't you tell me, Lily?" His voice sounds more frustrated now, exacerbating the tears that rush down my cheeks.

"Because you're Connor Wolfe!"

"SO?!"

His grip on my neck loosens, and seeing my shot, I push him off me, ducking under his arm so I can put space between us.

"Do you hear me?!" I ask incredulously. "You're Connor *Wolfe!* The second this city finds out you have a kid, he gets a target on his back!"

The features in his face soften a little when he realizes what I'm saying, but his menacing scowl quickly returns.

"That's bullshit!" He shakes his head.

"Is it?"

"Him being a Wolfe makes him invincible! Nobody will dare to touch him when they find out he's mine. He's a Wolfe!"

"Oh, really? So you think Emerson Jones wouldn't dare to threaten *your* son? To touch him? If you honestly believe that you're even thicker than I thought."

"Watch your mouth, *little girl*," he growls, taking a step closer.

"You watch your mouth, *big guy.* Call me whatever you want, hate me. Punish me for it, I don't care. But everything I've done for the last few years was to protect that little boy. *My* little boy."

"Oh, I'm gonna punish you for it all right." He takes another step closer, his eyes darkening in anger mixed with what seems to be a hint of lust. I take a step back, swallowing hard as I try to keep my head up, not wanting to cower under his gaze.

"If you hurt me, you will hurt Colin."

"You hurt *me.* By keeping him from me."

"And I'm sorry." He keeps walking, and I keep backing up until my ass hits the bed. I dart out towards the door to keep myself out of his reach, unable to guess what he may do. "But I did what I thought was best."

"That was not your decision to make!" he snarls.

"I'm his mother!"

"And I'm his father! We should've made that decision together, you fucking wench!"

"Shut up, you asshole!" I shout back before he lets out a growl, charging at me.

Thinking he may hurt me, my eyes grow wide as he pushes me against the balcony door.

He crashes his mouth against mine, roughly bringing my hands above my head, giving me nowhere to go as his body keeps me tight against the glass. I hesitate at first when I feel his bruising lips against mine until finally succumbing to the longing feeling between my legs that has been building for days now.

"I hate you," he groans, letting my mouth go for a split second while he roughly fists my hair, resulting in a burning sensation on my scalp.

"I hate you more," I huff out before I press my lips against his once more.

21

CONNOR

Forcefully, I fist her blonde hair.

"I hate you."

"I hate you more," she pants, then presses her plump lips against mine.

The move surprises me, even though it's everything I was going for, not for one second wanting to give her the option to walk away now.

I really do hate her.

I hate her for the decision she made. I hate her for denying me my flesh and blood.

I hate her for keeping Colin away from me. Keeping both of them from me. When she finally admitted the truth, I wanted to strangle her. To hurt her. To make her feel the pain that I've been experiencing for the last fifteen minutes, when Reign opened my eyes and made me realize what was right under my motherfucking nose. It's not a pain of 'what the fuck do I do now?' No, it's the pain of 'how much did I miss?'

It's a feeling I never prepared myself for and a feeling I never expected to hurt so much until it hit me in the face.

Lily punched me in the face without even touching me, and I hate her for it.

I don't get punched in the face. I'm the one who makes you face your greatest fears, the one who makes you feel pain like you've never felt before. Yet here I am, completely stonewalled by some perky blonde who once upon a time filled my bed for the night.

It's motherfucking ridiculous.

"You don't get to hate me," I snarl between kisses as I bite her lip, drawing a drop of blood. She winces from the sting, narrowing her eyes while she grabs my chin. I stare at her with what I hope is an evil smirk on my face, determined to let her show her true colors once again.

Because as much as I hate her right now, the ferocity in her eyes turns me the fuck on. The way her eyes change whenever she goes into lioness mode protecting her cub at any costs is the sexiest thing I've ever seen. It pushes away the innocence that holds part of her soul, and it puts her wild side on full display.

"I may look like an angel, but don't ever think you can tell me what to fucking do. Wolfe or no Wolfe." Her hands dig into my chin, making me chuckle at the powerplay she's trying to make. Without effort, I slap her hands away before grabbing her by the neck, throwing her face down on the bed. A screech escapes her lips as I push her cheek against the sheets, pushing my chest against her back.

"Don't lie, Lily," I whisper. "You like it when I tell you what to do."

My fingers push into the hem of her pajama pants, easily

pushing them over the swell of her hips before tugging them far enough for me to have free access to her behind.

"Stop touching me, you asshole," she snarls, trying to squirm her way out of my grip, resulting in my pressing her deeper into the mattress. My hands rub over the wet fabric of her panties, reflexively licking my lips in desire.

"Not a chance in hell, baby."

"I'm going to scream!"

"Oh, I plan on it." Unexpectedly, I flip her on her back before I push a finger inside of her, causing her to let out a desperate gasp while I turn her face towards me and her eyes grow wider.

She looks like a deer in headlights until her eyes roll back in their sockets as my fingers begin moving in and out of her tight pussy. Enjoying the warm, sticky feeling of her lust glazing my finger, I put my mouth flush with her ear.

"I'm going to make you scream so loud, they will hear you a mile away. Make you come so hard, you'll be thinking about me for the next twenty-four hours, and right when you start to forget about me… I'm going to do it all over again."

"You really are—" I push another finger inside of her, shutting her up as I curl them against her walls, and a desperate moan rings through the room.

"I'm the man who's going to make you forget your name, Lily." Biting her ear, I thrust my fingers into her pussy while she grinds against me with a scowl. Her stubbornness turns me on even more, and I laugh at her persistence as I feel her grow wetter by the second.

Slowly, I quicken my motions, until she starts to whimper under my touch, her closed eyes and guttural moans telling me how much she enjoys what I'm doing to her. When her little whimpers and groans become more desperate and her body completely relaxes beneath me, I pull out, and her eyes snap open in anger.

"What the fuck?!"

Ignoring her scowl, I roll her back on her stomach, then yank her hips up to point her butt in the air, pressing her cheek against the sheets of the bed.

"What are you doing?" she squeaks when she gets on hands and knees, clearly pissed about the sudden lack of touch.

I whack my hand against her ass, not holding back one bit.

"Shut up."

She cries out, throwing her head back before I do it again, the sound of my hand connecting with her round ass echoing through the room. This time the outline of my palm is clearly visible on her fair skin and I get on my knees while she opens her mouth again.

Tenacious little thing.

"You motherfucker, hit me again, and I will—"

My mouth covers her folds, digging my tongue inside of her like I'm thirsty, and the last drop of water is buried inside her hot cunt. She snaps her mouth shut, letting out a frantic whimper while I start working her into a frenzy. I feast on her freshly shaved center, exploring every inch while I keep her hips locked. Her hands branch out to her sides, spreading out over the bed, and from the corner of my eye I see her flexing her hands, holding onto the sheets every time I suck her clit like my life depends on it.

"If I knew this was going to be my late-night snack, I would've skipped supper."

"Fuuuuuck," she cries, pressing her center against my face even more. Eagerly, I lick up every drop of her wetness, coating my tongue with the delicious taste that is Lily Johnson. Tilting my head a little, I cover her clit with my lips as I push another finger inside of her, my thumb creeping down to tease her puckered asshole.

"You like that, don't you?" I lean back to watch my fingers at work.

Her skin is glowing with her own moistness, and just for the hell of it, I spit on her, spreading my saliva all over her folds with my tongue.

"Oh my god!" she shrieks, the sensation making her shiver underneath my palms.

Enjoying this way too much, I keep teasing the area around her sensitive nub in a torturous way, switching moves every time I feel she's getting close to climbing the peak she's dying to reach. Flicking my tongue over her clit, kissing her skin with a brush against the delicate flesh, sucking her folds into my mouth, all while alternating with my fingers digging into her center or my thumb testing how far I can get inside of her ass.

"You thought you could escape me, Lily?" I rumble while tormenting her as much as I can, enjoying every second of her ass in my face.

"Shut up, asshole!" she growls against the sheets.

"We'll get to your asshole another time, babe. Right now I want your cunt to remember me. To make you remember what you've been missing," I say between licks, my hands never leaving her body. "I know you remember how good I made you feel. Were you thinking about me when you were *fucking* anyone else? Did you pretend it was me when some other guy was plowing inside of you? Because I know no one ever fucked you better than I did." My moves become more aggressive, growing angry at the thought of someone else being inside of this tight body. "Answer me! Did you think about me?"

"Yes!" she shouts, frustration audible in her voice. "Yes! You asshole! I thought about you every single time I came in the last three years! NOW FUCK ME ALREADY!"

A weird feeling jams itself into my chest, and I get up, spinning her on her back.

"How many men came after me?" I pant, fueled by a possessiveness I've never felt before.

A ghost of a smile washes her face, laced with a wicked amount of sass.

"None."

I blink, stunned, as the arousal inside of me reaches that point of no return, that single word throwing out any left over restraint that was still there.

Lily Johnson is mine.

Leaning in, I press my wet lips against hers, pushing my tongue inside. Wildly, I start to delve into her mouth, feeling the need to leave my claim everywhere I can. Her hands roughly grab my hair, making my scalp burn and my dick lengthen in the already crowded space between my legs. She forces my head back, staring at me like a fucking Valkyrie.

"If you want to play the possessive motherfucker, stop stalling, take the goddamn plunge, and start *fucking* me, asshole." She shoves me up and I look down at her, amazed by her dirty mouth. I've had my fair share of women between my legs, but none of them matched the blunt demands Lily is spewing at me.

Straightening my body, I watch how she takes off her shirt, nice and slow, her deep blue eyes never leaving mine as she makes a damn spectacle out of it. I slowly start to unbutton my jeans, letting them puddle around my feet while

Lily drags her panties over the rest of her legs, letting the tiny scrap of material hang on her toes until she throws it against my face with an evil smirk.

I catch it when gravity brings it down to my chest, and I can help but breathe in the tainted fabric before letting it fall to the floor.

Motherfucker, I'm hooked.

She landed in my bed three years ago, and I quickly discovered she wasn't as well behaved as she looked to be. But looking at this enigma in front of me makes me realize I haven't even seen half of it. That night she showed me only a fraction of the devil who's really inside of her, the devil that's looking at me like she's about to devour me after a week of not eating, and I'm all here for it.

Tugging my boxers down, I lick my lips at the sight in front of me. Her legs are popped up, her knees open and wide, her cunt shining from the arousal dripping out of her, but what really gets me is the daring look in her eyes. The penetrating gaze that's enhanced by her blue eyes that are now laced with an undeniable craving.

"You want this?" I ask, fisting my cock as I rub my hand up and down the hard shaft.

She licks her lips, parting them while her eyes stay focused between my legs.

"You want this, Lily?" I repeat.

Closing her mouth, she purses her lips in a glare before her lips twitch. The look in her eyes turns mischievous as she says a line that's music to my ears.

"*Fuck* me, Connor."

22

A cheeky grin appears on his face, making him look more handsome than I've ever seen, when he grabs my ankles to drag me to the edge of the bed.

I yelp at the movement while I eagerly spread my legs even wider. Not wasting another second, he lowers his hips, pushing his hard shaft inside of me. He doesn't give me any time to adjust, stretching me wide with one big shove. Filling me in the most delicious way.

"Motherfucker," I mutter, feeling like my eyes will pop out of my head any second now.

His huge fingers wrap around my neck, squeezing in a dominating way while I look into his now dark green eyes.

"This is what you want, isn't it, *Lily?*" His voice is deep and hoarse, bringing me back to the last time he buried himself inside of me. He presses my throat, making it harder to breathe while I grow wetter with every thrust he makes. My eyes roll to the back of my head, loving everything he does with my body, enjoying being treated like a piece of meat. The few exes that I've had always treated me like I'm fragile, handling me with care, being sweet and gentle. They treated me with respect, dignity, and care.

But you know what the kicker is?

I want you to treat me with respect, dignity, and care outside of the bedroom. But when my clothes come off? I want you to fuck me against the wall until I don't know if I'm dead or alive. I want to be used for your pleasure like a whore, pleasing you in the most fucked-up way. I want to be used, devoured, spanked, bitten, and tormented until you're done, and then, but only then, do I want you to hold me against your chest, and stroke my back in a soothing way until I fall asleep. No one could ever do that. No one could ever give that to me.

No one except Connor.

Connor didn't treat me like glass when I ended up in his bed that first and only time, fucking me senseless like no one ever did, making me cross limits I've never crossed before. And yes, he was the one I was thinking about every single time after that when I got myself off after a long night at the bar. I've been dreaming about how I wanted him to ravage me while I screamed his name and how I wanted him to fuck me until I passed out in exhaustion.

"Is. This. What. You. Want. Lily?" Each thrust between words more painful than the other.

"Yes!" I cry out, relishing in the toxic combination of pleasure and pain. His hands press even harder, closing off my airway, making me lash out my nails against his ripped chest. I claw at him, pissed yet delighted about the lack of air getting access to my brain.

"That's it! Tear me apart, little devil." He loosens his grip on my throat when I rip his skin open, a satisfied look on his face while I gasp for air.

"Son of a bitch!"

"You gonna fight me, babe? Bring it!"

He pulls out, twisting me back onto my stomach before yanking me towards him, my ass and legs now hanging off the side of the bed. He roughly thrusts back in, slamming against my walls before he makes a popping sound with his lips. Moments later, I feel his saliva coated fingers start to work my throbbing clit.

"Oh, shit," I mutter.

"You want to fight this?" His free hand fists my long hair, pulling my head back until I'm looking up at the wall in front of me, my back arched, taking everything he wants to give me. He keeps pounding inside of me with slow yet explosive thrusts, making me whimper every time the tip of his cock smacks into my pussy.

"There is no fighting, babe. This body is mine. It was mine since the first time I've had it, and I'll fuck it anyway I please. I'll use it until you're begging me to stop." His fingers never stop flicking my clit, and I feel my orgasm building inside of me. "But you don't want me to stop, do you?" he groans against my ear. "You want me to fuck you like a whore, doing everything I tell you to. Don't you, Lily?"

"Yes," I admit with a cracking voice, at the point of combusting into flames any minute now.

"Say my name!" he barks when I feel my glutes tighten as my walls tense around his cock. "Say it!"

"I'm coming, Connor. Please."

"Good girl, take my cum." A few more circling moves around my clit and I explode, my mind balancing between heaven and hell while his thrusts speed up as he finds his own release.

"Aaaaah! Fuck!" I cry out while I ride an excruciating wave of ecstasy, slamming the bed with my hand, my legs trembling on the bed.

"Fuck!" he groans as he frantically plows inside of me. His hands dig into my hips, deep and painful while I hold still, unable to move because of my ultimate bliss as he unloads himself inside of me.

"Argh!" he roars when he reaches his peak before he collapses on top of me.

Deja-fucking-vu.

My body is completely worn out, not even able to smile as I enjoy the pink cloud he just launched me on. He heaves me onto my back, his breath fanning my shoulder before he lifts his weight, slowly getting off me. He pulls out, and instantly, the hollow feeling annoys me while his cum starts dripping out of my pussy.

A gasp leaves my mouth when his fingers push through my center, rubbing his cum all over me.

"Fuck, that looks sexy," he says before he slaps my ass and lifts the covers to get in.

I watch him with my head resting on my elbow while I bite my lip, still horny as fuck but too exhausted to do anything about it.

He places his broad body against the headboard, placing the sheets over his legs. When he catches my eyes, a smug grin tugs on his mouth.

"You want more, don't cha, you little slut?"

Many women would've been offended by his words.

I'm just wondering if he will eat me out again if I say yes.

I shrug, not denying or confirming.

"Come here." He reaches out his arms, and I crawl over to him, straddling his hips while he rests his hands on my thighs.

My thumb brushes the scar on his lip, the feature that makes him more menacing than any of the Wolfe brothers. But I have yet to feel fear for any of them, and it makes me wonder if they really are the worst of the evil in this city. Makes me wonder what would've happened if Damien started working for them instead of Emerson Jones.

Dragging his lower lip down a bit, I feel regret surging through my body, thinking about the question that pops into my head, a stressed flutter settling in my stomach. It's shit timing, but I ask anyway.

"Any news about my brother?"

He shakes his head, frustration visible on his face.

I push out a deep breath, pressing my forehead against his while I cup his face.

"I truly am sorry, Connor." I don't want to ruin this moment. I don't want to mess up the semi good mood he seems to have fucked us both into, but I feel like if I don't address this, if I don't address the hard parts, they will all keep hanging above our heads like big thunder clouds, having no clue when lightning will strike.

He closes his eyes, and I expect his face to return to its usual scowl, ready to be thrown off his lap. He has every right, but I'm silently praying he won't while my heart starts to race.

He lets out a deep sigh, closing his eyes.

"I'm still angry," he admits, even though his voice seems calmer.

"I know. I understand."

"I'll probably stay angry for a while."

"Okay." I nod.

"Fuck knows how this is going to work, but you can't keep me away from my son."

"I know. And I don't want to."

He rubs his face with a dazed look.

"Fuck, I have a son." His deep green eyes give me a puzzled look, as if the realization really just hit him now that his anger has somewhat simmered down.

I brush my thumb over his sharp jaw, hoping my coy smile will soothe him. I'm the one who has to put in the biggest effort to make this work between the three of us.

Whatever *this* may be.

"You do. You're his dad."

"I'm a dad." He speaks the words with awe, a slight question evident in his voice. "What the fuck." His eyes drift beside my head, and I stay silent, giving him a moment to think.

I had nine months to get comfortable with the idea of becoming a mom, so the second Colin got thrown on my chest, I was ready. Looking at his wrinkled little face, all dirty from getting pulled out of my body, I felt whole for the first time in my life.

I remember how I felt like I finally had a purpose even though it was scary as fuck. I can't expect Connor to feel like a dad right this second. He's gonna need time to adjust, and I need to give him space to do that.

"We're going to really need to talk about this." His eyes snap towards me, a frown creasing his forehead.

"We do."

"No more shutting me out."

I shake my head.

"I mean it, Lily. I'm still mad at you."

"I understand." I take a deep breath. "Will you stay with me tonight, though?" The words roll off my tongue before I can swallow them, unsure how he's going to respond.

He's a force field of a man, not the type of guy you pour your feelings out to, but for some reason, he makes me feel like I can be myself with him. Like I don't have to hide any part of who I am from him.

Staring at me intently, he licks his lips, dragging my lip down with his thumb, and my thighs instantly clench in desire.

Before I know it, his arms are snaked around my waist as he flips over, a screech escaping me.

Pressing his weight against my body, I look at his face hovering above me until he presses an affectionate kiss to my lips. It's sweet, it's soft, it's delicate, and it makes me swoon over him more than I should.

"You really thought I was done, little devil?" His mouth brushes against mine while I close my eyes, his hand cupping my cheek. He starts a trail of kisses along my jaw, and I let out a moan.

"I just got started, babe."

Fuck yeah.

23

CONNOR

Lily's light blonde hair is spread out over my chest, her arm laying across my stomach while her leg is tucked between mine. My hand starts to move up and down her spine, stirring her awake while my lips brush her hair. I breathe in the sweet scent of her hair that brings me a comforting feeling. I didn't plan on falling asleep in her bed, but after round three, my limbs started feeling heavy. I looked up at the ceiling while Lily slept in my arms. Enjoying the comfort holding her brought me, it didn't take long before I drifted off to sleep. Looking at my watch, I notice the time, and I hear Colin's faint voice followed by a giggle.

A weird jolt hits through my heart, and I freeze, a smile tugging on the corner of my mouth.

That's my boy.

"Good morning," Lily murmurs as she untangles herself from me, stretching her arms in the air.

"Does he know?" I blurt.

She lets out a yawn, giving me a confused look as I stare at her.

"What?"

"Does he know? About me?"

Rubbing her eyes, she blinks at me. She's wearing my t-shirt, and I can still see her perky tits through the fabric, turning me the fuck on.

"No."

"So what did you tell him?"

"Nothing. He's two. He hasn't grasped the concept of what a father is yet because he doesn't see a lot of kids. He's got me, and he's got Damien."

Damien.

I really hate the fucker for shooting Nigel, but now that I know he means something to Colin, hurting Damien is going to be a lot more complicated.

"Are we gonna tell him?"

"Now?" An incredulous look colors her face.

"Well, yeah? No? I don't know."

I don't know what's best for Colin. All I know is I'm his dad, and I'll be damned if she refuses to tell him.

"Connor."

"I want in, Lily," I sputter, a scowl on my face.

She places her hand on my arm, and I narrow my eyes at her, not in the mood to be smooth talked or hear whatever the fuck it is she's about to say. She better not be bullshitting me because I will storm downstairs and tell him myself.

"You're in, Connor. I promise. From now on, you'll be included. But let's do this in steps, okay? I'm used to being a single mom—"

"That's not my fault."

She sighs.

"I know. It's mine. I know that. But I've been doing this by myself for two years. I *will* include you. But can we please do this in baby steps? I have no right to ask you this, but can you give me a break? I did what I thought was best for my son, for *our* son. And as his mother, I'm asking you to think of him."

I know she has a point, and part of me trusts her judgment. She did everything by herself for the past three years, and she did great. But he's a Wolfe, and I'm not afraid to steamroll all over her if I think it will keep him safe.

I hate all the reasons she stated for not telling me. For not including me in his life, but I thought about it a lot last night while staring at the ceiling, and I do get it. I can't deny she's right. There is a big possibility that when this goes public, when the city finds out that the Wolfes now have a new heir… There will be a target on his head. He'll be the most wanted kid in the Boston area, in need of twenty-four-hour protection.

Lily included.

"What are you suggesting?" I mutter.

"Spend some time with him. With us. Get to know him a bit better. Make him more comfortable with you. Then in a day or two, we'll tell him."

The look on her face is genuine, making it hard for me to be a dick. As much as I love to fight with her, especially if it results in some angry fucking, she's Colin's mother. I have to make an effort, even if my primal urges tell me to do it differently.

"You're his father. I'm not gonna exclude you anymore. You can trust me." Her eyes are pleading, and the word *trust* puts me over the edge. If I want her to trust me to do the right thing, I have to be able to expect the same from her. I need to give her my trust as well.

"Fine."

"Thank you." She gives me a grateful look before giving me an unexpected hug. At first, my body freezes, feeling her hips resting near my morning wood, eager to do something about it. When I bury my nose in her hair and breathe her in, a potent mix of something sweet and sweaty, my arms automatically wrap around her waist, tugging her closer.

"Lily?" I grunt in her ear.

"Yeah?"

"If you don't want me to fuck you senseless again, I suggest you get off my hard dick."

Abruptly, she pushes off of me, her eyes flicking to the bulge in my boxers before she crawls backwards off the bed. I hold her gaze, allowing the craving I feel to show on my face. She's putting distance between us, silently telling me she doesn't want another round, but the lust in her eyes combined with her parted lips contradicts that.

"I should check on Colin."

"Yeah, I'll come with you."

"Y-yeah, sure." She keeps a close eye on me, grabbing a pair of gym shorts from her bag, then throwing a hoodie over her head while I walk past her in nothing but my boxers.

"I'm gonna grab some sweats from my room." I walk past her closely, whispering the words in her ear before I walk out of the room. When I get to my room, I can hear her jogging down the stairs like her tail is on fire.

A silent chuckle vibrates in my chest, enjoying the effect I have on her. Grabbing some gray sweats out of my dresser, I put them on before making my way downstairs and into the kitchen.

"Morning, ruffian!" Reign beams at me from the kitchen island when I walk in. Lily's holding Colin on her hip, giving him a tight hug that makes him giggle.

"How did you sleep?" Reign swallows a spoonful of his cereal, giving me that boyish grin, telling me I don't need to answer that.

"Shut up. Hi, big guy." I focus my attention on Colin, looking at me with a cheerful face.

"Hi!" He lifts his tiny hand in greeting, and I walk towards him and Lily, holding out my hands to grab him. Lily gives me a wary look while I wait in anticipation for Colin's response. When his arms reach out to me, a fuzzy feeling settles in my chest, and I grab him from his mother.

"Did Reign take good care of you?"

He nods his head.

"Cheerio!" He points at the box of cereal on the counter.

"He gave you Cheerios? So you already had breakfast?"

"Yes! Connor play vroom?" His eyes sparkle as Franklin walks in.

"Morning," he grunts, wearing the same clothes as the night before.

"*Franky.*" Reign nudges his chin in greeting, and I do the same.

Franklin looks at Colin in my arms before his gaze lands on Lily.

"Morning, Ms. Johnson. How are my brothers treating you?"

Walking over to the coffee machine, he looks at me with a straight face, but I can see confusion in his eyes. He's been at his penthouse in Beacon Hill for the last two weeks, since I gave Lily his bedroom, and I haven't really informed him that she's now strolling around the mansion whenever she wants.

Lily gives me a puzzled look, not sure how to react. My oldest brother can be intimidating if you don't know him, and with her knowledge of the Wolfe family, I can understand why she's cautious to answer.

"This is Franklin," I explain. "My oldest brother."

"I know who he is," she mumbles quietly. "They've been treating me well," she tells him, her voice loud and clear this time.

"Yeah, especially Connor." Reign smirks, and I quickly slap him over the head. He winces and an "ouch" escapes his lips, though his wide grin stays in place.

"How is Kendall?" I ask, trying to change the subject before Reign starts blabbering more shit.

Franklin turns around, leaning his back against the counter, taking a sip of his coffee. He looks tired and older, as if last night's events took a few years off his life.

"She's gonna be fine. The doc is keeping her asleep, for her own comfort. I'm heading back after I shower. She's coming home."

"Who's Kendall?" Lily whispers between Reign and me.

"His girlfriend," Reign pitches in.

"You mean like, *here*?" I question.

"Yeah, so since you hijacked my room," he says with a slight glare, "move your shit out, or move Lily to your room. But whatever you do, do it quickly."

I blink my eyes at him as we stare each other down, silently telling him this is too soon. I know he's not stupid. He heard about the familiarity between Lily and me that has been creeping in the last week, but I can't settle myself in her bedroom. Even if it isn't really hers.

"Scowl as long as you want, but I'm going to be back with

Kendall in two hours, and you're going to make sure a room is ready for her."

"What's going on?" I hear Lily mutter to Reign under her breath.

"Connor is going to move in with you." Reign casually takes another bite of his Cheerios.

"Wait, what?!"

"When Connor decided to kidnap you, he put you in *my* room," Franklin clarifies.

I can feel her head turn to face me, her glare burning a hole in my skin without having to look at her.

"Fix it, Connor," Franklin orders before turning his focus back on Lily, taking a step closer towards the island. "I apologize for my brother's savage behavior, Ms. Johnson. He can be a bit drastic, but trust me, he will keep you and your son safe." Slamming his knuckles on the cold surface, he moves his gaze back and forth between Reign and me. "Two hours, boys."

"What do I have to do with this?" Reign screeches as Franklin walks away.

"You're a Wolfe, Reign," Franklin replies matter-of-factly.

Lily's death stare is still locked on my face as I smile at Colin, trying to avoid her look.

"Reign, can you please take Colin for a minute?" she asks through gritted teeth.

Reign drops his spoon with a loud sigh.

Drama queen.

"Look, I love the kid already, and I'll happily be the fun uncle, but if the two of you are going to keep shoving him off to me to have sex, I'm gonna charge."

My hand reaches out to slap him once more, but instead, he ducks, lifting his hand up in a reprimanding way.

"Nah-huh! Just give me the kid, Connor. Your *wifey* wants a word with you." He smirks, grabbing Colin out of my hands.

"Shut up."

"I'm not his *wifey*." Lily turns up her nose.

"Keep telling yourself that, *sis*. Come on, little buddy. Let's get you dressed, then we'll go play in the yard."

"Yay!" Colin raises his arms as they walk out of the kitchen, and I rub my face before I turn to Lily. Her arms are folded in front of her body, lifting up her tits more than she's probably aware. The look in her eyes is filled with fire, turning me the fuck on.

"You got something to say, babe?"

"You put me in your brother's room?"

"You would've rather been dropped in my bed from the start?" My tone is dark as my eyes narrow.

"No," she blurts out, even though she doesn't sound convinced.

"You sure?"

"Shut up! Now what?"

"Now," I say, tracing her jaw with my finger, "I'm either sleeping on the floor with Reign or taking Killian's room." My mouth moves flush with her head as I whisper in her ear. "Or... I'll take residence in your bed. I prefer the latter..." I pull my head back, looking into her eyes that are now laced with lust. "But it's your call."

The desire is clear, though she's probably hesitant to voice this. Before she can shut me down, I make the choice for her.

"I'll sleep in Killian's room. I gotta go." I bop her nose with the tip of my finger, then walk off after grinding my body against hers.

"Where are you going?"

"Out. Got someone to hurt," I tell her without giving her a second glance, walking out of the kitchen.

IT'S A BRISK NIGHT, the type of weather I always enjoy when I arrive at our garage in the city. The door opens, and I watch Reign walk out.

"Where are you going?"

"I don't have to watch this. Besides, I want to check how the bar renovations are coming along."

"Yeah, okay."

I notice the troubled look on his face before he walks away.

"Reign?" I call to his back.

"Yeah?"

"You're cool with this? You on board?"

He lets out a sigh, rubbing a hand over his face before letting it fall against his leg.

"Of course, Con. Of course, I'm on board. But I just don't want to witness it. Saw enough shit in my life. Gonna avoid it if I can."

I nod.

"We cool?"

"Yeah, we're cool. I'm the hacker. You're the enforcer, we all have our jobs, right?" A playful smile lifts his lips.

"I'll see you at the house."

"Connor?" he calls when I'm almost through the door.

"Yeah?"

"Make him suffer."

I shoot him a smile before I walk through the door. Killian is standing in front of the soundproof window that gives full access to the garage, looking at the man tied up to a chair in the middle.

I know he enjoys this as much as I do. He likes to see those suffer who harm us in any way. He's just more in control of it.

Franklin is smoking a cigarette, leaning against a wall inside, listening to Emerson who is wailing through the garage. His face is bloody, his cheekbones and eyes already swelling up.

I look at Killian's bloody knuckles as he takes a sip of his whiskey.

"Had fun?" I chuckle.

An excited glint shows in his eyes.

"Just a little."

"You ready?" I grab his glass out of his hand, throwing the contents down the back of my throat before placing it on the ledge of the window in front of me.

"Let's go."

He follows me as I walk inside and I give a nod to the two guards situated in the corners before I look at Franklin.

"We taking turns tonight?"

"Do whatever. But he tried to kill my girl. I'm ending him." Franklin walks across the room to the small bar in the corner, taking off his coat, then pouring himself a drink before he drops back against the wall behind the bar while Killian takes a seat in front of the bar.

Do we have a bar for personal entertainment when one of us, meaning me, is torturing someone? Yes, yes we do.

It is fucked-up? Yes, yes it is.

But we don't take people back to the garage for no reason. If you get the honor of spending time in this building, you either fucked with our people, our family, or our business.

"What do you want to do, Kill?" I ask, rubbing my hands together as I walk towards the man responsible for my wrath the last few weeks.

Emerson slowly raises his chin, looking at me with a worn out expression.

"Connor. Nice to see you." His Southern accent echoes through the room, making goose bumps trickle over my skin.

I don't have anything against people with Southern accents; Kendall has one half the time, and I love her. But out of Emerson, it makes my skin crawl, like he's hiding behind fake hospitality when really he's just a motherfucking psychopath.

"Nice to see you too, buddy." I bend forward, placing my hands above my knees so I can look him in the eye. "How are you doing?"

"I've had better days." The asshole smirks.

"That's not hard to believe." Killian chuckles from the bar. "Considering this is your last."

The faint smell of blood enters my nose while I listen to the echoing voices resonating through the garage. I love this place. It's filled with raw energy. Primal feelings that are black and white.

Inside these walls, I don't have to consider what society thinks. I can have my way with someone, getting what I need from them without hesitation. It brings out the version of me I have to bury when I roam the streets of Boston. The side I have to contain most days. But inside this garage, I can let it all out. I can let that crude side of me out, which also ensures that I'm able to keep myself in check in public.

"Good point."

I have to admit, I admire his indifference, even though he knows he won't walk out of this place alive. He maintains his badass front as if he still has an audience, showing off his true sociopathic nature.

"You know what I don't get?" I begin. "Why Boston? You're bred and born in Alabama. Why would you travel all the way up here, settling in a city that's run by an organization whose reach goes far into New England?"

"I heard it was pretty." He shrugs.

The back of my hand swings against his cheek, blood spatter flying against the floor.

"Try again."

"I like the Red Sox?"

I repeat the move, this time with my other hand, his head swinging to the opposite side.

"I can keep this up longer than you can."

"I'm already dead, Wolfe boy. May as well have some fun before I meet my maker."

"Sounds like a plan," I snicker, walking over to the bar. "What do you think?" I look at the set of tools Killian spread out over the bar top.

"This one." Killian holds up the tongue-tearer, his face beaming with excitement.

"You're a sick fuck, you know that, right?" I smirk.

"You and me both, bro."

When I turn back around with the tearer in hand, Emerson's smile is replaced with a scowl, his eyes now filled with fear. His lips are firmly pressed together, and I can see his Adam's apple bob as he swallows hard.

"You want to try again? Why Boston?"

He doesn't reply, just keeps staring at me, trying to hide the angst that I know is running through his body.

"Wrong answer," I grouse at his silence. Before he can

even flinch, I place the tearer over his pinky, chopping it off in one clean cut.

A raucous cry reverberates through the room, the deafening sound hurting my ears.

"For fuck's sake."

"Help! Someone help me!" he yells maniacally, panic laced in his voice. His bulging eyes pan from his pinky on the floor to the door and back as he keeps screaming.

He shouldn't have called my bluff.

"Save it, Alabama boy," Franklin says from where he leans against the wall. "These walls are soundproof. You could have an Aerosmith concert in here, and no one on the street would hear a single beat."

Despair seems to wash over Emerson's face before he puts his brave front back in place, inhaling and exhaling excessively, presumably trying to calm himself down.

"Someone will make you pay for this," he spits.

He really has some balls.

"And what someone might that be?" I smile.

"You think I'm the only one who wants you dead? You have a lot of enemies, Wolfe."

"Tell me something I don't know. No one actually has the ability to do it, though. *Or the balls.*"

"If that bitch didn't screw me over, I would've." He smirks, referring to Kendall, and I throw my fist against his jaw.

"Watch your tongue. She's a Wolfe now."

He lets out a devious chuckle.

"Who's gonna take care of her when he dies?" He nudges his head towards Franklin.

"Who wants him dead?" I fold my arms in front of my body, towering over him.

"You're so quick to assume I'm the reason we all moved to Boston."

I narrow my eyes at him, trying to connect the dots.

"That's right, big boy. Let that peanut size brain of yours work for once." He grins.

Not willing to take his taunts, I lash out, grabbing him by the throat, cutting off his air supply.

"Speak, you idiot."

He gurgles, and I can feel his desperate need for air vibrating against the palm of my hand, forming a smile on my face.

"Okay!" he pushes out with difficulty before I let him go. He starts coughing like a madman and I give him a minute to get it back together.

"Speak." I hold up the tearer, silently threatening him.

"Okay, okay." His voice is throaty and cracking. "I'll tell you," he says, his face straight again. "We didn't move to Boston because I wanted to. One of us has unfinished business in this city."

"Who?"

I can see his lips tilt up again, reigniting the rage inside of me.

"I can't spoil *all* the surprises, right?"

A let out a roar, placing the tearer on his index finger to cut it off. He starts to scream uncontrollably, when his finger falls to the ground, clearly feeling more pain from this finger than the one before.

"Wrap that up," I command to one of the guards behind me when I see the blood gushing out of his hand. "Don't want him bleeding to death."

The guard grabs the first aid kit from under the bar to get

to work while Emerson keeps screaming like a pig being slaughtered until he finally passes out.

"Such a tough guy. He fucking screams like a little girl when he loses his pinky," Killian chuckles when I approach the bar to grab the bottle of whisky. I put it to my mouth, slugging a few sips before putting it back on the bar.

"Who do you think he's talking about?"

"He could be bluffing," Franklin suggests.

"You think Kendall will know?" Killian looks at Franklin.

"Doubt it. He pretty much kept her out of the loop the entire time. She was close to Josie, but she wasn't friendly with any of the other guys. She may be able to provide some history, though."

"Don't have to bother her with it. We'll get it out of him. Kendall has been through some wicked shit," I pitch in, then look at Killian. "Give me a hand?"

"Fuck yeah" Eagerly, he slides off the stool, grabbing a flame torch from the bar.

I look at Franklin who is shaking his head with a grin.

"The two of you are enjoying this way too much."

"I know." I smile, then follow my little brother back to Emerson who's slowly coming back to his senses. His hand is now wrapped up, slowing the bleeding from his missing fingers.

"Wake up, farm boy." Killian repeatedly slaps him in the face. "Hi, remember me? I'm Killian." He smiles.

Emerson keeps his head down, as if fatigue makes it too hard to hold it up.

"Are you going to good cop bad cop me?" He slurs his words a bit. "Let me guess. You're a good cop."

"Actually … I'm the bad cop," Killian retorts.

He flips the switch of the torch, dragging Emerson's shirt off to expose his stomach, and he starts to yelp once more.

"Connor likes brutal force. But I like it when the pain keeps lingering, nagging you until you can't take it anymore. Begging for relief." He starts to draw a letter W with the flame on Emerson's chest. The smell of burned skin fills the room.

"Argh!" Emerson cries out, his face crumpling. "Fuck you, you little bitch! I'm not telling shit."

"Fine by me. Means I get maximum fun out of this," Killian snickers, turning his head towards me. "What do you think? Forehead? Neck? Maybe if we melt his skin, blood will start seeping out. Would probably be a pretty cool sight?"

"Sounds good. I just need to cut this first. I can't have him flipping me off." I cut his middle finger off, and this time, instead of screaming, he lets his head hang and starts sobbing in agony like a baby.

Killian and I go at him for another fifteen minutes, me moving to his toes while Killian burns his skin in various places. He wails with everything we do, begging us to stop, but never giving us the answers we want.

"I think I'm gonna do this a little differently now," Killian announces. He pulls his knife out of his pocket, making a clean cut on Emerson's arm, then loosens the skin with the tip of the blade. Emerson is grinding his teeth, his nostrils flaring, trying to stay quiet when Killian places a piece of his skin between his fingers.

"Who helped you with the horses? Who gave you access to the tracks?" he asks, slowly peeling the skin off Emerson's arm. I'm watching in awe while Emerson's chest starts to heave, doing his best to control the pain as Killian keeps going.

"A girl!" he finally shouts. "A girl!"

Killian stops, giving me a confused look.

"What girl?"

"A girl walked into the bar one day saying she could help us overthrow you guys. Said she knew you from way back and had some shit to sort with you." The defeat in his voice is palpable.

"Knew us from where?"

"She wouldn't say. But she gave me information about your early years that checked out, so I decided to believe her. She helped me fuck with the horses and seduce your accountant, Callahan, blackmailing him in to giving us information."

"Who was she? What does she look like?" I grunt, my volume ramping up with every question.

"Bella! Her name is Bella! Brown hair, gray eyes. A real cunning little bitch!"

"Where does she live?" Killian frowns, probably already thinking about our next move.

"I don't know," Emerson whimpers, pathetically. "She pops in every now and then, but she barely shares any information about herself other than the fact that she loves Cary's cock."

"Where does she live!?" Killian shouts only an inch from his face.

Emerson sobs.

"I don't know, man, I swear. She's not from Boston. She doesn't talk like you guys."

"Why did you move to Boston? Who has unfinished business here?" I try again, grabbing the loose skin on his arm and giving it another firm tug, making him squeal again.

"No," he bites out through the pain. "That's not my story to tell. You'll have to kill me."

"Gladly," Franklin booms behind us, and we all put our focus on him. He grabs a knife from the bar while he makes his way over to us with a menacing glare on his face.

"Franky?" Killian questions.

"He's not gonna give us shit. He pretends to be a big guy, but he's just a pathetic little shit." Franklin crouches down to look up at Emerson, bringing his hand up to place the knife at his throat.

"Wait!" The sound of my voice makes him halt. "Where is Damien Johnson?"

Emerson's eyes darken, a knowing grin appearing on his battered face.

"Who knows?"

"Tell us!" Killian places the torch on his cheek.

"He was a liability."

"Is he dead?" I press.

"I guess you'll never know." He shrugs.

"Argh!" Killian hits him over the head with the torch before throwing it through the room in frustration. "Kill him. He's useless."

Franklin gives me a questioning look, waiting for my confirmation.

When I nod, he turns back to Emerson.

"I'm glad you're not talking," Franklin begins in a deep, malicious tone. "It will be the perfect opportunity to show the rest of the city what we do with people like you. And once the rest of your minions get the message ... we will send pictures of your violated, dead body to your mother, making sure she'll never forget what a scumbag her son was. Then and only then, I will happily get on a boat and feed your Alabama

ass to the sharks in the Atlantic. I'll see you in hell, Jones."
Before Emerson can respond, Franklin slits his throat, and he
gurgles with his eyes practically bulging out of his head.
Blood floods out of the veins on his neck until finally he
collapses, and the life leaves his body.

We share some looks when Franklin gets up.

"What fucking girl?" I finally ask.

"No clue." Killian shrugs.

"Get Reign to find that out. I'm going to the office for a
few more hours."

"Yeah, sure."

Franklin looks frustrated as he walks back to the bar and
grabs his coat, then gives us a final nod before he heads out.

"I guess this isn't over yet." Killian purses his lips in
annoyance, shaking his head.

"I guess not." I rub a hand over my face before snapping
my fingers at a guard. "Pay off the cops. I want this body in
front of his bar for at least two hours. Then I want it
shredded into fish food. Let's go, Kill." I walk out of the
garage with some relief, knowing the bastard responsible for
Nigel's death is no longer a threat.

"You going to the house?" Killian asks when we step into
the night. The streets are quiet, with no one around other
than Killian's chauffeur waiting for him. I don't have one. I
like to drive. I like maintaining control over where I'm going.
Not to mention being alone sometimes. There is something
relaxing about just sitting in my truck and driving.

"Yeah. Are you?"

"Nah, gonna hit up a club I think. Score some ass. I'll
probably sleep in the city."

"Good. Because I'm sleeping in your room."

Killian's eyebrows pop up in surprise, then he laughs.

"I guess Lily isn't ready to 'sleep' with you yet?" He makes air quotes, causing me to roll my eyes with a grin.

"She'll come around."

He examines my face for a few seconds.

"You want her to?"

The question throws me off guard, not really knowing what I want. She turns me on like crazy. And now that I know she's my baby mama, I want us to get along, but do I want more? Do I want her to share my bed?

"I don't know." I shrug.

"You'll figure it out." He smiles before we both go our separate ways.

24

I'm finishing the chocolate frosting on the cream pie in the kitchen when I hear the front door open and close with a loud thud. Out of habit, I drop the knife to wipe my hands on my jeans, staying quiet to listen to one of the brothers coming home.

The first time I was wary, wondering if I'd be safe from whomever would walk through that door, but I soon found out that this estate's security is off the charts. After Emerson and his crew, including my dumbass brother, crashed Killian's birthday party, they doubled their security. Though the guards rarely share the room with me, giving me my privacy, I know there is one covering every room in the house even when I can't see them. The yard has even more, covering every yard of the estate's grounds. Colin stared at them in awe the first time we went to play outside.

'Look, Mommy! Soldier!'

'Those are not soldiers, sweetie.' I'd replied to his confusion.

Well, they are, they just serve a different kind of army. I couldn't bother to explain, so since that day, Colin has been calling them soldiers.

The sounds of heavy boots in the hallway are coming closer, and I don't even have to wonder who it is. My eyes stay focused on the door with a smile, like the little tramp that I am. My mind keeps telling me the son of a bitch kidnapped me, not to mention the fact that he left my two-year-old son unsupervised because he was on a rampage, but I can't help but forget about that every time I'm reminded of how he feels between my legs.

And I'm sore, so that has been pretty much all day.

I've been walking around the house like a horny teenager for the last twelve hours. Connor walked out of the house looking all fresh and clean with his white t-shirt, and I wanted to grab him and drag him back upstairs. From that moment on, everything was torture. As soon as Reign offered to watch Colin so I could grab a shower, I eagerly ran to the bathroom, giving myself the quickest release I've ever pulled off. I don't know what it is with this man, but he has me craving him like mad.

I want to feel him eat me inside out.

I want him to fill me up and stretch me wide.

I want him to spank me like a little girl.

And most of all, I want him to make me crash and burn until I can't speak.

I feel obsessed, and it's making it impossible for me to even remotely try to keep up an indifferent front.

It shouldn't even surprise me since I've been using him in my imagination ever since the first time we hooked up. I guess I had expected myself to have at least a little more restraint after our fight last night. Or in general. Even though I never pretended he wasn't hot, I sure as fuck had been feeding my own mind with reasons why I shouldn't tell him about Colin. Telling myself it was better and safer to not allow him into our lives. Being involved with a Wolfe was bad news. Something I should stay far, far away from.

Been there once, can't go there twice. But the second his scarred lip touched my face, I knew I wanted more.

I still want more.

He finally walks through the door, and my face instantly falls, my lust replaced with horror as worry races through my body.

His once crisp white shirt is covered in blood, making my eyes grow wide when he approaches me with a smirk on his face. His blonde hair is brown from the blood that is sticking to his scalp, and there are dark smudges on his arms.

"What happened?" I gasp.

He slowly closes the distance between us before grabbing my hips and spinning me to face him. He crowds my space with my ass against the counter as I look up at him with what I hope is a fierce scowl in place.

"Hey, babe. Did you wait up for me?" he rumbles casually.

When he places both hands beside me, giving me no out, he leans in, moving his face only an inch from mine. His breath smells like caramel and whisky, and I press my lips into a firm line to prevent myself from diving in.

"Wanna tell me what happened?" I counter.

"Not really."

"Connor."

He looks beside me on the island.

"What the…? Is that a cream pie?"

"Yeah."

"You made this?" He runs his finger through the chocolate before putting it in his mouth, licking off the dark sweetness with a suggestive look.

"Yeah?"

His brow shoots up in surprise, a sparkle in his eyes that makes me chuckle.

"What the hell, woman? You said you baked cookies. Not complete cream pies."

I shrug.

"I like to bake for Colin. I'm not a chef or anything, but I know my way around the kitchen."

"You really are full of surprises, aren't you?"

"Am I?"

"Yeah," he muses, wiping the flour off my cheek with his thumb.

His touch has me parting my lips. It feels like a box of butterflies is emptied in my stomach when I look into his green eyes. They are both intimidating and hypnotizing at the same time, completely drawing me in.

"What else surprised you?" I let out a desperate breath, and he drags his teeth over his lower lip, his nostrils slightly flaring. I can feel the tension rising, and I'm enjoying every second of it.

"The lack of fight you put up yesterday." His thumb brushes my lips. "I'd expected you to give me a hard time. Shut me out. I expected you to punch me between the legs when I kissed you. But instead, you launched yourself at me like a little bitch in heat."

I push out a deep breath, my tongue darting out to lick my lips, briefly touching his fingers.

He's right. I can't help myself when it comes to this man.

I have been imagining the day Connor would walk back into my life for the last two years. I knew it was inevitable. He was gonna find out who Colin was eventually, either because I had to tell Colin the truth or because you can't keep secrets in this city forever.

I could've moved. In fact, I should've moved. Found a nice place somewhere in the Midwest where criminals stick to car theft and burglaries. Somewhere the Wolfes don't control the city.

But even though the thought crossed my mind numerous times, I never seriously considered it. This is my city. This is where I was born and raised, and this is where I want Colin to grow up.

He clears his throat. "You wanna play, don't you, *Lily?* Your mind is telling you to push me away. That I'm bad. That I will hurt you. That I will hurt Colin. That I will hurt *Damien.*" His finger moves down my collarbone in a scorching way, and all I can think is how I want more.

More of his touch all over my body.

He frustrates me.

But I frustrate myself even more.

I want to hate him for disrupting my life.

Twice.

But I can't.

"I hate you," I lie in a whisper.

"You keep saying that. But I call bullshit. You don't hate *me.*" His finger moves down, drawing circles around my pebbled nipple, peeking through my shirt before slowly migrating towards the hem of my shorts. "You *want* me. And you hate yourself for it." He brushes his fingers between my legs, pushing the fabric aside to run his finger along the seam of my panties.

I swallow hard, staring into his eyes, longing for him to go even farther.

"You want me to torture you." He lifts me up to the counter, placing himself between my legs. His hand moves back to my center, the other one keeping me in a firm grip. "You want me to devour you." His lips start to leave a trail of kisses down my neck. "You want me to eat you alive. And burn you like you know only *I* can." He says the last two words while simultaneously sliding his finger through my folds, making me whimper at his touch. He strokes it up and down, coating his finger with my juices.

I let out a moan right before he stops, moving his head back to look me in the eyes.

There is an arrogant grin plastered on his face that's pissing me off, but I ignore it because of the hunger he has ignited inside of me.

"What do you want, *Lily?*" His tongue runs over his scar, and all I can think is how I want his tongue to lick me like I'm a fucking popsicle.

My hands are still beside me, aching to run over his rock-hard chest. To claw him and leave my mark on him for everyone to see, but I hold back, not wanting to play into his hands.

He rubs his hands over my bare legs, softly massaging the muscles, then moving them to my hips. He presses his fingers deep inside , the arrogant look on his face never changing.

"Answer the question, babe."

I hold his stare, my breathing steady, though my heart feels like it will pound out of my chest any second now.

"Answer the question, and I'll make you feel everything I know you've been craving all day. Keep your pretty mouth shut, and I'll be off to bed, stroking my dick while I think of you."

I can't hold in the gasp that leaves my throat, imagining the picture he just painted. Not only does it turn me on, it irks me, causing the muscles in my cheeks to tense. The smirk on his face grows wider, making me shake my head.

The son of a bitch has me exactly where he wants.

Wrapped around his dick like I have no backbone.

An obsessed little cunt.

"What's it going to be, babe?"

I lash out, grabbing his blood-stained shirt with a tight grip, pulling him close to my body. His heft feels good against my chest while I brush my nose against his, my voice gruff.

"I wish I never laid eyes on you."

"Oh, stop kidding yourself, babe."

Done playing games, he crashes his lips against mine, his tongue pushing roughly inside of my mouth. His arms snake around my body, pulling me tight against him, making me arch my back while my hands hold his face in place so I can explore his mouth.

I pull his shirt over his head, momentarily disconnecting our faces before our frenzied kissing resumes. Heat flashes all over my body, desire curling my toes.

God, I want this man so bad.

His fingers delving into my body is the best feeling in the world, and I'm not sure I can go without it another day. The very first time seemed like an event I made bigger in my head, the dream I'd let myself remember when I thought about my baby daddy. But the last twenty-four hours made it clear that the real thing is even better than the dream.

Connor Wolfe makes me come undone with his hands like no man ever has or ever will.

My nails dig into his shoulders, and a grunt leaves his lips as he forcefully grabs my face with his hands.

"You wanna brand me, baby? Make it *stick*. Gotta dig deeper than that."

Surprised by his reaction, I kiss him while scratching the skin on his back. An approving rumble vibrates against my tongue, and I bite his lip in answer.

"My baby likes it rough. I still remember that," he breathes against my lips, then lifts me a little off the counter with one arm wrapped around my body as he starts to drag my shorts and panties off my hips. "Best memory of my life."

Quickly, he throws the pieces of fabric on the floor before getting down on his knees, making me whimper before he even touches me.

He rapidly pushes my legs as wide as possible, a screech leaving my lips while I look down at him.

It's the sexiest thing I've ever seen, watching this beefy piece of man on his knees in front of me, looking up like I'm the most beautiful thing he's ever seen. There is a greediness in his eyes that turns me on even more, wanting to clench his head between my thighs.

"This..." I throw my head back with a moan when he pushes a finger inside of me. "I have been thinking about this since I walked out the door this morning. And you know what I decided when I walked into the kitchen just now?"

Without waiting for my reaction, he moves my ass to the edge of the counter, giving him full access to eat me out like a fucking animal.

I shake my head, biting my lip.

"It's mine. Your pussy is mine. You want to brand me? Leave your mark? I'm claiming *this*." He runs his tongue from my asshole all the way up to my clit with a flat tongue. "It's mine, *Lily.*"

I lean back on my elbows next to the unfinished cream pie that is now the last thing on my mind. The cold marble chills my ass cheeks while my center burns to the core from this man's tongue, a delicious combination that has me panting for air.

"Oh, you taste so good," he rasps, bruising my skin when his fingers sink into my ass with force. He starts to flick my clit interspersed by his flat tongue dragging from my center all the way up, giving my clit just enough pressure for me to want to combust into flames. I can feel the muscles in my ass tighten, and I cry out, knowing I'm close.

"No." Connor gets up, leaving me wide-eyed and legs spread. "You're coming around my dick," he announces, pushing off his jeans before stepping out of them.

When he's standing in front of me, all naked and glorious, he takes a few steps closer, his hand snaking under my shirt. He licks his lips in a seductive way.

"You need to taste yourself."

He runs his tongue along the seam of my lips, and I softly push my own out, meeting him halfway. Grunting, I taste my saltiness, loving the thought of him covered in my heat. Unexpectedly, I feel the tip of his shaft pressing against my center, teasing me, then he pushes in until he can't go any farther.

My arms are wrapped around his neck, and I rest my teeth on his shoulder, softly biting into his skin while he starts to thrust inside of me. A shattering jolt surges through me every time he hits the wall inside of me, as if he's determined to tear it down.

All I can do is hold on for dear life, needing him to fuck me rough and hard like it's his last day alive.

"Fuck me harder, Connor," I encourage when I feel my orgasm start to grow like a balloon ready to pop.

He softly bites my neck in response before he starts to plow inside of me at a frantic pace, taking my command. He's holding me tight against his body which is completely at his disposal while I hang onto his neck, completely surrendered. I want this. I want to be used by him. I want him to lose himself inside of me like I do every time he touches me.

On his next push, I let out a desperate moan, my lips forming an O while my eyes grow wide from the force that erupts inside of me.

"Fuuuuuuck!"

"That's it, baby. I want you to still feel me when you wake up in the morning." He licks his thumb then presses it against my clit, and my legs start to shake while a flood drips out of my pussy onto his cock. "Fuck yeah! Give it to me!"

When my body goes almost limp, he keeps driving inside of me until a roar vibrates against the skin on my neck, and he unloads inside of me. He gives it a few more pumps until he stills, keeping me in a tight hug pressed against his body, my legs wrapped around his waist as I rest my forehead on his shoulder. I close my eyes in satisfaction, holding onto Connor like he's my lifeline, and I'm not ready to let go while he seems to be doing the same.

We are both panting against each other's heated skin when I hear the front door. Instantly, I stiffen in his arms.

"Shit," he mutters. I try to wriggle out of his grasp, but he tightens his grip even more. "Sssshhh. It's okay."

I look into his eyes which are soft and laced with something I can't define. Regardless, they're comforting, so I nod in agreement, showing him I trust him.

"Franky?" Connor calls out towards the kitchen door.

"Where you at, Connor?" Franklin replies while I hear his leather shoes move closer.

"Don't come in!" Connor shouts at the same time the swinging door flies open.

Afraid to turn around, I keep staring at Connor's rugged, but beautiful, face. His eyes close for a second before a coy smile appears on his face.

"For fuck's sake, Connor. Hi, Lily."

"Hey," I respond, feeling awkward as fuck now that Franklin has a clear sight to my bare ass on his kitchen island.

"I've been living here for the last few years while the three of you have been cooped up in your apartments most of the time. Don't come at me when I wanna fuck my girl in the kitchen, okay?"

"Connor!" I slap his chest.

"What?!" He shrugs with a questioning look pointed at me before he turns his focus back to his brother.

"Kendall and I are going to be staying here for a while. Please don't fuck *your girl* in the kitchen we all eat in, okay?"

Hearing Franklin repeat Connor's words makes my heart jump in excitement. You know in movies when the hero wins one of those gigantic stuffed animals for his girl, and she hugs the thing all giddy with love struck eyes?

That's me right now.

"Fine," Connor scoffs. "Can you go now?"

"Bye, Lily."

"Bye," I chuckle, staring at Connor, waiting for him to face me again.

When Franklin's footsteps are only a faint sound in the foyer, he finally does.

"Sorry about that."

"It's okay." I burst out in laughter.

"What?" He grins.

"This kitchen will never be the same again."

He snickers then reaches behind me before turning to face me with his finger covered in chocolate, all while still situated between my legs.

"You're the first one to make a Boston cream pie in this kitchen. It definitely will never be the same again," he jokes, then places his finger in front of my face.

Eagerly, I place my lips over it, sucking off the frosting, keeping my eyes locked with his while I stare at him through my thick lashes.

"Do you want me to have a heart attack?" he groans, pulling out his finger with a pop, then pressing another kiss against my lips.

"I'd never," I reply in faux shock.

"Time for bed, babe."

The sound of that makes my face fall, realizing Colin is sound asleep upstairs. He must notice my hesitation because he presses his forehead against mine, holding my neck.

"I'll go to my own bed, don't worry, angel."

"It's just... I don't know how he'll react if we're in bed together."

"It's okay. You don't have to explain." He gives me a comforting look, turning into a sweet teddy bear. To my surprise, I can feel disappointment seeping out of him. He takes a step back, and I hate the cold feeling I'm left with.

I watch him as he grabs his jeans from the floor, putting them on, then throwing his ruined shirt into the trash can.

"Connor."

"Lily." He grabs my face, this time with his signature scowl in place. "We're good. Everything is fine. Don't make this bigger than it is. I'm going to take a shower. I'll see you in the morning." His lips find mine in an affectionate kiss, warming me inside.

"Okay." I give in when he presses his forehead against mine. "Goodnight, Connor."

"Goodnight, babe." He shoots me a wink that almost has me sliding off the counter as I watch him walk out of the kitchen with his bare chest. His toned back is clawed up like I'd intended, covered with scratches. I press my lips together with a smile as pride fills my chest. Like he can read my mind, he turns around when he reaches the door.

"Enjoying your work?" He smirks.

"Hmm."

He laughingly shakes his head before he disappears out of my sight, and I'm left alone with my naked ass still plastered on the counter. I slide off, taking a paper towel to clean myself before I put my clothes back on.

Turning around, I take in the cream pie that's still only half frosted, laughing before rubbing my hands over my sweaty face.

I've been fooling myself all these years, thinking Connor Wolfe was nothing more to me than a one-night stand that became a permanent reminder because of the gift he left me with. But now I know the feelings I felt that first night were real. Connor and I, we have a connection. An undeniable chemistry that links us not just by Colin, but by everything that we are. I felt it the first time, and I've felt it again since the day he stormed into my apartment like a crazy person.

Connor Wolfe craves me just as much as I crave him, like a junkie living from fix to fix.

I just can't get enough.

Connor seems to know my body even better than I do, and I can't help wondering what life would be with him in it.

Still enjoying my natural high, I push my thoughts away, washing my hands before I finish the frosting on the cream pie. When I'm done, I start cleaning the kitchen with a smile still in place. After I run the last cloth over the counter, I make my way upstairs. My hand reaches to the doorknob of my bedroom, but I linger, staring into the hallway. The distinct sound of a shower is coming from Killian's room, and I feel my heart start to beat a little quicker.

The desire to spend the night with Connor is lurking in the back of my head, fed by the memory of the warmth of his arms on my body. Waking up in his arms this morning was a feeling I'd like to relive again, but knowing Colin is sleeping in the same room tells me I can't. Making a decision, I push the door open, walking into the room as I close the door with my foot. I glance at my baby boy, safe and sound, on the right side of the bed. The middle of the bed is filled with pillows, while Reign and Killian's improvised gate on the right side prevents him from falling out. I give him one last kiss on his hair, brushing his cheek with the back of my hand before I crawl in bed right beside him.

TWO HOURS.

I've been staring at the ceiling for two hours, thinking about the man in the next room.

My pussy is still sore in the best way, but the ache keeps

reminding me I'm in bed alone when really I want to be wrapped in his arms until the sun rises. I've been overthinking this every possible way, thinking of every possible scenario.

But they all have one thing in common: I will have to tell Colin who his father is.

I already came to terms with that, but I can't seem to explain to myself why I should wait any longer if that means that Connor could spend the night with me.

Finally, I'm done.

I throw the covers back, tiptoeing out of the room and into the hallway.

My heart starts to race when I'm standing in front of Killian's room, wearing nothing more than a tank and my panties, praying Franklin doesn't catch me roaming the house dressed like this. I take a deep breath, trying to control my nerves as I open the door, letting my eyes adjust to the darkness.

The room is set up the same as the other rooms, but this has a more modern feel with glassy art and black furniture. A typical man's bedroom.

Blinking a few times, my eyes finally notice Connor, sound asleep in the middle of the bed. He's on his back, his hand folded on his chest, bringing out the muscles of his arms.

This man even looks like a beast sleeping. It's ridiculous.

I feel the soft carpet under my toes as I slowly walk over, not wanting to scare him. His breathing is heavy until suddenly it stops, and I hold my breath, frozen in the middle of the room, waiting for him to freak out.

"What are you doing here, Lily?" His voice is throaty, his eyes still closed.

"I can't sleep."

He opens his eyes, tilting his head towards me. The

moonlight from the window is shining into his green eyes, making him even more intimidating, even though there are a few yards between us. Like a wolf, lurking in the shadows.

Propping up on his elbows, he moves his body up until it's rested against the headboard.

"What do you want me to do about that?"

I awkwardly hug my arms around my body, clearing my throat before I take the last step to reach him. Grabbing his hand, I stay beside the bed, not saying a word as I tug him to get out. To my relief, he gets out of bed without hesitation as I start to guide him out of the room.

We walk back to my bedroom, but when I open the door, he gives me a soft pull. I turn on the spot while he plants his hands on the small of my back, hugging me against his chest.

"Are you sure?" He dips his chin, brushing his lips against mine.

"Yes."

A silent understanding forms between us, and he gives me a sweet peck before we walk in, and I crawl into the bed. Connor watches how I'm waiting for him to join me as he closes the door, then gives Colin a glance.

"He won't wake up?"

I shake my head, raising the covers for him. He gets in beside me, then opens his arms. With a content feeling, I settle against his chest, holding him tight against my body.

"Thank you, angel," he whispers against my hair.

"Don't need to thank me, Connor." I press a kiss on his chest.

I mean that. I'm grateful he's willing to do this at my pace. It only makes me want to give it to him faster. I don't want to lie to anyone anymore.

Connor is Colin's father, and they have the right to spend time together.

If it means I can spend some time with the beast of Boston as well, I'll take it.

"Goodnight, babe."

"Goodnight." His hand softly strokes my back while I listen to the beating of his heart. It doesn't take long before I drift off to the best sleep I have had in years.

25

CONNOR

L ily's still wrapped up in my arms when I feel some movement next to me, and I slowly open my eyes.

"Hey, buddy." My voice sounds hoarse as I crack out the words , noticing Colin sitting next to me. He's on his knees, still wearing his dinosaur pajamas, with a big smile on his face. His green eyes still look sleepy, telling me he hasn't been awake for long. He holds on to his teddy, Boot, with his pacifier between his teeth.

He looks fucking adorable.

"Hi!" he waves, then glances at Lily who is still sound asleep. I bring my finger up to my mouth.

"Ssssh let's not wake up, Mommy."

"Mommy sleepy."

"Yeah, Mommy still sleeping."

When I try to wiggle from beneath her body, she starts to wake up, and Colin giggles.

She pushes off of me, pulling her head from my chest, stretching her arms with a loud moan.

"Oh, shit. Hi, baby," she mutters, then plasters a big smile on her face before glancing awkwardly at me. I can't help but smile as I watch her insecurity make her indecisive over what to do. She reaches for him, and he hops over me as if my sleeping next to his mom is the most normal thing in the world. He throws his little arms around her neck, and she settles against the headboard.

When I turn to my side to look at them, a warm feeling forms in my chest. It's the same feeling I've had every time I've looked at them these last two days. The concept of family has changed completely for me. For longer than a decade, my family was me and my siblings. Nothing more and nothing less. I liked that Kendall had made my family expand. I didn't expect our family to continue expanding, at least not so soon. Even though I have no clue how Lily and I will make it work, now that we share a tiny person, Colin is my blood. Lily is his blood. They are family.

"Conno sleepy!" Colin smiles, his pacifier still in his mouth. He drops his head against his mother's chest.

"Yes. We had a sleepover. Isn't that fun?" She shoots me a look, telling me to play along. Right, like that is going to work. He may only be two, but I'm sure he doesn't understand that something is different about this situation.

"Sleepover. Nice," I mumble with a smile.

"Pajama party," Colin giggles. "Again?"

Well, okay. I guess a sleepover is a good enough explanation for him.

"You want me to sleep over again?"

He nods, his chunky face fixated on me. I glance at Lily, still a little unsure about it all.

I don't want to push her into a situation she doesn't want to be in, so I wait for her to give me any kind of hint to go on. She dragged me out of bed last night, clearly for reasons other than sex, because she could've gotten that in Killian's room without waking up Colin. But instead, she wanted me to *sleep* with her, and even though that tells me that this isn't just an itch she needs to scratch, I'm also not sure what it is that she wants.

When she doesn't say anything, I take matters into my own hands.

"Yeah, we can have a sleepover tonight."

"Yaay!" His arms lift in the air, then he launches himself at me, cuddling into my chest like he did with Lily. I gently brush his blond hair, enjoying the feeling of his tiny body against mine.

I think I've grown on him the last week. The first few days after I brought them here, he was cautious, eyeing me skeptically every time he saw me. He never seemed scared, more like he just wasn't quite sure what to make of me. I don't give off an approachable vibe like Reign does. I'm big, broody, and the permanent scowl on my face doesn't help butter up any toddlers. Yet I managed with Colin. When I come to find him after dinner, he's usually already waiting for me, and he's becoming real chatty with me. But him wanting me to hold him when his mom is only a foot away? That makes me feel more satisfied than I expected.

"Mommy." He points at Lily.

"You wanna go to Mommy?"

"No," he firmly shakes his head. "Mommy!"

"Yeah, that's Mommy."

"Mommy," he repeats, then pokes his little finger into my chest. "Daddy."

Lily's eyebrows shoot up, releasing a tiny gasp.

"Daddy? Connor Daddy?" she asks Colin.

"Yes, Connor my daddy?" He gives her the sweetest smile before pressing his body even closer. I breathe in his fresh scent, giving him a tight hug when I realize what he's asking.

"Pweez," he begs when we don't reply.

"You want Connor to be your daddy?" Lily asks for clarification.

"Yeah!" It leaves his lips so quickly, with the easy tone only a child can possess. The simplicity of a kid who just flat-out asks for what he wants. I stare at Lily, giving her the chance to take the lead. We have a silent conversation, both unsure what to do right now. Lily seems overwhelmed, not sure what to do, yet I'm not willing to let this moment pass. I place my hand on her cheek, giving her an encouraging look. Hoping she understands my silent plea to go through with this.

I'm not going to fuck it all up for her. I'm not going to waltz all over her parenting routine or whatever shit it is you need to do when you become a parent. But I want in. And I want Colin to know who I am. Who I really am.

Finally, Lily leans into my touch, giving me a small smile before she sighs.

"Well, sweetie. Connor *is* your dad."

"Yes!" Colin responds, pointing at his mom, then poking his finger into me once more. "Mommy. Daddy." He looks proud and smug, as if he asked his mother for candy at eight in the morning, and she complied.

"You want me to be your daddy, little guy?"

"Yes. Connor Colin Daddy." He looks up at me, his hopeful green eyes unleashing a whole wave of emotions inside of me. He's like the mirror of the young boy I once was. Before Reign and Killian were born and everything was still semi-peaceful at home. When I still held the innocence I see in Colin's eyes. It's right then and there that I truly realize the meaning of being his father, and I silently vow to him to do better. To do better than my father did. To protect him for as long as I can, making it my primary mission to help him stay innocent for as long as possible.

"Yeah. I'm your dad."

Lily gasps for air, and I look up to watch a tear run down her fair skin.

"What's wrong?"

"How? I didn't…? What just happened?" She shakes her head incredulously.

I shrug.

"No clue. He must have noticed how handsome we both are. Seeing the resemblance."

She slaps my arm with a grin.

"Shut up, you tool." She falls silent again, a satisfied look on her face. "I guess telling him was easier than I thought."

"You didn't do shit."

"Neither did you. And don't say shit!"

"Lily."

"Yeah."

"Shut up." I grab her neck, tugging her towards me to give her a sweet kiss.

We cuddle against each other, just the three of us, and I haven't felt this content in my life. Never expecting this feeling to be in the cards for me.

Colin startles in my arms when a loud knock sounds on the door, and I curse under my breath.

"Connor!" Reign bellows through the door, and I look at the clock on the nightstand.

What the fuck is this tool thinking, banging at my door at seven in the morning?

"Reign!" Colin bellows.

"What?!"

"It's Kendall. The doc is gonna wake her up."

I sigh with relief.

"I'll be right there."

"Kendall? Franklin's girlfriend?" Lily looks up at me.

I nod, putting Colin next to me to get off the bed.

"What happened to her?"

My eyes roam over her questioning face before I grab my phone from the nightstand. Her blonde hair is messy, but with the lack of makeup on her face, she looks perfect in the morning light. Like the purest of angels.

"She hit her head pretty bad. The doctor kept her in a medically induced coma for a few days."

"How did she hit her head?"

"Not the right time for a story, Lily." I glance at Colin, then watch as a scowl appears on her face that makes me laugh. "Don't be like that. I will tell you another time. *Alone.*" My mouth presses against hers while my hand rests on her neck. "I'll see you later, okay? Bye, buddy." I give Colin a high five before I walk out the door, hearing her mutter behind me.

"Bye, jackass."

"Bye, angel," I chuckle without looking back.

26

CONNOR

It's a few hours later when we all walk into the mansion office.

"She looks good. Tired, but good," Reign points out.

The doc took her off the meds this morning and by the time my brothers and I were surrounding her bed, she slowly woke up. She looked like she could use a vacation, but other than that, she'll probably be on her feet in no time.

"Not good enough." Franklin sits down behind his desk, pouring himself a glass of whisky from the bottle in his drawer even though it's only nine in the morning.

The room is stuffy and still smells smokey from the amount of cigarettes Franklin used to smoke in here before Kendall came along. With the dark wood of the furniture and the books filling up the shelves, along with some boring paintings, it looks like the place where old men drink liquor and plot world domination.

In reality, this is where we sit with a box of Dunks ninety

percent of the time, hashing out who needs to do what that day.

"She'll be fine in a few days, Franky," I reassure him.

He chugs down the contents of his glass, then slams it down on his desk.

"What the hell was that bullshit yesterday?" he grunts, referring to the shit Emerson Jones spewed before we bled him out.

"What bullshit? Did I miss all the fun again?" Reign moves his head between the three of us with a cocky grin. We all know he's not the ruthless type like the rest of us can be, so we know he's full of shit.

"If by 'fun' you mean burning and skinning Emerson Jones, then yes. You missed all the fun." Killian laughs.

Reign pulls a face of disgust, his hair flopping in front of his forehead.

"You skinned him?"

"Oh, don't forget about all the fingers Connor chopped off."

"You two," he says, pointing his finger back and forth between the two of us, "are nasty."

"Whatever." I shrug.

"So what did the bastard confess?" Reign looks at Franklin.

Since Kendall joined our little fucked up family, Reign seems to get along with Franky better. He'll still piss Franklin off any chance he gets, but the amount of snarky comments has gone down to a minimum, and I can't deny I'm enjoying it. It's a welcome change after Killian and I tried to get them to sort their differences like a million times.

When we were younger, the two of them were two peas in a pod with Reign looking up to our oldest brother. Franklin was his hero. We all knew our father was never gonna fill that role, yet Franklin was there for us. But that all changed when Franklin got arrested. With a dead mom and a father nowhere to be found, the rest of us were thrown in to foster care. Reign, being the little whiz kid that he is, found a way to hack the police station, tampered with some files, and got Franklin's charges dropped and out within a week. Innocent until proven guilty.

I've always known Franklin wasn't innocent, but I also knew that the kid he hurt deserved everything my brother did to him. Luckily, Reign made sure there was no evidence. But Reign didn't know what our oldest brother did, and foster care fucked him up. Franklin did everything he could to get full custody of us when our dad left, but by the time Franklin got out of shackles, it was already too late for us. The three of us had been separated and placed with different families. It took an additional two months after Franklin was released until he was able to get me out of that hellhole. After that, it took us two years to get Killian out, but we couldn't get Reign out until he was sixteen. All was well when the four of us were finally back in one house, but Reign, still thinking Franklin was innocent, freaked when he found out that wasn't the case. After everything he'd witnessed in whatever fucked up family they'd put him in, he put Franklin in the bad guy corner, and he has hated his guts ever since.

He never turned against him, but Reign made it real clear he wasn't happy with Franklin in the slightest. It pissed Franklin off more than anything, but our oldest brother is a proud man. He refused to tell the truth to Reign if he, in turn, refused to ask him what happened that night. After Franklin also swore Killian and me to secrecy, the matter was pushed under the rug, and we formed a united front to present to the city.

"Some shit about some girl out to get us," Killian answers Reign.

"Some girl?"

"Yeah," I chime in. "He said some girl walked into the Anchor one day, saying she had information about us that could help him overthrow us."

"Pissed off any more *damsels*, Reign?" Franklin scowls, leaning back in his chair.

"Me?!" he yelps, then points his thumb at Killian. "Ask the man-whore over here. He's the one picking up a new piece every Friday. Not me."

"He's not wrong." Killian nods.

"Focus, shitheads." Franklin shoots both of them a reprimanding glare. "He said something about not being the one who wanted to move to Boston. *What makes you think I'm the one we moved to Boston for?*' That's what he said. How many of them moved from Alabama to Massachusetts?"

"Maybe Kendall can help?" I suggest.

"Not in the state she's in now. But she has mentioned that she moved here with Josie, Emerson, and a few of his friends. Find out who else moved up here with them. I want to know names, family, friends, everything."

"What am I looking for?" Reign asks.

"Anything that could be a connection to Boston, I want to know. One of those assholes is out to destroy us, and I want to know why. Emerson gave me the impression it was personal." Franklin lets out a weighted breath before turning to Reign, changing the subject. "How is the bar coming along?" Franklin changes the subject, referring to the bar Reign and Killian are going to run once it opens.

"They'll be done renovating by the end of the week. We had some wicked setbacks, but we planned the opening for two weeks from Saturday." Reign shares a look with Killian, who nods in agreement.

"You have to give us a list of people you want to invite, and we need to hire some more security for that night," Killian suggests.

"Sounds good. The two of you make sure the bar is ready, and arrange some extra security, Connor," Franklin orders.

We all nod in agreement, and I get up, ready to leave to find Lily and Colin.

"Hold up," Franklin calls out to me, then points back to the chair I just vacated. "Sit."

A smug grin spreads across his face as he grabs three more glasses out of his drawer and pours two fingers of whisky into all of them before he hands them out to us one by one. We all take a glass while I shoot him a confused look, wondering what the fuck this is about.

"These bastards," Franklin nudges his chin towards Reign and Killian, "told me their suspicions a few days ago, but it came to my attention that it's official now?"

"What the fuck are you talking about?"

"We have a new Wolfe joining the pack?" He smirks, cocking one brow in question, and I suddenly realize what he means.

I let out a huff, the corner of my mouth curling.

"Not sure if I want him to join 'the pack.' Four of us fucked-up souls are more than enough, don't you think?"

"Either way, he's a Wolfe now," Killian chides.

"Yeah, he's a Wolfe," I admit.

"Whoop whoop!" Reign waves his hands in the air, dancing while sitting in his chair.

"Congratulations." Franklin raises his glass, and we all mimic his move. "She finally admitted it, then? Does Colin already know?"

"We told him this morning. Or actually, he found out," I say with pride.

"He found out?" Reign questions.

"Sorta. He asked if I wanted to be his daddy when he found me in bed with his mother this morning." I take a sip of my whisky, avoiding their smug grins.

"You dirty fucker," Killian chuckles.

"I didn't fuck her next to the boy, if that's what you're thinking."

"No, you already did that with her ass plastered on the kitchen counter," Franklin retorts.

"Right."

"Oh, for fuck's sake. You fucked her in our kitchen? I eat in there," Reign whines like a damn toddler before we laugh in unison.

"You know what this means, right?" Franklin starts. "He's a Wolfe. Lily is his mother. Not sure what your relationship is with the girl, but they're family now."

I nod. I wouldn't want it any other way. I push out a troubled breath before I mention the pink elephant in the room.

"It also means we need to find Damien Johnson."

I feel my younger brothers' eyes on me, but I keep my focus on Franklin who tilts his head a little.

"Are you cool with that?"

"Not gonna lie, I hate the bastard. But that's her brother. And Colin's uncle. For them, I'm willing to settle for a good beating."

"All right, then that's what we do," Franklin agrees, bringing his glass to his lips.

We sit in silence for a few seconds before Reign opens his mouth again.

"I'm a bit disappointed that Colin would want you to be his dad. I mean, it's clear I'm the fun one." I slap him over the head, and he lets out an "ouch," between chuckles.

"I'm kidding," he snorts.

"Shut up," I scold.

Damn tool.

27

I watch how Colin places the cookie cutter over the dough that I spread out on the counter. We can't really go anywhere, so we've been baking every day for the last week. I asked Connor if we could just go home now that Emerson is in custody of the Wolfes. He reminded me that even though we are no longer his prisoners, we're not allowed to leave either… There is still a threat out there because they don't know who took over Emerson's crew.

Or where my brother is.

I've been trying to ignore the bad feeling I have about my brother, but at least once a day I break out in tears, hoping, praying he's all right. I trust Connor. I believe him when he says he won't hurt him anymore, but I have a feeling the Wolfes are not the ones Damien and I have to worry about.

It's frustrating because I don't want this life. I feel safe within the Wolfe mansion. In fact, I haven't felt this safe in my entire life. But I know wherever the Wolfes go, violence follows them. Connor walking in with his bloody shirt last week was proof of that. It's the main reason why I decided not to tell Connor when I found out I was pregnant with his son.

"Good job, baby. Now carefully put it on the plate." Colin beams at me as he slowly starts to peel the dough off the counter, wrecking half of the flower shaped cookie before putting it on the plate.

"Hi."

I look up into a set of big baby blue eyes. Her hair is a soft chocolate brown, framing her pretty face as she gives me a friendly smile.

"Hi. You must be Kendall?" I wave, feeling a little awkward.

She nods, slowly approaching the counter and glancing at Colin.

"Who are you?" Her voice is smooth like honey, and I have a feeling there is not an ounce of bad inside the heart of this girl when she places herself next to Colin, softly petting his blond hair.

"Colin." He then points at me. "Mommy!"

"That's your mommy?"

"I'm Lily." I brush the flour off my hands then hold them up apologetically since they are still covered with white dust. "Sorry."

"Don't worry about it. I'm Kendall."

"Nice to finally meet you. How are you feeling?"

She sighs.

"Tired. I'm not sure if it's because of the hit on the head or because I have to process what the fuck happened the last few months." She slams her mouth shut, pressing her hands over her mouth as she looks at me with wide eyes.

"Sorry," she mutters. "I'm not used to being around kids."

"Don't worry about it. His dad can't seem to stop saying *shit*. I've decided I'm gonna stop trying."

"Fair enough," she chuckles.

Colin takes advantage of my lack of attention, popping a piece of dough into his mouth with a smirk.

"I saw that, you little sneak!" My hands tickle him, and a burst of giggles leaves his mouth.

"Oh, I want some!" Kendall looks at Colin with a pleading face, and Colin looks at me with a beaming smile before he slowly tears a piece off the dough.

"Don't do it, boy." I fake scowl. "Don't you dare."

Kendall opens her mouth, frantically nodding her head to encourage him. He gives me one more glance, then he quickly places a piece of dough on her tongue before I grab him off the counter, tickling him until he screams in joy.

"Not listening to your Mommy! How dare you?"

"Ooh, cookies!" We all look up when Reign walks into the kitchen like a ray of sunshine. He's wearing a dark green t-shirt and some black jeans, looking fine as always. But it's his floppy, honey brown hair combined with his contagious smile that makes it impossible to not be happy when he's around.

Colin wiggles himself out of my grip to run to Reign.

"They still have to go into the oven. But *someone...*" I emphasize, looking at Colin who's now giggling in the safety of Reign's arms, "keeps eating the dough."

"You're eating the dough again, little man? So your tummy is full? Like too full for ice cream?" Reign pushes a finger into Colin's stomach with a questioning look on his face. "No. No, I'm pretty sure you still have room!"

"Reign Wolfe, it's not even noon," I reprimand.

"And this is why you are the mother, and I'm the fun uncle."

"Don't you dare, Reign."

"Whaaat?" he drawls. "I'm not doing anything."

He whispers something in Colin's ear, and both their mouths twist into wide grins before he puts Colin back on the floor and grabs his hand.

"You're so full of shit, Reign," Kendall chuckles, still standing next to me.

"One, two, three," he whispers, looking at Colin, then they take a bow, and Reign leads Colin out of the kitchen. "It was a pleasure, girls. The boys need some man time now."

"Reign!"

"Bye!" They both run off, ignoring me, and before I know it, they are out of my sight. I just shake my head with a grin on my face. Even though I don't agree with ice cream at eleven in the morning, I do appreciate the amount of time Reign spends with his nephew. Every free minute he has, he comes looking for Colin to play with him. Colin is crazy about his uncle, and it kinda compensates for Damien not being around.

"So he looks like a prince, and he's good with children... I think I fell in love with the wrong Wolfe," Kendall jokes.

"Tell me about it. I've got the scowling one."

"He looks scary, yeah. But he's not as bad as he seems, is he?"

"No, he's not," I admit, even though he probably won't want me telling the world about his soft side. Connor is not the brutal man he wants everyone to believe. He cares deeply for the people in his small circle, and I love that about him. He can be ruthless and is unapologetic when it comes to protecting the people he cares for. I have yet to see that he's ruthless for no reason.

"Tell me…" Kendall leans a little closer with a smile, lowering her voice. "Is he secretly one big teddy bear?"

"A very moody one, but yeah. You can put it like that."

"Reign told me what happened." She pushes her finger through the leftover flour, not sure where to look. "Sorry that happened."

"What part?"

"Well, everything. But mainly the part where he basically abducted you and held you prisoner like you're freaking Belle, and he's the beast. That must have been scary."

"It was. Especially when I realized he didn't take Colin with us. That was when I really freaked out. Other than that? Connor Wolfe doesn't scare me. He hasn't treated me badly other than the one time he burst through my door. And to be honest, I can't blame him for doing that. He told me you were there that night?" I ask carefully. "When Damien shot Nigel."

Kendall pushes out a deep breath, her face falling a little.

"Yeah, it's imprinted on my retinas. I've seen people die before—if you date a psychopath for seven years, it kinda comes with the territory—but those were people I didn't know. Emerson always painted them as the bigger evil. But Nigel… I knew Nigel. He may have been a Wolfe, but he was a good kid."

I place my hand over hers, and she looks up at me.

"I'm really sorry my brother killed Nigel. I didn't know until Connor told me a few days after he took me. But I swear, my brother is not a coldhearted killer."

"I know." Kendall places her hand over mine, giving it a small squeeze. "Emerson told him to. The look on your brother's face made it clear that he didn't enjoy doing it. Not like when Cary goes to torment someone else."

"Cary?"

"Yeah, he's Emerson's right-hand man. I know him from back home. We all went to high school together. Cary always creeped me out. Anyway, have they found your brother yet?"

I shake my head, a tightness forming around my ribcage. My gut keeps telling me he's fine, hiding out somewhere, but there's a feeling growing in my heart that he's laying in a ditch. My eyes well up, and Kendall wraps her arms around me, resting her chin on my shoulder. I met this girl ten minutes ago, but it feels like she's been my friend for a long time. She's sweet, she's kind, she's genuine, and she makes me feel like I'm not alone, stuck in this mansion filled with testosterone. Every single one of the Wolfe brothers has tried to make me feel welcome, spending time with Colin, asking me if I need anything. Even Franklin came to check on me the other day. But sometimes you just need a girlfriend to connect with. Someone who will listen to you without looking for solutions.

"It will be alright," Kendall muses.

"I sure as fuck hope so." I wipe away a tear that escaped the corner of my eye.

"I'm sure it will. Now that Emerson is dead, the rest of the crew will fall apart soon. They're terrified of the Wolfes. I'm sure we will find Damien soon."

The cogs in my head are turning, thinking back to Connor telling me it's not safe to go back home yet.

"Wait, hold on." Kendall lets go of my shoulders and looks at me when she hears the confusion in my voice. "Emerson is dead?"

Her eyes grow wide.

"Yeah."

He told me I couldn't go home because of Emerson.

"That son of a bitch," I mutter as I take off my apron and start washing my hands.

"Everything all right?"

"Peachy. Do you know where Connor is?"

"He just left to do his rounds in the city. He said he'll be back before supper."

"Perfect," I seethe, wanting to punch the fucker senseless.

28

CONNOR

P arking my truck on the driveway, I get out of the car, ready to head upstairs to look for Lily and Colin. When I walk through the door, Reign is running around the house with Colin in his arms like he's an airplane making a humming sound.

"Daddy!" Colin screeches in joy while Reign keeps him in the same position.

"Hey, big guy." I ruffle his hair before Reign continues their game, running through the house.

"Have you seen Lily?" I call out to Reign's back.

"She's upstairs!"

I watch how they disappear through the dining room before I make my way upstairs with an excited feeling. Reaching our bedroom door, I lean against the post, my arms folded in front of my body. She's walking across the room, throwing clothes into a bag, looking sexy as fuck. Her slight curves strut around the room, her blonde hair bouncing along with every move, grabbing my dick's attention until I realize something's wrong.

"What are you doing?"

She snaps her head towards mine, frustration dripping off her face.

"What does it look like? I'm leaving. *We* are leaving."

Something breaks inside of me, and rage floods my entire body, my scowl back on full display.

"Excuse me?"

"We are leaving. Do you need me to tell you in Spanish? Irish? We are leaving. We are gone. We are going back home."

"The hell you are."

"You can't stop me."

"Watch me." I take a step forward to slam the door shut behind me.

"What are you going to do, Connor? Kidnap me? Tie me to a chair?"

"As much as I'm dying to do exactly that, I prefer that kind of shit when you're naked."

Heat flashes in her eyes for a second before she turns her head and keeps packing.

"Three seconds, Lily," I groan, grinding my teeth together.

"What?" The tone of her voice is bored, pissing me off even more.

"You've got three second to explain what the fuck is going on before I tell Reign to look after Colin, and I do exactly that." My dick gets uncomfortable inside of my jeans, liking the image that is now stuck in my head, even though my heart is pounding in my chest with anger.

"Do what?" She frowns.

"Lock this door. Take off your clothes and tie you to a chair."

Her lips part, and her chest slowly moves up and down while the features in her face show the desire she's feeling inside right now. My tongue darts out to lick my lips while I take a few steps forward with narrow eyes.

"You'd like that, wouldn't you?" She swallows hard when I close the distance between us, pushing her against the wall next. My hand cups the front of her neck with slight pressure, the other digging into her hip. "For me to have my way with you like you're my personal little doll to abuse." I brush my lips against hers, and her eyes shut. "To eat you until you can't move an inch, completely surrendered to my touch. You want me to tie you up, baby?"

She breathes out, fanning my face as her nostrils flare before her eyes open again.

"You already kidnapped me, isn't that enough?" She pushes me off of her with a glare, trying to walk past me. I throw her back with one hand, slamming her against the wall forcefully.

"What is wrong with you?" she shouts angrily. Her tone is sharp, but her eyes don't match the trash that's leaving her mouth.

"What the fuck is going on, Lily?" I growl, her lashes fluttering as I look down at her.

"Nothing! I just want to go home."

"You're not going anywhere. It's not safe."

"Bullshit! I know about Emerson. I know he's dead. Meaning there is no fucking reason to still keep us locked up in your ivory tower! Is that why you didn't tell me, you sick fuck? So you can keep me locked up for as long as you want? To treat me like your personal sex toy?"

My eyes move back and forth, feeling both amused and pissed about the accusations she's spewing at me.

"Oh, let's not pretend you don't love being my personal sex toy, baby."

"Fuck you!" she spits, and I press her even harder against the wall.

"Gladly, but it seems like we have some issues to work out."

"We don't have *anything.*"

I flash her my teeth, trying not to shut her up by sticking my tongue inside of her, even though it's what I'm dying to do. At least that would shut her up. Well, aside from making her scream in six different ways.

"*We* have a kid together, so you don't get to walk out on me like you did for two years. Never again, babe."

"You lied to me," she states, the tone in her voice now more disappointed than angry.

"I did," I sigh. "Just because Emerson Jones is being eaten by the sharks in the Atlantic as we speak doesn't mean it's safe for you to walk outside of these gates. Like you once told me with your smart ass, when they find out Colin is mine, he'll immediately have a target on his head. The same goes for you."

"I mean nothing to you."

"You are the mother of my son. It doesn't matter what I think. People will see you as valuable enough to use you against me. Or hurt you. I can't let that happen. Until this shit is resolved, you and Colin are staying here. End of fucking discussion!"

"You can't stop me," she sasses back, hands planted on her hips.

"I swear to God, Lily, don't test me."

Her scowl is still in place, but her eyes are laced with lust. I really want to push my lips against hers and kiss her senseless, hoping it will knock some sense into her, but I have a feeling it will only work against me today. So instead, I close my eyes and plant a lingering kiss on her forehead.

"I'm not a sweet guy. But I will do anything to keep you and Colin safe. Don't ever fucking doubt that." I turn and walk away, leaving her stunned, standing against the wall where she will hopefully cool off.

As I walk back down the stairs, Reign calls out, "Connor!"

"What?" I bark, agitated, as I walk into the kitchen.

"They found Damien," Reign announces.

"Where?"

"Facedown in the Charles." I stop in my tracks, running a hand through my hair.

"Shit," I mutter.

"Yeah. Franky is expecting us at the coroners in thirty minutes."

29

The son of a bitch left me flustered against the wall, both horrified and horny at the same time. How is it that one minute I want to punch him in the face, and the next I want to beg him to fuck me? Especially when he mentions shit like tying me down. Any normal girl would feel concerned when a guy starts talking like he owns her, like her sole existence is to please him whenever he wants. But for some fucked up reason, it just turns me on.

Great, I'm officially Connor Wolfe's hoe-bag.

Well, fuck that. Connor Wolfe doesn't control me. He doesn't dictate what I do. Yes, we have a kid together, and we can decide *together* what is best for Colin. But I'll be damned before I let that arrogant Wolfe push me around like he does the rest of this city.

He doesn't scare me. *The beast of Boston.* Pff, whatever.

I'm horny for him all the time, but I sure as fuck am not afraid of him.

Determined, I stomp through the room, packing the rest

of our things before the ding of my phone tells me my Uber is here. Throwing the bag over my shoulder, I put my sweater on and head downstairs. Colin is playing with Reign and his teddy in the living room near the front door.

Thank fuck.

"Come on, baby. We need to go." I quickly scoop him up, opening the front door.

"Hey." I turn around to look at Reign who has a confused frown on his face. "Where are you going?"

"Home," I say, closing the door behind me, then trot down the steps towards the car waiting for me. I wave at the driver before I put Colin in the backseat. I've got him all buckled up when I hear the front door open behind me.

"Reign, get Colin!" Connor orders his brother, then continues to storm towards me. My heart feels like it stops. He looks even bigger than usual, his energy swirling around him like a fireball ready to burn everything that comes within a two-foot radius.

"Where the *fuck* do you think you're going, baby?" he sneers, looking even more malicious than normal.

"I'm going home!" I throw my bag in the trunk, but before it connects with the bottom, he yanks it out of my hand and throws it onto the steps of the circle driveway.

"What the fuck, Connor?!" I notice Reign pulling Colin out of the car in the corner of my eye before carrying him back inside while I try to keep glaring at the infuriating man in front of me.

"What the fuck, *Connor?* What the fuck, *Lily?*" he emphasizes my name. "Did you not hear me just now when I told you it's not safe?"

"I heard you, I just don't believe you!"

"So you decide to leave and take my son from me?

217

Again?" A vein on his forehead pulses, and the accusation kills me. I know I gave him enough reason to fear that I'll cut him out of Colin's life—two years to be exact—but it still hurt to hear him say that.

"I'm not taking him from you! We are going home! Home. Where we live. You can visit whenever the fuck you want, but we don't belong here."

He takes a step forward, pulling my upper arm until I'm flush with his body.

"Because you belong in Roxbury? You think I'm gonna let my son stay there for another day? Think again, babe."

Feeling his heat against my skin makes me flustered, distracting me from the point I was trying to make. What was it again?

"I don't want to do this, Connor. Be part of Colin's life? Fine. Make decisions about him together? Fine. But never did I agree for you to fuck up our lives. For you to fuck up *my* life."

"Fuck up your life? You think you didn't fuck up my life when I found out I had a kid walking around for the last two years?" The features on his face harden even more, his green eyes darkening like he's ready to kill me.

"Yes, you're right," I fire back, sarcasm painting my words. "I'm a bitch. I took your kid from you. You gonna keep throwing that in my face until he's eighteen?"

"Probably."

"Great, sounds like a fucking blast. All the more reason I don't want to stay here, serving as your toy who you like to fuck every once in a while."

His brows shoot up as my words hit him, and I purse my lips, glaring.

"Are you fucking kidding me?" He looks up at the sky,

218

blowing out a heavy breath before dipping his chin again. "That's what this is about?"

"What?!"

"For fuck's sake." He lets go of me, walking up to the passenger door before he yanks it open. He reaches into his back pocket, then throws a few bills at the driver.

"Get out of here," he barks, then walks back to me, dragging me with him by my arm.

"What are you doing? Let me go, asshole." I try to pull my arm free, but with his huge hand wrapped around my slender arm, I don't stand a chance.

While I try to get loose, he leads me to a small gazebo in the rear of the yard. I hadn't seen it before, so for a second, I notice all the pretty roses around me, forgetting he's taking me against my will. It's a colorful display, the roses completely shielding the gazebo from outsiders. He yanks me up the steps, then throws me against the railing before placing his hands on either side of me, caging me in.

"Ouch, dickhead!" I snap, pinning him with a glare that hopefully expresses how angry I am.

"I'm telling you this one more time. You better listen because next time you pull a stunt like that, I'll be keeping you in the basement just for my own entertainment."

"There's a basement?"

"Shut up." He forces a bruising kiss on my lips, then pulls his head back to lock his eyes with mine, effectively shutting me up. "I'm pissed at you for not telling me I have a son until two weeks ago. I'm pissed at you for trying to take him away from me. *Again.*"

"I didn't—"

"Shut up," he interrupts. "But the two of you are here

now, and I'm not letting you out of my sight. Ever. The two of you are mine. Mine to protect. Mine to take care of."

"I can take care of myself."

"I know you can. You've been doing it for the last two years." I can't help the faint smile that curves my lips, appreciating the acknowledgment. "But that's over now. You. Are. Mine. Now. Lily. Both of you," he growls.

The defiant yet insecure bitch inside of me can't help the eye roll that sneaks through, wondering what that even means. Don't get me wrong, I like the promise of being protected by a Wolfe because yes, being around them comes with a lot of risks. But the cat's out of the bag now anyway, so sooner or later, people are gonna find out about Colin and me. Having the most powerful crime lords of Boston in my corner at least puts my mind at ease. But it's the obsessed girl in me who wants more.

I've been trying to ignore it, pretending that whatever we have is just lust. Just a desire I've been dreaming about for too long, a craving that I need to fulfill before we can get to the part where we can co-parent and co-exist. But the more time I spend with Connor Wolfe, the more I'm convinced it's so much more. My attraction to Connor has nothing to do with Colin. I've known about it since the first day we met. It was intense, it was brief, but it was all I'd ever wanted. My mind never could let go after that one night that changed my life. My heart has been full since the day Colin was born, but whenever Connor is around, I feel like everything is how it's supposed to be. That all the puzzle pieces fall into place. I could tell myself it's because he's Colin's father. I mean, what girl doesn't want a relationship with her baby daddy? In the end, we all want that fairy tale, right? That happily ever after, even if the story unfolds out of order.

I'm in love with Connor Wolfe, and I can't deny it anymore. Not to myself, anyway.

"I'm not your sex toy, Connor," I sneer like a goddamn child since he has not once called me that or treated me like I am.

"Jesus, woman! You piss me off so bad," he groans incredulously. "When have I ever made you feel like a booty call?! Stop fishing! Just tell me! If you want anything else from me, this is your time to open that snarky mouth of yours before I fuck it out of you right here. But I sure as hell am not going to engage in your girly way of communicating. I'm simple as fuck, Lily. If you want something from me, you lay it out, baby." His voice softens, and the sincerity in his hypnotic green eyes has tears stinging my eyes. The smell of his fresh aftershave mixed with a hint of sweat makes it hard for me to think while I do my best to scrape out every ounce of bravery I have to tell him how I feel.

"Just say it, baby." The back of his hand brushes my cheek in the most endearing way, melting my heart even more.

"I want you, Connor," I finally confess. "I have wanted you since that first night. I don't want you to just be Colin's father. I don't want to just co-parent. I want it all. I want you."

A smile brightens his face, and he grabs a hold of my chin.

"Good girl," he coos. "Was that really so hard?"

"Stop torturing me."

"I want you too, Lily," he replies before his face turns stony again. "My attraction towards you never stopped. I want to make this work. Make *us* work. Be a family."

His words spark my confidence, and I open my mouth once more before I lose my nerve.

"Connor, I think I'm falling in love with you."

The smile on his face disappears, instantly making me wish I'd swallowed my words. I can see how his eyes are sparkling with pain, telling me he can't say it back.

"Lily, I care about you, and I want to make this work. But I can't promise you I can give you everything you deserve. Do you understand?"

I want to cry. I want to cry my eyes out, but I clear my throat before swallowing the tears away.

"I am..." He pauses, rubbing the back of his neck. "My life has been complicated. I don't think I can offer you anything more than what we have now. I don't know—"

I press my fingers against his lips.

"Ssssh. It's okay. Just give me you. Exclusively. That's all I want."

"You got me, baby. You and Colin." Our lips connect, and I can feel my heart settling in my chest as a curtain of comfort showers me.

He may not be the happy ending in that fairy tale I'd hoped for, but I'll settle for the beast he's willing to give me.

30

CONNOR

We're all in the coroner's lab, standing in a circle around the dead body that was once Damien Johnson. He looks battered. Like someone beat the shit out of him before they decided to stab him to death. I was tempted to tell Lily before I left, but I decided to wait until I got back. Now that I've seen the body myself, I'm pretty sure Lily will end up with nightmares if she sees him before they put all the makeup on his face to make him presentable.

"Did he drown?" Killian asks the coroner, staring at Damien's face. Or what's left of it.

"No. I'm 99% sure he was dead before he got dumped in the Charles. He's got twenty-five stab wounds, severe bruising on the skull, and a few bones broken in his arm and upper leg. The bruising to the skull being what killed him."

"Jesus." Reign is deathly pale, holding his hand in front of his mouth to avoid throwing up.

"Someone must have really wanted to hurt him." I look at Franky who raises his brows in agreement with a small nod.

"Actually," the coroner counters, "there is more." He pulls the sheet off, exposing the rest of Damien's damaged body. His torso is covered with red cuts, his skin torn and red. The stab wounds and the purple-blue bruises on his ribs show he endured a lot. But it's the carved message on his leg that has us all wide-eyed. I cock my head to read the words etched down the length of his scrawny leg.

"What the fuck?" Reign mumbles.

A life for a life.

"A life for a life?" I repeat, a little dumbfounded. "Why the fuck would those tools want to avenge their psychopath leader by killing one of their own? Killian, any word on the street who took over?"

"Cary took Emerson's seat officially as soon as we dumped his body in front of city hall. Apparently, he and his girlfriend are calling the shots now."

"Girlfriend?" Franky narrows his eyes, glancing between the three of us, stopping when his focus is on me. "Didn't Emerson mention that Cary was fucking the girl he got his info from?"

"Yeah, he did," Killian answers for me.

"Right. You think that's the same girl?" Franklin glances at the coroner. "Anything else we need to know, doc?"

"No, nothing of significance. His blood was clean other than some THC."

"Good. Can you give us a second, then?" Franklin gives him a smile that doesn't meet his eyes.

The coroner doesn't move a muscle, shooting daggers at Franky.

"You realize this is my lab, right?"

"My brother asked you a question, doc," I rumble, taking a step forward with my shoulders back.

"Fine," he sputters. "You have five minutes."

"Thank you, doc," Franklin answers as we watch him walk out of the room. Once the door closes behind him, Franklin snaps his head towards us again. "Reign, you need to do a background check on every single piece of ass we ever slept with. Long term, short term, one-night stands. If one of us fucked them, I want to know everything about them. Where they are from, where they live, where they went to school, who their parents are, every single fucking thing."

"Are you kidding me? Do you know how many women there are?"

"Nope, dead serious."

"Franky, if you take Killian's list alone we are talking about at least a hundred women."

"I don't care," Franklin seethes. "There is a bitch somewhere in this town who knows one of us from the past and is trying to fuck us over. I want to know who she is. Today."

"Yeah, you can forget about that," Reign scoffs.

"He's right, though, Reign. We need to know who she is," Killian says.

"Well, why don't we just find out who Cary's girlfriend is?" All three of them look at me as if I just suggested burning the city down. "What?"

"You know we're in deep shit when the ruffian starts making sense."

I roll my eyes at Reign before Killian makes a valid comment.

"Yeah, sounds good. But one, we haven't seen her. Ever. She's good at flying under the radar. Two, we won't be able to get close to their crew without getting a bullet through the head, and we don't have anyone we trust not to jump ship if Cary gives them a better offer."

"It's pissing me off that some chick is fucking messing with us." Franklin drags a hand over his face in frustration. "Think! Which of you broke someone's heart?"

"What makes you think it's about a broken heart?" Reign counters.

"Because it always is when women go mental."

"He's not wrong," I agree, thinking about how Lily threw a fit when she thought I was keeping her around for her ass. I am definitely keeping her around for her ass, but it's not the only reason.

"Look, I only dated Sienna and Callie. Other than that, we're talking casual flings, nothing special. Not even second drinks or anything." Reign throws his hands in the air.

"What are you looking at me for? You know I don't do girlfriends," Killian defends when Franklin pins him with a stare.

"Yeah, that's exactly the reason I'm looking at you," Franklin retorts. "Any chicks you fucked more than once?"

"One."

"Who?" I ask.

Killian lets out a deep sigh, clearly not keen on sharing.

"Emma."

Franklin and I keep a straight face while Reign's jaw falls to the floor.

"You slept with Emma? *My* Emma?"

"She wasn't *your* Emma," Killian argues. "She was my friend too."

"And you never told me?"

Killian shrugs.

"It was just sex."

"Wait…" I grin, suddenly realizing the ages Killian and Reign were when they were friends with Emma. "Did she take your v-card?"

"Oh, for fuck's sake," Killian mutters, letting his head hang. "Yeah."

"You dirty little bastard," I chuckle.

"Can we please stop this and not taint the memory of my dead best friend?" Reign pinches the bridge of his nose with a dramatic sigh.

"Yes, please," Killian replies.

"Well, fine. We can rule her out," Franklin says dryly.

MY FEET FEEL heavy walking up the stairs when I get home. With each step I take, it becomes harder to move, Reign following behind me.

I hated Damien.

I've hated him for weeks, wanting to hurt the fucking guy for killing someone I cared about. I thought about all the numerous ways I could torture him before I'd finally slit his throat. I knew he was just a kid taking orders, but I didn't care. Damien had to die. Preferably with a lot of agony. I hadn't been able to sleep well, needing to see fear in his eyes. The same fear that filled Nigel's last expression, one I will never forget.

But when I took Lily and Colin, I was forced to see Damien as human. As a boy forced in to a shitty situation. The love Lily felt for her brother made it impossible for me to kill him, knowing she'd never forgive me. And even though this outcome was completely out of my hands, I'm not looking forward to giving her the news she's been dreading for weeks.

When I walk into the room, Colin is playing with his toys on the floor while Lily runs a brush through her wet hair.

"Daddy!" He jumps up, launching himself against my body. I pick him up to give him a tight hug.

"Hey, big guy. Did you have a good day?"

He nods his head, then spreads his arms.

"This good!" He beams.

"That good, huh? That's great, buddy."

"Hi Reign!" He enthusiastically waves at Reign, waiting in the doorway. Reign copies the action, showing him his boyish grin.

"I need to talk to Mommy. Can you go downstairs with Uncle Reign for a minute? When I come downstairs, you can tell me all about your day."

"Kay!" I put him down as Reign reaches out his hand to guide him down the stairs.

"Come on, buddy. Let's see if your mommy has any more sweets hidden in the kitchen."

The second they close the door behind them, Lily walks over to me, wrapping her arms around my neck before she hungrily kisses my lips.

"Did you just use your brother to have sex?" She cocks an eyebrow in suspicion, though her lips are curled in an amused smile.

"I wish, babe." She frowns when she sees the grim look I'm wearing.

"What's wrong?" Her eyes go from lustful to panicked in the blink of an eye. I place my hand on her neck, hoping to keep her calm.

"They found your brother."

"Oh god," she whispers, her hand flying to her mouth. "Is he … dead?"

I press my lips together, not wanting to voice it. She moans, pushing her face against my chest while grabbing my shirt in a tight grip.

"No. No. No. No, it can't be."

My hand cups the back of her head, holding her close while my lips brush over her hair.

"I'm sorry, baby. I'm so sorry." She sobs in my arms for several long moments. When she finally looks up, her face stained with grief.

"Where?"

"They found him in the Charles."

She shakes her head as her knees buckle down underneath her and I pick her up to carry her to the bed.

"Nooo," she wails. "He's all I've got. He's the last family I have."

Cradling her against my chest, I hold her in my lap while she cries uncontrollably in my arms, her grief surging through my body like venom. It's an unfamiliar feeling, a feeling that extends even further than the pain I feel for my brother's past struggles in life.

I knew I cared for Lily within the first twenty-four hours of keeping her hostage in my house like the asshole I am. I wasn't going to admit it to anyone, but when I saw the look of distress on her face when she didn't know where Colin was, it did something to me. I brushed it off, waved it away like it was just a nuisance. But when look of terror was replaced with a gaze of love when she was holding her boy in her arms again, I knew I was fucked. I didn't ever want to see that pain on her gorgeous face ever again. I silently vowed to do my best to not make her cry ever again, and it's killing me right now that I can't take her grief away.

"Sssh, I'm here. I got you," I whisper against her blonde hair as I rock our bodies from left to right. "I'm not going anywhere."

We stay like that for God knows how long, glued together as one, until she finally starts to calm down. My fingers gently stroke the skin on her arms while I do my best to be there for her when all I really want to do is go and hurt someone.

Hurt anyone.

But the little bit of rational thinking I have in my body keeps me from doing that, sensing she needs me to just be with her. To comfort her. To reassure her she's not alone.

"Can I see him?" Her voice normally sounds sweet, like honey, but this time it's fragile and meek.

"No," I state firmly.

"What do you mean *'no?'* That's my brother." She wiggles herself out of my arms, jumping off the bed, putting distance between us while she pulls a face I haven't seen in a while, wiping her tears with the back of her hand.

The one where it's clear I'm the villain in her story.

The beast.

I clench my jaw, annoyed, then run a hand through my hair.

"Look, I'm not trying to be an asshole, okay? But your brother was beat up pretty bad. I don't want that to be the last image you have of your brother."

She folds her arms in front of her body, popping her hip defiantly.

"That is not your decision to make."

"It's my responsibility to keep you safe and happy. Seeing your dead brother as a corpse in the morgue isn't the way to keep you happy!" I tell her this a bit more aggressive than I'd intended.

"Nice, Connor! Real nice. Geez, you're such an insensitive dick!" I push out a frustrated breath, seeing that tears are streaming down her face again.

"I warned you I'm not some kind of storybook hero! You've got the wrong brother. I can't give you that."

"I haven't got the wrong brother!" she shouts. "Just don't be an ass!"

"I'm just trying to look out for you. What more do you want from me?"

"To not be a fucking asshole?"

"Yeah, well, tough luck with that," I mutter, averting my gaze.

She shakes her head.

"I want to see him, Connor. I *need* to see him," she pleads.

I sigh, then get off of the bed to close the space between us. Rubbing her arms, I stand before her as she looks up at me with her big blue eyes, the whites now tinted red.

I want to protect her from this. From the image of her dead brother that's now embedded in my head. I'm not fazed by dead bodies, but I'm pretty sure that the last image I have of Damien Johnson will not do my girl any good. But I also know she's right. It isn't my choice.

"Are you absolutely sure?"

"Yes." The tone in her voice is resolute, and I keep my eyes locked on hers for a moment.

I can't blame her. If this was one of my brothers, I'd want the same. I'd have to see for myself that it was really them.

"Okay, let's go."

31

My eyes keep glancing at Connor behind the wheel as he drives us into the city. I watch the buildings slide by on Downtown Crossing in silence, thinking back to the last few days.

Connor was right.

I should've listened to him when he told me not to go and see Damien's dead body.

His body was covered in bruises in many different shades while his skin was gray and bloated, hardly looking like the vibrant boy I'd partially raised. The first night I had a nightmare, waking up screaming because Damien's face kept haunting me in my sleep. Connor kept me close, and soon I found myself unable to sleep if his hands weren't wrapped around me. After the funeral, it got a bit better, but I still feel like my head is in a constant cloud, making it impossible for me to truly function.

The other day, I tried to get my mind off things and bake a cream pie, but when the cake came out of the oven looking like one big-ass cookie, I cried my eyes out until Kendall came to the rescue. She ran me a hot bath and took Colin off my hands until Connor came home and stayed with me.

They all have been amazing, to be honest.

The day of the funeral, Kendall stayed with Colin, and all four brothers stood by my side while I said my last good-byes to my baby brother at South End South Burying Ground. Franklin made sure there wasn't a soul in sight, both for security reasons and for my own sake, knowing I didn't want to have small talk with people I didn't care about.

It was quiet and weird, watching the casket disappear into the ground with four Wolfes standing guard behind me. But even though I was overwhelmed with grief, I'd also never felt safer in my life. There is something about being in the presence of those four brothers, working together like water, earth, fire, and air, that makes me feel untouchable.

"Where are we going?" I finally ask, sick of my own thoughts.

He turns his head towards me with a straight face before his hand reaches out to brush my cheek with the back of his fingers.

"Wherever you want to go." He winks at me.

"What do you mean?"

"I'm gonna park the car at a private lot on Huntington Avenue, and then I thought we could just walk around the city for a bit and spend some time together? Maybe go to Chinatown, have some food?"

"Really?" Surprised, my weeping heart leaps for a second, feeling a little spark of joy run through it as I take in his words.

He rolls his eyes at my amazed gaze.

"Why are you looking at me like I'm going to kidnap you?"

"Wouldn't be the first time."

He lets out a full belly burst of laughter that brings a smile to my face.

"You need a break." He shrugs as if it's the most normal thing in the world to say. "You haven't been out of the mansion for something fun in weeks, and you need a break. I want to give it to you. Just take it, okay?"

"Okay." I shoot him a grateful look, then turn my head back to the window, watching the city of Boston pass by until he drives us into an underground garage to park his truck.

When we exit his truck, he grabs my hand, leading us onto the street, followed by two of his men who tagged along in a separate car. A spark of joy pinches me in the heart when our hands connect, and for the first time in a week, the dark cloud in my head seems to let in a little ray of sunshine.

"Where do you wanna go? Are you hungry?"

I suck in the fresh summer air, enjoying the sweet smells of the different bakeries in the area as I tilt my head to look at Connor.

"Not yet. I can pick whatever I want?"

"Whatever you want, baby."

"I want to go to Brattle Bookshop."

His eyes widen.

"You can go anywhere you want, and you want to go to a bookshop?"

"Not just any bookshop!" I reprimand. "One of America's oldest and largest antique bookshops."

His face tells me he's not impressed as I tug him with me.

"Come on, grumpy."

A chuckle escapes his lips, and I realize that he's been doing that a lot more the last few weeks.

Smiling.

It makes me wonder if Colin and I have something to do with that, or if it's just because he's getting more comfortable around us.

"You're really into books, aren't you?" We walk down the street, the sun warming our faces.

"I love books. When I was still in Harvard, I used to study in the library all the time just to be surrounded by books."

"You went to Harvard?" His brows knit together, and I press my lips together with a smile as I nod in confirmation.

"Yeah. Got a full ride, too. I wanted to be a lawyer."

"You didn't finish?"

"When I was nineteen, my dad got arrested. I had to take care of Damien." Saying his name makes my eyes prick, so I exhale and inhale a few times to push the tears away.

"It's okay, baby," Connor comforts me, kissing my hair.

"No, it's a beautiful day. I don't want to cry today. I've cried enough."

"You can cry as much as you want." Hearing his words, I thankfully grab his upper arm with my other hand, pushing my cheek against it as we continue strutting down the street.

"Thank you. But I don't want to today. Anyway," I continue, "I had to drop out when my dad got arrested. Damien was only thirteen. I couldn't go to school and earn enough money to provide for him. So I stopped. Found a job as a legal assistant for a new lawyer who didn't want to pay more for a grad student. The plan was to go back when Damien went to college."

When Connor stays quiet, I peer up at him.

"You okay?"

"Yeah, it just reminds me of Franklin."

"He became your legal guardian when you guys were teenagers, right?" I look up at the bright lights of the movie theater as we walk by, waiting for his response.

"I was fifteen, almost sixteen. Killian and Reign were fourteen and twelve. Because I was almost sixteen, Franklin got me out really quick. But Kill and Reign had to be in foster care for much longer."

"How long?"

"Killian two years, Reign four."

"Did you have a nice family, at least?"

"Oh, no," he huffs with disdain rolling off his tongue. "I got stuck in a house with eight other kids. It wasn't awful, but it was far from great considering the fact that we were hungry all the time. They only gave us dinner, and even then it was a fight to get a decent portion. When Franklin picked me up after three months, I ate Dunks for a week."

"What about the other boys?" I wonder while we turn left to the Brattle Bookshop.

"They don't talk about it. Killian told me little snippets of how he was well fed and well clothed, but every day was a game of manipulation. They had one son, and Killian and he were being trained to steal shit whenever they went out. Like their own set of pickpockets."

"It's unbelievable how people can treat their children. Or use the system like that to benefit themselves instead of helping the kids. What about Reign?"

"He doesn't talk about it." We stop in front of the book-shop, and I turn my head towards Connor, waiting for him to finish. "We tried. I know he had it the worst out of all three of us, you can just see it in his eyes. But he refuses to talk about it. Says it's all in the past anyway."

I let out a sigh, staring at his chest, imagining Reign as the same age I was when I became responsible for Damien. Breaks my heart to hear that as a teenager, he didn't have the safe haven every child deserves.

"Anyway, go on. Get your books." Connor places his hand on my ass, giving it a small squeeze, and I let out a squeal before he nudges me towards the outdoor section of the shop. With a smile splitting my face, I eye him, then dive into the shelves, running my finger along the book spines. Most of them are ragged and damaged, giving me a rich, nostalgic feeling, like taking a step back in time. I love the feeling of holding a book that was published years ago and has endured so much time. It reminds me that like I'm in a world that changes so fast, one that never stays the same.

"What's your favorite?" Connor asks behind me.

"Peter Pan."

"Peter Pan?" I can hear the curiosity in his voice as my fingers continue running down the shelves. "The one from the Disney movie? They made that a book?"

"Tut, tut," I chastise playfully. "Disney turned the book into a movie, yes, as have a number of producers. But the original story is by J. M. Barrie."

"Well, excuse me, miss," he teases.

"That's okay." I pat his arm. "Your sexy body makes up for your lack of classic book knowledge."

He rapidly pulls my body flush with his, rumbling into my ear, "You want me to show you what my body can do?"

The hairs on the back of my neck stand up, and arousal pulses through me.

"Connor," I hiss. "We're in public."

He glances around before letting me go with a groan, pursing his lips in annoyance.

"Buy your books. I'll wait for you outside."

Hunger is dripping off his face. I blow him a seductive kiss, and a muscle in his jaw jumps. Laughing, I turn around to check out the rest of the books.

After a few minutes, I settle for a poetry book and a historic romance novel written in 1980 that I'm excited to dive in to when we get home. I smile when I've paid for my books and meet Connor on the street, feeling lighter than I have in days.

"You done?" He grabs the bag out of my hand when I nod before he hands it over to one of the security guys. "Good."

His hand circles around my arm when he starts to drag me down the street like he's on a mission.

"What are you doing?" I ask when we walk past the restaurant next to the bookshop.

"Fucking you."

I gasp in shock, stunned by his bluntness when he turns right into the nearest alley. My jaw drops when I take in the wide alley, a few cars parked behind the bookstore.

"You can't be serious?" I ask incredulously.

"Dead serious."

"Connor, we're on the street."

"I know. And I don't care." He shoves me behind a truck, shielding me from the main street, as he backs me up with a lustful glare. He licks the scar on his lip, and I swallow hard when my back hits the cobblestone wall.

"Conner, don't," I try again, even though my voice doesn't sound convincing at all.

"You want this, Lily. You always want it. You look like an angel, but you fuck like the devil."

238

He crowds my space, his breath fanning my face as my eyes move down to my lips.

"You can't get enough." He reaches for the button of my jeans, undoing it so he can glide his finger through my folds. "Your slick pussy tells me you want me."

"What if people see us?" I know it's futile, but common sense tells me I need to make one last effort.

A devilish smirk twists his lips, and I know there is no way back.

"Let them."

I reflexively suck in a deep breath when he yanks my jeans off my ass. Getting down on his knees, he helps me step out one side, then he throws my leg over his shoulder, giving him full access to my wet center.

With two fingers sliding through my center, he wets every area until he reaches my clit, and I feel my other leg falter under me. He presses one hand against my stomach, holding me up against the wall while I patiently wait for more.

When his mouth covers my pussy like I'm his fucking dinner, I cry out in pleasure, completely forgetting my surroundings. His tongue swirls through my folds, alternating with soft sucks of my clit, torturing me in the most delicious way.

"Fucking hell, Connor," I grit out.

My hands fist his short hair, pulling it hard enough to make him groan while I hold on to it like I'm riding a bull.

"That's it, baby. Ride me," he commands as if he can read my mind. My hips start to move in conjunction with my desire, completely using him as my own personal pleasure device as I start to chase the eruption I'm after. I gasp when he continues his tongue movement while dipping two fingers inside of me, fingerfucking me before pulling out to use my juices to slide over my asshole. I cry out when he softly and gently pushes a finger in at the same time he bites my clit, loving how he fills me up in the best way. With his finger up my ass, his thumb circles around my entrance, keeping his tongue over my clit.

"Oh, fuck," I pant, overwhelmed by the sensation coursing through the different places between my legs. "This is so good. Keep going. Keep going, baby." I look up at the sky, noticing the clouds pass by with the occasional bird flying over my head, and I wonder for a second if I died and went to heaven.

When I feel like I'm about to pass out because of the orgasm that's lingering under the surface, he pulls his finger out, leaving me with a hollow feeling before he gets up with a smirk. His pink lips are coated with my cream, looking shiny as fuck. I yank his head towards me, feeling the desperate desire to taste myself on his mouth.

I moan when the saltiness of my core hits my tongue as he undoes his jeans and pushes them over his hips. Breaking our scorching kiss, I pull back, cupping his face in my hands.

"Fuck me, Connor. Fuck me like there is no tomorrow. Make me scream your name."

His eyes darken with greed, pulling my leg up to hold it above his hip before he roughly pushes his hard shaft inside of me. Giving me no time to adjust, he opens me up, making me throw my head back to let out a deep moan.

His hand covers my mouth to keep me quiet as he starts to thrust inside of me like a man on a fucking mission, and I close my eyes to enjoy the excitement of being fucked by this man in an alley in broad daylight. He explores my boundaries, making me cross them, and every time I do, the next time is even better than the one before.

"I fuck you where I want, when I want. Do you understand?" he grunts in my ear, gently scraping the skin on my neck with his teeth between thrusts. His hand is still covering my mouth, so I make a noise to agree with him.

"Good girl. Now be quiet." As if the minutes before this was just an appetizer, he starts plowing inside of me like he's digging for gold, ready to retrieve his treasure.

My mouth opens, wanting to moan, but he's literally fucking me silent because no sounds leaves my throat. He's using me, fucking me, like that's my sole purpose on this earth, and I'm loving every second of it.

His moves go faster every few seconds, and his fingers dig into my ass as if he's trying to slam his dick through me, no matter the consequences. When his face goes rigid, I push my hips a bit more forward, giving my clit that last push it needs before an eruption blazes through my body at the same time Connor cries out an animalistic roar.

He dumps his load inside of me, giving a few final pumps, then drops his forehead on my shoulder while my hands rest on his neck.

"We should go book shopping more often," he ultimately says, and all I can do is laugh.

32

My eyes are glancing around the bar, the heels I strapped on for the occasion tapping on the wooden floor.

"Wowww." I look around in awe with Colin on my hip, holding onto Boot.

The wood throughout the entire room is shiny like ice, giving it a luxurious feel. The middle of the bar is stacked with bottles of liquor with a big blackboard above it, listing numerous cocktails in a classy font. The other walls are decorated with old pictures of Boston through the years, starting somewhere in the 1800s.

It's the perfect balance between laid back and chic.

"Guys, this looks so good." I beam at Killian and Reign, who are hanging out behind the bar.

Reign lets out a whistle, eying me from head to toe.

"Indeed, girl. You look smokin'."

He glances up and down my body, covered by a gray denim skirt and a tank top. Tonight is not the opening, but

Connor told me we would have a few drinks with Kendall and his brothers, and I figured it was the perfect moment to change my regular jeans and a sweater for something more feminine.

I shake my head, rolling my eyes, but before I can tell him to shut up, a voice rumbles behind me.

"Stop flirting with my girlfriend, or I'll rip your head off."

Colin snaps his head to his father with wide eyes, then looks at Reign, shaking his tiny little head with worry on his face.

"No, Daddy. I like Reign head."

"Connor!" I scold while Reign and Killian start to laugh.

"No, no, little man." Connor smiles, trying to reassure his son. "I was just kidding. I won't hurt Reign," he promises, giving his brother a dirty look.

"Thanks, little man." Reign comes around to the front of the bar, placing a chaste kiss on my cheek, then pulling Colin out of my arms. "I like your head too. Want to come check out this place with me? When you're sixteen, you can come help your uncle behind the bar."

"Twenty-one," I correct, cocking an eyebrow.

"Isn't that what I said?" Reign chuckles then walks them both behind the bar where he grabs one of the colorful cocktail stirrers for Colin to play with.

"This looks great, Kill." Connor wraps his arms around my waist, pulling my back against his chest, and I tilt my head to lean into his touch.

Something changed between us that day when we walked around the city together. It's like we bonded, sharing our lives together. And since that day, I've noticed Connor being more affectionate with me. He steals kisses wherever he can, brushing his hands over my body when he walks by me. The sex seems to get better every single day, and he has even confided in me about his daily frustrations. For someone who told me he can't give me what I want, he comes damn close.

"Thanks." Killian raises his glass. "Now we just need to make some good money."

"Are you ready for the opening tomorrow?"

"As ready as we'll ever be. Sorry you can't be there," Killian says with sympathy.

"That's okay. Someone has to keep an eye on the little guy. I'm not comfortable leaving him with a babysitter yet. Even if that babysitter is holding a gun," I joke, glancing at one of the security guys walking through the bar.

"Yeah, I get that." Killian smiles as he takes a sip of his drink.

"Boss." We all snap our heads towards one of the security guys coming from the stockroom with a stern look. "You need to see this."

Killian and Connor share a look, both with frowns and creased foreheads. Connor lets go of me, following the guy who's on his way to the back while Killian slides off his stool to trail behind his brother. Looking back, I steal a glance at Reign and Colin, completely wrapped up in each other, before I follow the men.

"What the hell?" Connor booms.

Connor and Killian are standing at the rear exit, their attention fixated on something outside. My feet feel heavy the closer I get, but my curiosity keeps me going until the pool of blood on the cobblestones outside makes me gasp for air. They turn around at the sound of my arrival, giving me a clear view of the dead body outside the door.

"Is that...?" I stumble. "Is he dead?"

"Yeah, pretty much," Killian deadpans followed by a punch from Connor. "What?"

"Baby, just get back."

I glance at Connor, peering into his troubled gaze. I know he usually doesn't bat an eye when looking at a dead body. Chances are, most of the dead bodies he's seen are caused by himself. No, he's worried for me, not wanting to scare me with the fact that there is a dead body two yards away from me. A nauseous feeling forms in my stomach, but instead of listening to Connor, I take a deep breath and take another step forward.

"It's okay." I give him a reassuring smile before I take a closer look at the dead body. With a heavy heart, I see that he doesn't look a year older than twenty, reminding me of Damien. He's wearing ripped jeans with a black shirt, his face still intact other than the bullet hole in the middle of his fore-head. I tilt my head, feeling my heart race inside my chest, when I notice the piece of paper pinned to his chest.

"Is that a note?"

Killian squats down, pulling the piece of paper off.

"The past will always catch up with you," he reads it out loud. "What the hell does that even mean?" Killian looks up at his brother.

"Means someone's not done fucking with us." The anger is audible in Connor's voice, and I notice him ball his hands into fists.

"We should call the cops," I suggest, my attention still fixed on the blood on the ground.

Killian and Connor share a look, keeping quiet for a moment until Killian opens his mouth.

"If we call the cops, this place will be locked down as a crime scene. We won't be opening for another two weeks."

"Which is exactly what they wanted when they dumped the body here," Connor points out before he turns his head towards me. "Baby, get Reign, will you? Wait for me inside the bar."

I nod, then make my way back.

"Call the cleaners. We need this body gone within the hour. *Without* witnesses," I hear Connor order someone as I walk into the bar.

"Reign, you gotta go meet your brothers," I call out.

He snaps his head up.

"Everything okay?"

I shake my head, going behind the bar to grab Colin from where he's sitting with Reign.

"That bad, huh?" Reign frowns.

"Yep, that bad."

A FEW HOURS LATER, the cleaners are gone and Kendall and I are having a few drinks at the bar.

Disappointed our night got canceled, Kendall and I wanted to go and have some drinks downtown, but as soon as our plan reached Franklin's ears he gave us a simple *'think again'* with no room to negotiate. Not to mention the raging scowl Connor gave me. But Reign stepped in, offering to hang out with us here with a few guards to keep us safe. Franklin and Connor weren't keen on the whole plan, but eventually we convinced them we deserved a night to relax and they took Colin home.

Picking up the bottle I've been drinking from, I refill my glass, my eyes falling on the two security guys keeping guard a few yards behind us.

I can't get used to having those people around all the time. I get why it's important, but I'm not exactly happy with it.

"Well, that was an eventful afternoon," Reign mutters, glancing between Kendall and me.

"I can't believe how I'm not freaked out by a dead body." I take a sip of my pink vodka.

"Pff, you and me both, girl. At some point, you get used to it. Dating a psychopath taught me that. Although I could never get used to the torture when they were still alive," Kendall confesses, taking a sip of her drink, her upper body leaning onto the bar beside me.

I turn my head towards her, not hiding my shock from my face.

"You watched them get tortured?"

"Emerson forced me to watch, yeah. Told me he needed me there for support when really he just wanted to show me what would happen if I didn't comply with him."

"Damn, that's twisted."

"Yeah, you got great taste in men," Reign adds with a grimace.

"I'm dating your brother." Kendall's eyebrows arch up.

"Yeah, I know," he snickers, pouring himself a shot, then throws it down his throat.

"Don't you have a big opening tomorrow? Shouldn't you be sober?" I ask.

As much as I love filling my days with Connor by my side, I like spending time with Reign. Out of all four brothers, he's the fun one, the lighter one, compensating for his brothers' constant broodiness. He makes everyone laugh, even when shit hits the fan.

Like this afternoon. You know, with the dead body on their rear doorstep.

"Yeah, Franklin will be pissed off when you're hungover tomorrow." Kendall gives him a warning look over the rim of her glass as she takes a sip.

"He's always pissed off. Besides..." he sits up straighter, "no offense, girls. But it takes a bit more than a bottle of..." he glances at the bottle with disdain on his face, his nose scrunching as he continues, "pink vodka to get me even remotely drunk."

"And also," he adds, pointing his finger towards Kendall. "You, sweetheart, are not *dating* my brother. You're caught in his web, doomed to be a Wolfe forever."

"What?" she screeches. "Take it easy, we're not married."

"Yet," he counters. "You're not married *yet*. But trust me, you will be by the end of the year."

"Now you're just talking shit, Reign. No one is getting married. I love your brother, but we've only been together a few months. I doubt he's ready to get down on his knees. Hell, I don't even know if I'm ready."

"Pff." He waves her away, clearly amused. "As if you have any say in the matter."

"Well, I do still have free will," Kendall chides.

"Oh, puh-lease. You know my brother doesn't take no for an answer. Like how he tricked you into working for him. Then he quietly moved you in to his penthouse, and now look around." He opens his arms. "You moved into the mansion. Face it, Kenny, you're a Wolfe."

I let out a laugh because of his matter-of-fact tone. I haven't got to know Franklin well enough yet, but every single time I've seen him with Kendall by his side, one thing was very clear: he's crazy about her. Taking in the fact that he isn't the kind of man who takes no for an answer, I have to agree with Reign.

"Same goes for you." Reign snaps his head towards me when he hears my amusement.

"What do you mean?"

"What? You think you have anything to say about the matter? As I recall, my brother dragged your ass back into the house a few weeks ago when you tried to bolt."

"Oh, yeah, that was a fun story," Kendall mumbles, averting her gaze.

"That's because we have a kid together." I wave a hand in the air, brushing his words away.

"Bullshit. That's part of it. But my brother is crazy about you, and hell will freeze over before he'll let you walk out of that front door ever again."

"He is not *crazy* about me."

"No, you're right. He's madly in love with you."

"Connor is not capable of love."

"Is that what he told you?" Reign snorts. "Connor has the biggest heart there is. It's charred, but it's there." He leans back with a satisfied grin, stretching out his arms.

"Maybe." I shrug.

"Nope, definitely. You think he would've already got you a birthday present if he doesn't love you?"

"My birthday isn't for another two months!"

"Exactly!" Reign says, turning his head when there's a knock on the door.

"Ooh, pizza!" Kendall cheers before she gets up to open the door and grab our dinner for tonight.

"Look, Lily." Reign leans in, his voice low. "I know he acts like a tough guy, and trust me, he is most of the time. But my brother loves you. He's just too much of a dickhead to admit it. But he does. I can see it in his eyes. Like I can see it in yours." He grabs my hand, then gives it a small squeeze, and I reply by offering him a smile.

"Oh, this smells so good," Kendall moans. She locks the door behind her, then walks back to where we're seated at the bar, setting the pizza box in front of us.

"Fuck yeah." Reign opens the box with an excited spark in his eyes, like a boy on Christmas morning, until he freezes. His face pales, his cheeks instantly losing all color, and his mouth opens in shock.

"What? What is it?" I yelp, feeling my heart rate speed up again.

He reaches into the box, holding up a small swan made of folded white paper.

"Hey, that looks like the one I got at the races!" Kendall chirps until she notices the horrified look on Reign's face. "Are you okay?"

"Fuck. We need to leave. NOW!" He quickly gets up, his face a mask of seriousness I'd never seen or thought him capable of wearing. Kendall and I share a stunned look when moves to the door.

"NOW!" he shouts, his raised voice startling both of us.

His behavior makes me nervous as fuck, seeing how this is the complete opposite of what's typical for Reign. He doesn't get mad. He doesn't raise his voice, and he sure as fuck doesn't panic easily.

"What the fuck?" Kendall mouths at me, looking as baffled as I am, before we both slide off our stools, leaving the pizza where it is.

33

CONNOR

I've just put Colin to bed and am walking down the stairs when Franklin enters the foyer from the kitchen. We share a surprised look when we hear a car door in front of the house.

Franklin looks at his watch.

"I didn't expect them to get home before midnight."

I have no time to reply before a pale Reign bursts through the door with Kendall and Lily right behind him. Confused, my gaze connects with Lily, who gives me a small shrug.

"It's Aubrey!" he shouts, distress marring his face as he runs a hand through his messy hair.

"What are you talking about?" I demand while we all keep staring at him as if he's lost his mind.

"This!" He holds a white piece of paper in his hand, looking like a bird.

"Okaaay," I drawl, skeptically. "What is 'this'?"

"Girls, can you please wait in the kitchen? We'll be right there." Franklin takes a step away to make room for them to pass, and they do as he asks while shooting both of us worried glances. We wait until they pass through the kitchen door before we turn our attention back to Reign, who still looks completely flustered.

"Come on, let's go," Franklin commands as he heads into the office and we trail behind him. I close the door behind us as Reign takes a seat while Franklin trudges over to the liquor station to pour a drink before he hands it over to our youngest brother.

Reign eagerly grabs the glass, throwing the brown liquid down his throat, then hands it back to Franklin as he reaches out his other hand towards the bottle still lingering in Franklin's hand.

"Give me the bottle."

Franklin's brows raise a little, hesitating before until he hands the bottle to him. Reign places the bottle to his lips, taking a big slug that seems never ending. When he's downed a large portion of the bottle, I step in, snatching the bottle out of his hands.

"I think that's enough for now."

He wipes the corner of his mouth with the back of his hand, then slumps into his seat with a troubled gaze that's fucking unsettling.

"Speak, Reign," I growl, placing the bottle on the desk while Franklin and I wait expectantly.

"It's origami."

"What is?" I frown.

"The bird," Franklin explains while Reign pulls the piece of paper out of his back pocket. "Kendall explained it to me."

"Right," Reign agrees. "When Kendall showed me the swan she got from that boy at the races a few weeks ago, I thought it was a coincidence. I mean, a lot of kids are into crafts and shit, right?" He closes his eyes as if he's fighting his emotions, and I feel my jaw harden at the sight. "But the girls and I ordered pizza at the bar tonight, and this came with it." He holds up the paper folded into a bird. "It's an origami swan," he explains.

"What's the deal with it? Why is it important?" I wonder, not understanding where this is going.

Reign rubs his chin and sighs.

"The oldest daughter of my foster parents," his voice cracks, "she used to make them while…" He stops, pinching the bridge of his nose with his head hanging.

"What is it, Reign?" Franklin asks, concerned.

Reign sighs again, his hand dropping to his leg as he turns to stare out the window, like he doesn't want to look at us.

"She used to make them while shutting out the world. She would put on headphones to drown out the noises that came from the rest of the house."

We all stay quiet for a moment, and Franklin and I share a confused look, unsure of what we should do. When Reign finally came home at age sixteen, he was scrawny, looking like shit, but still walking around Franklin's penthouse with a satisfied grin on his face. Yet almost every other night, we'd find him on the balcony, staring into the night, completely zoned out.

For weeks, we tried everything to get him to talk, but he refused to say a word. Giving us some crappy Buddhist shit like 'the past is the past.'

After a few weeks we gave up, since neither of us are real chatty guys anyway, but I can't deny I've always wondered what the hell happened to him.

"What noises?" I ask softly, not wanting to startle him now that he's finally opening up.

He lets out another deep sigh, and I can feel the weight of his struggles filling the room. He's our playful little brother, the charmer and the playboy, all at the same time. And it kills me to see him turn into this meek little boy whenever his past catches him off guard.

"It was a brothel."

"What?" Franklin barks at the same time I mutter, "Holy shit."

"What are you talking about, Reign?" Franklin seethes, slamming his fist on the desk.

"It was a brothel!" Reign shouts this time. His face is clouded with pain, as if saying the words out loud physically hurts him. "It was a brothel. The bastards only took in girls so they could sell them for the night in the basement. It was a brothel." His eyes shine with unshed tears, and I can feel my anger moving up to the surface, my blood surging through my veins at lightning speed.

"Who?! Who are *they*?" I demand. "Did they..." I swallow the words back as horrendous images of my brother in some whorehouse enter my head. The thought alone makes me sick to my stomach.

"Did they... Did they hurt you?" Franklin chokes.

"Did they sell me for the night? Rape me? Is that what you want to ask?" Reign's jaw is set, clenching and unclenching his hands. He looks devastated, reminding me of the time he found out Franklin wasn't innocent after all. He'd blasted through the house like a hurricane, breaking every-thing he could find while expressing his grief at the top of his lungs. I felt helpless when my brothers and I got separated the day we all got dumped in foster care. And I felt helpless the day he found out Franklin wasn't his hero after all. But neither of those days compare to how helpless I feel now, knowing my brother spent four years of his teens in the hands of a psychopath who whored out innocent kids.

"Y-yeah," Franklin stammers, wrecked.

"No. No, they didn't. They beat the shit out of me on a daily basis. But they never touched me. Not like that," Reign clarifies, and we both let out a sigh of relief.

"Why didn't you tell us, Reign?"

"And risk one of you getting arrested again?" he cries. "I took care of it."

"What do you mean, you took care of it?" I don't like where this is going.

"I took care of it."

"Quit with the half stories, Reign. How did you take care of it?" I push, getting more frustrated by the second.

"I blew a bullet through his head."

"No-suh," Franklin mumbles next to me, shock written on his face.

"Ya-huh." He shrugs right before Killian enters the room.

"What's going on? The girls are in the kitchen, pacing and wringing their hands." He closes the door behind him, then looks from Franklin and me to Reign and back. We all stay quiet, tight jaws, flared nostrils, and tight muscles.

"Okay, seriously? The three of you look like you ate jalapeños and are putting on brave faces. What's doing?"

Silence hangs over the room until Reign turns his head towards Killian.

"They know."

Killian's eyes widen before he slowly nods his head.

"You knew? He told you?" Franklin rushes towards Killian like a raging maniac.

"Right," Killian says, turning around and reaching for the doorknob. "I'm gonna go check on the girls. They seemed pretty startled." He opens the door, and I wait for Franklin to lose his shit.

"Close the door, *Killian.*"

Killian's head drops as he expels a big, dramatic sigh. He then turns around with a fake grin on his face, his usual five-o'clock shadow covering his jaw as he tries to act casual about the matter.

Nice try.

Killian is the one who serves as Franklin's right hand. The two hotheads plot most of our tactics and invest both money and time deciding the next step we will take in order to grow our empire. I can completely understand why Franklin is fuming beside me right now. Not only does he hate it when he doesn't have all the information, but Killian is the last one he'd expect to keep information from him.

"What?" Killian finally speaks, throwing his hands in the air.

"How long?" Franklin growls. "How long have the two of you been keeping this from me?"

He glares at Killian and Reign, his finger moving between the two of them.

"I made him swear not to tell you," Reign says.

"You didn't think this was too important to keep to yourself?" Franklin charges forward, grabbing Killian by the throat, his eyes shooting knives at him.

Killian roughly pushes him off his chest with a scowl, and I grab Franklin's shoulder to force him to step back, trying to make sure neither goes too far.

"It's not my secret to tell, Franky! Who am I to tell you the shit he's been through? If he doesn't want to tell you, he doesn't want to tell you. I'm not going to force him, and I sure as fuck am not going to tell you shit that is none of your business."

"Everything you do is *my* business!" Franklin roars. "At least the fucking important shit. And knowing my little brother was stuck in a whorehouse for four years and apparently whacked someone for it seems pretty important to me! We don't keep secrets, not between us four! You should've told me!" he explodes, throwing the nearest glass within his reach across the room.

"Franky!" I pull him back, placing my body in front of him. "Calm the fuck down!"

"Well, maybe if you would've told him your secret, he would've wanted to share his!" Killian raises his chin in challenge, his gaze locked on Franklin. I can feel Franklin's chest heaving up and down under my palm as he remains mute.

"Look, how about we all just calm the fuck down, and Reign can tell us the rest of the story."

We're all quiet until they both nod in agreement.

Franklin shrugs my hands off his body, then takes a seat on the desk again while Killian takes the seat next to Reign.

"Speak, Reign. And don't leave anything out," I order calmly.

He glances at me as he starts to talk again.

"The house I was placed in was owned by a couple who had two daughters. We had to call them Mr. and Mrs. Brady. I never even heard their real names. Anyway, they wanted to reenact their own version of the Brady Bunch. Sick, right? Besides their own daughters, they had four foster girls living with them. Well, most of the time. It felt like a new girl left or arrived every few months. I was the only one that stayed the full four years. The oldest girl, Aubrey, was two years older than me. She helped me as much as she could. She hid me when her dad was on a drunken rampage, and she nursed my wounds if there wasn't enough time to hide."

Franklin pushes out a deep breath next to me, clearly having a hard time coping with everything Reign is saying.

"It wasn't until I was there for a few months that I noticed how strange men would come by the house at night and then disappear into the basement for a few hours. It didn't take me long to realize what the hell was going on. When I asked Aubrey about it, she shrugged her shoulders, as if she had accepted the situation she was in. Aubrey and her sister, Nova, didn't … they didn't go to the basement often. But when Nova was forced to go every now and then, Aubrey would spend that time folding a shit-ton of those swan things to keep herself busy."

"How old was Nova?" I'm afraid to ask the question, but I have to know.

"Ten."

"Holy shit," I hiss.

"Yeah. I tried to stand up to them, but Aubrey told me to shut up when her dad started to threaten to find me some clients to start working for the roof over my head. This went on and on for years, and the only thing that kept me sane was going to school. I was a punk kid, but school was my escape, so I made sure not to fuck that up. A month before my sixteenth birthday, it was Nova's turn to 'work.' But the sick bastard who paid for her didn't only fuck her in every single way until she was covered in blood, he also choked her while doing it. By the time he was done … it was too late."

My stomach turns, and I can feel bile pile up in the back of my throat. I suck in a deep breath, doing my best to keep the contents in my body where they belong while I stare out the window.

"You think it's that Aubrey girl who's out to get you? To get us?" Franklin suggests with a strained voice, though I can hear his effort to sound unaffected.

Reign shakes his head.

"Aubrey killed herself six weeks after you got custody of me. Kill and I drove back to Providence because I wanted to pull her out of that hellhole. One of the girls opened the door, telling me she wasn't there, so we went by the high school. A girl from her class told me she drowned herself in Greenwich Bay. That's when Kill and I rode back to the house. I waited until past midnight, knowing everyone would be in their rooms, and the drunk bastard would be passed out on the couch. Then I snuck in and blew his brains out." The look on Reign's face is completely vacant, as if this doesn't affect him one bit, but I know deep down inside he's dying. He's not the violent type.

He doesn't back down—he's very much an alpha, just like the rest of us—but Reign would never resort to violence if there is any other option.

"What makes you think this has anything to do with us?" Killian turns his head to Reign.

"This." He holds the origami swan up in the air once more. "It's too much of a coincidence."

"Okay." Killian nods. "But Aubrey is dead, and so is her dad. Who would want to avenge them? And why you? Why us? Why now?"

"I don't know. Maybe one of the other girls? Maybe the mother?"

"What happened to the mother?" Franklin asks.

"Right after Nova died, she supposedly went to stay with her sister in Idaho for a while. Never saw the woman again."

"She probably didn't give a shit either. You can't if you pimp out your kids," I mutter, cracking my knuckles. I never sugarcoated our time in foster care, but I had a fucking breeze in comparison. Sure, it was a shithole and often felt unbearable, but my suffering didn't move past having an empty stomach for three days. Right now, that sounds like a fucking dream compared to Reign's foster care experience.

"You think this is connected with the dead body? With Cary and the rest of Emerson's crew?" Franklin glances between the three of us, asking for our opinions.

Killian clears his throat, looking at Franklin.

"I wouldn't rule it out, but to be honest? I don't think it's related. Someone is fucking with Reign, giving him stupid paper birds to make him remember his past. That sounds personal. Dropping a dead body on our doorstep is just a way to fuck with our businesses."

"Maybe…" I cock my head a little. "But it sure as fuck is a big coincidence. Did we find anything more on that Bella girl Emerson was talking about?"

"I asked around. Apparently, she was just a fuck buddy. Nobody has seen her for the last three weeks. My guess? She's just a mafia whore looking for some attention."

Our heads snap towards Franklin when we hear his phone ring in the pocket of his jeans. He pulls it out, a frown forming on his face when he looks at the screen. He shows us what it says.

Anonymous.

"Well, speak of the devil," I say, already knowing who's on the other end of the line.

Franklin rolls his eyes, then presses the speakerphone button.

"What?" he barks.

"Franky! How are you doing?" Cary asks on the other side of the line. "I heard Kenny made a swift recovery. I have to admit, I didn't take you for a country girl lover. Although, I did hear she gives some serious head."

Franklin's face flushes red, hearing Kendall's name. I quickly grab the phone out of his hands, taking over the conversation.

"What do you want, tool?"

"Is that you, Connor? Sorry about Nigel. I had nothing to do with that. I do have something to do with the dead boy behind your bar. Like what you guys did with the place," Cary rambles. "Nice ambiance. Good location. It's a smart move, great way to launder all your dirty money, right?"

"Do you always talk this much?" I glare at the phone. "Because I have shit to do."

"Watch it, Connor. You'll turn green before you know it."

"What do you want, Cary?" Franklin seethes from over my shoulder, still fuming.

"Simple. The same as Emerson wanted. Bow. Bow and admit your reign is over. Oh, and half your business."

"This is getting old, Cary." Killian sounds bored and unimpressed, and I share his feelings. "You can't overthrow us. This is not a playground where you can steal our marbles and we go crying to Mommy to kiss it better."

"You see, that's the problem with you Wolfes. You think no one can touch you. That you're invincible."

"We are invincible," I counter.

"No one is invincible. Emerson was an arrogant ass. But trust me when I say, I have more patience. I'm smarter. I will hit you where it hurts the most. Destroying each one of your businesses, your influences, until the city can no longer turn the other cheek."

"You do realize we own Boston?" Killian rebukes, rolling his eyes.

"For now. But all good things eventually end. And when it does, I'll be there to pick up the pieces." Before we can say anything else, the line goes dead and I turn my head towards Franklin, still grinding his teeth in annoyance.

"I want him dead," he snarls.

"First chance I get," I reply, meaning every word. I'm sick of these Southern boys trying to rule our city. Threatening our livelihood. It's time we put an end to it.

"Reign, you okay?" Franklin nudges his chin to Reign, who is still slumped in his chair.

"Yeah. I'm all right."

Franklin nods awkwardly, probably still feeling uneasy about what Reign finally shared with us.

"Right… See if you can find the names of the girls who were living in the house with you in Providence. Maybe one of them pops up that might have some personal issue with you." Franklin then turns his attention to Killian. "You check the politicians we own. See if any are likely to flip if Cary offers them the right thing. I want a list of potential liabilities. And you." His gaze lands on me. "Set up personal bodyguards for Kendall, Lily, and Colin. I want them protected at all times." We all agree in unison before he walks out the door, followed by Killian. As Reign gets up out of his seat, I trail behind him.

"Reign."

He turns around to face me, fatigue clear in his features,

as if it took a lot of energy for him to share that part of his life with us.

"I'm sorry that happened to you."

"I know." He smiles. "It's not your fault. It's not anyone's fault."

I sigh.

"I know I'm not … well, the one you go to for a good talk. But I'm here for you, okay?"

He nods with a grateful look in his green eyes.

"I know, Con. Thanks," he says before he walks out of the office.

34

CONNOR

Lily is sitting against the headboard with a book on her lap when I enter our bedroom a few hours later.

"Is Reign okay?" she asks as I walk through the door.

"To be honest? I don't know." I saunter over to the edge of the bed then crawl towards her to yank her underneath me, a screech leaving her luscious lips.

"Connor!" she chuckles.

"It's been a day, babe. I just want to bury myself inside of you."

"Your son is right there." She points her head to the other side of the bed where Colin is sound asleep between a bunch of pillows.

I sigh.

"He needs his own room."

"He does?" Her brows raise up in surprise, a smile forming on her beautiful face.

"Well, yeah. We're not going to keep sleeping with him

between us for the rest of our lives, right? I mean, I love him. But I'm not sure I want to share you every single night."

Her face lights up at my words, and I frown, not sure what I said that made her glow like a damn Christmas tree.

"You don't want to share me?"

"Oh, you like hearing that?" I snicker, dropping a kiss on her lips.

She cups my face, pressing her forehead against mine while I hover above her.

"I love hearing that," she purrs, bringing my dick to full alert. But then her face grows stern, and I let my head fall in defeat.

"Don't kill the mood, baby," I groan.

"Sorry," she drawls.

Letting my body fall next to her, I prop up on an elbow, laying on my side to face her.

"What do you want, angel?"

"Why did Reign freak out?" The concern on her face is genuine, like she truly is interested in the welfare of my little brother, and I know she is. It's impossible not to love Reign. I don't even have to ask to know he has both Lily and Kendall wrapped around his little finger. I'm hesitant to share his story, though, knowing technically it's none of her business. But the thing is ... I really want to make this work with her. To build a life with her and Colin. To be a family. Though Franklin and Kendall haven't been together for long, I like seeing what they have together. That undeniable bond. I want that. I want a partner I can share my shit with, a wife I can seek comfort from.

I let out a deep sigh, placing my hands on her hips as I tug her a little closer so our faces are only an inch apart.

"Apparently, the origami reminded him of his time in

foster care. It was worse than we'd expected. Turns out his foster parents were running a brothel in their basement with the girls they took in. Including their own daughters."

Lily gasps, placing a hand in front of her mouth.

"Yeah, it's bad."

"Did they abuse him?"

"Sexually? No." I shake my head. "Physically, yeah. But we all got beat up in foster care."

"Even you?"

"Even me. But my time in foster care was a walk in the park compared to the shit Reign had to endure for four years. How he's still so cheery half of the time beats the hell out of me."

"He's one of the good guys," Lily gushes as she strokes my cheek with the back of her hand. "You all are."

"Pff," I snort. "I'm *not a good* guy."

"Yeah, whatever, tough guy. You may be a stone-cold asshole ninety percent of the time, but I see the other ten. You can't hide it from me." She states this as factual. There is no playfulness in her voice, no hidden messages. Sincerity is tattooed in her eyes, causing a weird feeling to bloom in my chest.

"Does Reign think his foster parents are trying to destroy you guys? Leaving dead bodies behind bars and shit?" She changes the subject.

"No. Both biological daughters are dead, and so is their father. Their mother is missing, but Reign doubts she has anything to do with it. He's gonna try to find the names of everyone else who lived in that hellhole during the four years he was there. Besides, Cary just claimed the dead body."

"Cary? Is he the guy who replaced Emerson? Did he kill Damien?"

"No, that was Emerson."

She's quiet for a moment, worrying her lip while staring at my chest. I brush my thumb over her eyebrow in what I hope is a soothing way.

"Lily…" I start. "There will be times when I can't tell you everything."

"I know."

"Will you trust me when I say I won't keep anything from you if it's not in your best interest? Or Colin's?"

"Hmm, I trust you, Connor," she proclaims, before she covers my mouth with hers. "Always."

I take her into my arms, trailing kisses along her jaw. She moans every time my lips connect with her skin, and I feel her melt into my touch. I can't believe how much this girl has grown on me in the last few weeks. When we first met that one night, I knew she was a girl I'd always remember. One of few women who'd caught my attention in a very long time. But when I burst through her door, not once did I expect her to become what she is to me now. A part of me, a part of my life.

Family.

Sliding my ass off the bed, I keep her in my arms, cradling her against my chest as I walk us into the hallway.

"What are you doing?" she screeches with an excited grin.

"Taking you to another room so our son doesn't wake up when I make you scream my name when you come." I wink. "You know, keeping his childhood traumas to a minimum."

35

Glancing at all the tasty food around the table, a warm feeling forms inside of me.

The table is covered with enough food to feed a small army, but then again, looking at these four brothers, I guess that's exactly what they are.

"Oh my god, Lily. You did all this?" There's awe in Kendall's voice as we all take our seats around the large dining table.

"I love to cook." I shrug, helping Colin into his booster seat before I sit down beside him.

"She's a pro at cream pies." Connor takes the seat next to me with a big smile on his face. "Looks great, angel."

"You outdid yourself, Lily," Franklin offers with a wink, and I give him a grateful smile.

I still don't have the same lighthearted relationship with Franklin as I have with Reign and Killian, but since Kendall came home, I realized that's just who he is. Kendall is the only one who gets the fun and playful version of Franklin, while the rest of us get the brooding crime lord, the head of the Wolfe family. I'm cool with that, but it's still nice to get a compliment from him.

"Should we say grace?" Reign asks once everyone is settled in their seats.

"When the fuck do we ever say grace?" Killian rolls his eyes, grabbing a piece of chicken off the platter in front of him.

"Kill. Language." Connor glares, then shoots me an apologetic look.

"Oh, please. I give up. Dig in everyone," I blurt, my eyes on the ceiling.

Eagerly, everyone fills their plates, and for a few minutes, the room is silent except for the clattering of cutlery against plates.

"I can't believe you're graduating tomorrow, Kendall! And how you managed to do it with so much shit going on…. I'm so proud of you," I say when my plate is almost empty.

She lets out a satisfied sigh while Franklin grabs her hand and gives it a small squeeze.

"I know, I can't believe it either."

"Believe it, pretty girl. You worked hard for it," Franklin murmurs.

"Can't deny that. Sorry you can't come to the ceremony, Lily. It's stupid we can't bring Colin." Kendall offers me a regretful smile before taking a sip of her wine.

"Oh, don't worry about it. A graduation is no place for a toddler anyway. He'd probably babble through the whole ceremony. Besides, we still don't want him out in the open too much, right? We'll see you afterwards."

"Yeah, that's true," she agrees, turning her attention to Killian. "How is the bar doing?"

Killian drops his fork, chewing on his last bite.

"Like shit."

"How come?" I ask, surprised by his response.

"We barely get any customers. At this point, it's costing us more to stay open than closing down."

"I don't get it, though. You're the Wolfes. I'd expect some people coming in to at least see your bar every night."

"I know. But I guess Cary's doing a good job of convincing the city to boycott us."

"Should we reach out to Sienna?" Connor leans back in his chair, looking at Killian. Reign freezes, giving his brother a glare.

"No," he answers before Killian can.

Killian shrugs his shoulders and rolls his eyes, but he keeps his mouth shut, clearly not feeling like getting into whatever reason Reign doesn't want to ask Sienna for help.

Whoever she may be.

Reign suddenly lets out a loud, "Yum", scaring the shit out of Colin. He then stretches his arms in the air before he drops his hands on his stomach. He slouches down, a smile tugging on the corners of his mouth.

"That. Was. Amazing. Lily. No wonder Connor is head over heels for you. If you weren't already taken by my ruffian brother, I'd probably snatch you away myself."

We all laugh while Connor slaps his brother over the head with a scowl.

"Shut up, tool."

"What?!" he yelps. "I'm just saying I understand why you love her. Oh, wait? You haven't told her yet?"

An awkward hush settles over the table, and Kendall and I share a curious look.

"What is it with my brothers being unable to admit their feelings? Has Franky said it, Kenny?"

"That. Is. Private. *Reign*," Franklin growls from the head of the table, his face grim.

"What? There is nothing wrong with admitting you love someone. Besides, it's not like we don't already know it."

"Oh, like you and Sienna?" Connor challenges, making Reign scowl at him from across the table.

"I have no issue admitting that I love Sienna. But she doesn't love me, so move on."

"Who's Sienna?" I finally blurt out, unable to control my curiosity, resulting in a simultaneous response from three of the boys.

"His ex," Killian voices at the same time Connor replies with, "The love of his life," followed by Franklin mentioning, "The best event manager in the city."

The room goes silent once again as Kendall and I look between all four of them. Finally, she opens her mouth.

"Well, which one is it?"

Reign's face hardens.

"All of the above."

THE NEXT DAY, Connor and I decide to enjoy the summer day by taking Colin to one of the playgrounds in the city.

"So what happened to Sienna?" Connor and I are sitting on a park bench, watching how Colin climbs up the small slide, then glides down to do it all over again. The sun burns on my head, but I'm enjoying it, absorbing the natural vitamin D while keeping an eye on Colin.

"When Reign found out Franklin wasn't innocent,

Franklin decided it was best if Reign went away for a while. He sent him to New York. The Distuccis needed someone to help dig up dirt about some politicians, and Franky still owed them a favor. Reign broke up with Sienna, saying he needed some alone time, that he would be back within two months, and they'd go from there. But Reign stayed in New York for a year."

"A year? Why?"

"A girl. Callie Reyes. I never understood why he stayed with her and kept working for the Distuccis when Boston has always been his home, but now that he came clean about what happened all those years in Providence, it makes sense."

My eyes are looking for Colin's dark blue t-shirt, and I freak for a second when I can't find him before his blond head pops up behind the wooden playhouse in the middle of the playground. I sigh in relief, glancing at Connor.

"How come?"

"Callie was sold by her brother. Reign saved her while she was getting raped at a strip club. After that, he took her in, and they bonded. I guess he felt like at least he saved her when he couldn't save the other girls."

I push out a breath, blinking, my heart feeling for Reign once more.

"What happened to her?"

"I haven't asked. But after a year, he walked through the door like nothing happened."

"Did he get back together with Sienna?"

Connor snickers, tugging me a little closer against him.

"Sienna found him in the bar below Franky's penthouse and gave us a full show at the busiest hour of the day."

"No-suh!"

"Ya-huh, she even punched him with a wicked shiner. I

laughed about it for weeks. Nowadays, she avoids the places she might run into us, but I still see her every now and then. She's a good girl."

I rest my head against him, settling into the warmth of his body. I like how comfortable we've become with one another. He says he can't give me everything I want, but he sure seems to spend every minute trying.

He makes me coffee in the morning, holding my hand every chance he gets, taking care of Colin so I can run a bath and relax with a book.

It's the little things that do it for me, and he doesn't even realize it.

I love him. And I think he loves me. But I'd be stupid to force the words out of his mouth before he's ready. Don't want to rattle the Boston beast.

His big hand lands on my thigh, giving it a squeeze.

"Do you know where Colin is?" To most, his voice would sound calm and composed, but I can hear the uncertainty in it. My head snaps frantically between the playground equipment, searching between the slide, the playhouse, and finally the swing, before I do it all over again when I still can't see him.

"No," I reply, getting up. "Colin?" I call out, holding a hand in front of my forehead to cover my eyes from the sun.

When I don't see him, I turn around to look at Connor. He frowns, then gets up.

"Colin!" he booms, loud as fuck.

"He was just there," I say, quietly. My heart starts to race, and panic grips me by the throat.

"Calm down, he must be out here somewhere." He turns to one of the security guards who followed us here. "Do you have eyes on Colin?" he calls out.

The man shakes his head, then says something in his earpiece while his eyes search the area. My feet start to move quickly, my head turning every few yards in a different direction while calling out his name.

"Colin! Colin, where are you?"

"Colin! Get out here, buddy!" Connor shouts.

"Colin! Colin! Colin!?" About half a minute passes, and tears start to soak my eyes, knowing he would have responded by now.

"Where is he, Connor?" I cry, desperately gripping his shirt.

"We will find him, babe." I want to believe him. I want to be one of those moms who overreacted because within the next few seconds, my boy will dart out of some bushes, wondering what all the fuss is about. But a brick develops in my stomach because my mother's instinct tells me something is wrong. That something is off.

"Do you see him?" Connor barks, this time with more force.

The team of security guys jog around the park, looking everywhere for our boy, and I break down in Connor's arms when they return empty-handed.

"Colin!" I shout once more, even though I know it's futile.

Grunting, Connor pulls one arm from my body to get his phone out of his pocket.

"What are you doing?"

"Calling Reign. I need him to tap into the system to check the cameras of the area around the playground. See if he wandered off."

Yeah, okay, that makes sense. Colin is not the kid who

wanders off, but he's getting older. He could be getting more adventurous, maybe?

"Shit. His phone is off," Connor mutters, his jaw tight. I can see the stress he feels on his face, and I'm glad he's here with me, that we can share our concern for Colin together.

"I'll try Franky." He starts to tap the screen when a frown creases his forehead, his top lip raising in displeasure as he looks at the screen.

"What?! What is it?"

"No. No. No," he chants, wildly shaking his head as his eyes go glassy before his pupils dilate to the point that barely any green remains.

"NO!" he roars, making me flinch while grabbing the attention of the security guys still searching for Colin.

With long strides, he walks away from me, and I follow him like a confused puppy.

"Take her home, now!" he bellows to the nearest guy on his team. "You, you, and you." He points. "Take her home and don't let her out of your sight. If anyone so much as blinks at her, you shoot them. Got it?" The three men give him firm nods. "The rest of you, follow me."

"Connor! What the fuck is going on?!"

He turns around, a pained expression in his eyes, as if he doesn't want to tell me.

"They took him. They took Colin."

36

CONNOR

When I storm through the door of the kitchen at the mansion thirty minutes later, my brothers and Kendall following on my heels, I feel like a ticking time bomb. I felt anger when Nigel died, rage, a feral need to tear everything apart that crossed my path, but it doesn't even come close to the mania that's blazing through my body right now.

They took my boy.

When I opened the photo they sent me on my phone of an unconscious Colin in the back of a car, it felt like the whole world crumbled beneath me.

"Where is he?" Lily jumps up, looking like hell just took her and spat her out. Her cheeks are tinted red from the tears that probably have been racing down her face, her usually perfectly straight hair now a disheveled mess on her head.

"Kendall, can you take Lily to the bathroom for a second? Freshen her up?" Franklin turns his head to Kendall, giving Lily a sympathetic look.

"The hell I am!" she roars, taking a step forward, ready to get into Franklin's face. "This is *my* son we're talking about! I'm not going anywhere." I circle my arm around her, holding her weight, my eyes locking with Franky's while I gently speak into her ear.

"You don't have to go anywhere, baby."

Kendall quickly darts towards Lily, holding her head in her hands while I keep my arms around her.

"Franky!" she scowls.

My words are returned by a questioning look from Franklin, silently asking me if this is the best idea, and I nod my head even though it probably isn't. If we want to get Colin back safe and sound, we will have to be smart and tactical, leaving no room for emotion. A grieving mother is not going to help with that, but what can I do? She's his mother. I can't exclude her from something this important.

"Okay." Reign jumps in, taking over. "Give me your phone. Maybe I can track the number."

Still holding Lily in one arm, I can feel her legs trembling as I pull my phone out. Handing it to my brother, I keep her close, then wrap my other arm around Lily's waist to keep her on her feet.

"A life for a life? *Again?*" Reign mutters, his brows lifted in surprise. He pulls out his second phone, which is connected with a shit-ton of apps he uses to track whatever we want as soon as possible. "Cary would really take a toddler because of Emerson?"

"Makes no sense," Killian proclaims. "You would've thought he'd be happy to take over for Emerson. Were they close?" He turns his attention to Kendall, whose hand is stroking Lily's hair, trying to comfort her.

"Not particularly. They knew each other for a long time,

and Cary was Emerson's right hand. But Cary didn't mind going against Emerson's wishes."

I notice Franky giving Lily a side glance, his worried gaze flashing to me before turning to Kenny.

"Do you think he's capable of killing a toddler?"

"Oh god," Lily gasps, letting her body completely fall against me, as she starts to cry uncontrollably.

Kendall is quiet for a moment, her eyes laced with horror.

"I-I don't know," she stammers.

"Don't worry. We will find him. *Alive*," Reign emphasizes, glaring around the room before he continues tapping on the screen of his phone. "Wait. I don't think we need to."

"What do you mean?" Franklin questions.

"They just sent another message. It's a meeting point."

"What does it say?" Killian takes a step closer to Reign, stretching his neck to look at the screen. "Evergreen Cemetery. One hour."

"All right, let's go."

Reign halts me, lifting his hand.

"I'll stay with the girls. I can track you from my laptop. Have some back up at every corner."

"Sounds good," Franklin agrees, turning towards the door.

"I'm coming with you!" Lily announces, making Franklin stop in his tracks, looking at her.

"Lily," I plead.

"Don't you fucking dare, *Wolfe*. I'm coming."

We all wait for Franklin to tell her no, but instead, he just looks at her in understanding, and I'm not sure if I want to applaud him or kill him when he makes a decision.

"Let's go."

37

CONNOR

Having Lily come with us to the meeting point gives me even more anxiety than I'd anticipated. My heart is racing, and I don't feel as calm as I normally do when we have to deal with this kind of shit now that I have not one but two people to protect.

Franklin walks onto Evergreen Cemetery followed by the rest of us and two security guys. The rest of the team is strategically situated all over the cemetery, some visible, some hidden, with an extra team spread out on the streets around the burial grounds.

It doesn't take long before we see Cary, accompanied by six of his men, standing outside of one of his SUVs. He's leaning against the hood of his car, with his leg popped up on the bumper while a cigarette dangles from between his lips.

"Evening, boys," he says, taking a drag of the smoke then pointing it at Franklin. "You want one?"

"I quit."

"Right. I heard good old Kenny made you a reformed

man." His arctic eyes peer down at him with a smug grin. "How is she? Is she doing good?"

"Where is my boy?" I snap, unable to continue with the small talk.

"Connor Wolfe, always straight to business, or the *beast* will be unleashed." He mockingly shakes his hand in the air. "Yikes!"

"I have to admit, I'm surprised you feel the need to avenge Emerson. I thought you'd be thanking us for the job opening," Killian remarks.

"Oh, that's cute," Cary chuckles. "You thought that was about Jones? No, you're right. You did me a solid with that one. But let's talk about the boy. In all actuality, he wasn't the life I wanted. Although, he was a nice surprise."

"Well, just tell us who you want, and give us the boy."

"Not yet," he retorts.

"Where is he?" I grind out.

"I'll show you." He throws his cigarette on the floor, walking onto the burial grounds as we trail behind him. I glance at Lily, giving her a reassuring look before turning my attention back in front of me. He leads us past a wide pine tree, an empty grave in front of it, and I gasp when I notice a girl sitting in front of it with Colin in her lap.

"Colin!" Lily screeches. She starts to run towards him, but when Cary turns around with a threatening look on his face, Killian circles her waist to hold her back.

"Not so fast, sweetheart. I still want something in return. A life for a life, right? Give me what I want, and Bella here will safely hand him over to you. Fail, and he'll be buried alive in front of your eyes. Have you met Bella?"

The girl gives us a wave, sitting cross-legged on the edge of the grave with Colin still unconscious in her lap. Her hair is honey brown with small curls, while her dark red lips stand out against her fair skin. She gives us an amused smile, her eyes looking manic as fuck. She looks like a fucking psychopath.

"I have to say, I'm a little disappointed. I thought we'd get all four brothers to join us," she pouts, petting Colin's blond hair. The sight of her touching my son like he's her puppy makes me sick to my stomach.

"Stop touching him!" Lily barks, as if she can read my mind.

"Tut-tut," she chastises. "Don't push it, *Lily*, is it?" The words leave her red painted lips with disdain, making me wonder how much she knows about us. "We don't want sweet Colin to take a nap six feet under, do we?"

"What have you given him?" Killian glares, asking the one question I was afraid to ask.

"Nothing much, just some Nembutal. Don't worry, he'll be fine in an hour."

"What do you want?" Franklin's voice is laced with impatience, and I quickly glance at him, seeing the grimace on his face.

"I'm disappointed, Franklin. You, of all people, should know what I want. You don't remember, do you?" Cary asks, his beady black eyes narrowing at my oldest brother.

"Remember what?" he seethes, taking a step forward.

"That." Cary points at the tombstone next to the empty grave, and it isn't until that moment that I notice the name on the gray stone.

Declan Cole Murphy.

"Fucking hell," Killian mutters beside me while Franklin visibly swallows before securing his gaze on Cary once more.

Franklin's eyes narrow at Cary, his hands clenched into fists beside him.

"Who are you?"

My oldest brother is always the composed one. The one who holds his temper, keeping the rest of us in line. But in this moment, his neck flushes red, and I know without asking, he's going back to that dark place he found himself in when he was eighteen.

The one moment he couldn't keep his cool.

The one moment that was detrimental for all of us.

"Ah, see, here comes the good part! Story time! Drumroll, please." Cary dramatically drums on his legs, a grin splitting his pale face. "My mother's name was Noreen Baker. Once upon a time, she met a banker, and they hit it off, but he was married. You know how this story goes. She got pregnant out of wedlock, and because said banker didn't want anything to do with her once she got knocked-up, she moved back to Alabama. Had a beautiful boy, blond hair, blue eyes. A real stunner."

"It was you," Killian states.

"Ding, ding, ding! You win!" He does a little victory dance then freezes. "But here comes the grand finale! Because my father's name was…"

"Murphy," Killian finishes his sentence, pursing his lips in distaste.

"Right again! You are on a roll, Wolfe!"

"Declan was your brother?" Killian asks for clarification, then looks at Franklin and me with confusion. I shrug, not sure what the fuck is going on. Franklin keeps staring at Cary, silent as a rock.

"He was. I only saw him once a year, but I was planning on moving to Boston after High School. Still did, just for different reasons. A life for a life, Wolfe." Cary glares at Franklin, now fuming. "You killed my brother. It's only fair I get one of yours."

"That shithead deserved to die!" Franklin yells.

"Your brothers aren't innocent either, so trade one of them for the boy, and we will call it even, cool?"

"Connor," Bella offers, blinking with wide eyes, reminding me of one of those old porcelain dolls. "We want Connor. Makes sense, right? You would give your life for your sweet boy, wouldn't you, Connor?" She bats her lashes at me, running her hands through Colin's hair.

"In a heartbeat."

There is no hesitation in my words, no second thoughts. If I need to give my life to save my son's, they can have me.

"Connor." Killian gives me a wary look. "What are you doing?"

My heart starts to pound so hard, I wouldn't be surprised if everyone could hear it, but I mean every word.

"That's my boy, Kill."

"NO!" Lily panics when she realizes what's happening. "No, Connor, you can't do that!"

Cary grabs the gun out of his waistband, pointing it at the two men next to Bella.

"Go to them. Come on, move."

"Not until Colin is safe."

"Fine. You, blondie," he barks to Lily. "Grab your boy and skedaddle. And you two," he says to Killian and Franklin. "Don't get any ideas. She grabs the boy, you back away slowly while we take the big guy out of here. You got it?"

"Franky," I plead, and he gives me a rigid look.

"Fine," he complies as I hear Killian let out a growl.

"Lily, go." At my command, she quickly marches past me,

her blue eyes swimming in tears. She walks towards Bella, then crouches down to scoop Colin out of her hands with a vicious glare, cradling him tightly against her chest. When she's about three yards away, Killian shelters her with his body, and I hear her cry in despair.

"Get them out of here, Kill," I order.

I keep my chin in the air, while my heart feels painfully heavy, wanting just one more moment with the two people I love more than anything. But I refuse to risk their safety.

I refuse to risk their lives.

38

"Get them out of here, Kill," Conner exclaims.

Killian pushes me forward, obeying his brother, and we break out in a jog towards the safety of the car parked just outside of the cemetery. I hold Colin close to my body, scared someone might snatch him out of my sight again, feeling a sense of relief when the SUV comes into sight. Picking up the pace, we both make a run for it until we reach the door of the car and Killian yanks it open.

"Get in!" He shoves me inside with Colin still in my arms, then slams the door shut as he jumps into the passenger seat. "Drive!" he yells at the security guy behind the wheel.

"NO!" I shriek. "We can't leave them, Killian. We can't!"

"My brother is giving his life for the two of you. We need to get you to the mansion. Franklin will worry about Connor."

"And do what?!" I counter. "Cary thinks he won. He'll take Connor to a second location where he will torture him until he's done, and we get his body back in pieces! He can't leave the cemetery!"

Killian snaps his head towards me, glaring at me with a conflicted gaze in his eyes.

"What the hell do you want me to do, Lily?"

I reach out for the seatbelt, wrapping it around his body as best as possible before clicking it in. Then I hold Colin's head between my hands. Laying a kiss on his forehead, I swallow my tears away, giving him a final glance, praying I'm making the right decision. My eyes look into the rearview mirror, meeting the eyes of the security guy behind the wheel.

"Bring him to the mansion. If he gets hurt, I will hunt you down." I wait until he nods with a glint of surprise mixed with respect. "Do you have an extra gun?" He reaches into the glove compartment then hands me a gun with a straight face as Killian watches our conversation in silence. I check the bullets, counting ten, before my eyes find Killian's.

"Let's go."

A proud smile forms on Killian's face.

"Yes, ma'am." He turns to the guy next to him. "No stops. I want confirmation that my nephew is safe and sound at the mansion within fifteen minutes, or I'll come for you. You got it?"

He nods again, then we exit the car and start jogging back to the grave of Declan Murphy. We keep our bodies low, moving from tombstone to tombstone while Killian signals shit to the men who are still hidden throughout the cemetery.

"Okay, so what's the plan, Lara Croft?" Killian whispers once we are crouched behind a mausoleum about thirty yards away from where Franklin is still in conversation with Cary.

"Shoot the crap out of them?" I glance at Cary's men who have circled Franklin and the rest of their crew. Bella is still sitting at the edge of the grave, looking bored as fuck while Cary is holding Connor in a headlock with a gun against his temple.

"Come on, Cary. It's me you want. Not Connor," Franklin tries to negotiate.

"But it's more satisfying if we take your brother," Bella explains. "To watch you suffer when we take your family, one by one. Until finally, you'll be begging us to kill you because there is nothing left to live for."

Franklin frowns at Bella's words, but he apparently decides to ignore her, his focus returning back to Cary.

"You know you don't give a shit about Connor. It's me you want to torture until I'm screaming at the top of my lungs. I'm the one who killed your brother. I beat the shit out of him, right before I put him out of his misery and pumped a bullet through his head." Franklin's tone is menacing, sending chills down my spine.

"Seriously, Lily. What is the plan?" Killian hisses, keeping a close eye on his brothers.

"I'm a good shot."

"You're a good shot?" he whisper shouts, doubt coating his words.

"I'm a great shot, actually."

"Why is that not comforting?"

"I just need Cary to let go of Connor so I can get a clean shot," I explain.

"Come on, take me, Cary. Let him go," Franklin says, doing his best to convince Cary.

Cary looks like he's considering Franklin's words, and we all wait patiently for his answer.

"Fine!" he relents.

"NO!" Bella lets out a dissatisfied screech.

"Get closer," Cary barks at Franklin, motioning urgently with the gun in his hand. "Don't try anything." Franklin holds a hand in the air in surrender, slowly walking towards Cary and Connor.

"Please don't shoot one of my brothers, Lily," Killian whispers to me as I try to focus on my shot as he holds his own gun aimed at Bella to back me up.

"Shut up." I keep my eyes fastened on Cary, making sure I don't miss my shot.

His head moves from Franklin to Connor and back, as if he's realizing he won't stand a chance if Connor tries to fight him before he has Franklin in his hands.

"Stay there! On the count of three, you step closer," Cary snarls to Franklin before turning to Connor. "Once I have Franklin, you get the fuck out of here. If you don't, your brother will be laced with bullets. Got it?" Both men nod in compliance, and my heart clambers against my ribs as I anxiously try to control my breathing, waiting for the perfect moment. My eyes stay totally concentrated on Cary's forehead as I slowly move my finger to the trigger.

"One. Two. Three."

Cary roughly kicks Connor's legs from beneath his body, making him drop to his knees. Cary then takes a step away from him, quickly moving towards Franklin. He reaches out his arm, but Franklin is not close enough for him to reach without having to take one more step. For a split second, time seems to freeze, and I see the perfect opportunity. Cary stands in the middle of the two brothers, leaving enough space between them to make sure my bullet hits its target and only its target.

I breathe out, pulling the trigger with a steady hand.

Bang!

I watch, holding my breath as Cary's head falls back as the bullet pierces his neck. Blood splashes in the air before it starts to gush out, and chaos erupts around us.

"Shit!" Bella yelps when Cary falls to the floor in front of her, scrambling up to start running.

Not wasting another second, I aim the gun at one of Cary's guys.

Bang!

He falls to the floor, and his partner ducks down, frantically looking around, trying to decipher where the shots are coming from while Killian and I remain hidden behind the tombstone. When Killian jumps up, firing shots at the rest of Cary's men, Connor and Franklin both scramble behind the pine tree, guns cocked as gunfire echoes around the graveyard.

"Stay down!" Killian commands, his gun now aimed at the men hiding behind their SUV.

"Get the girl!" Franklin shouts to Killian from where he's squatting behind the tree. Killian's gaze follows Bella, running over the graveyard, and he stumbles forward before he breaks out in a run, chasing her.

Connor's head peeks out from behind the tree, and his eyes lock with mine. I can see the panic in his eyes.

"Stay there, Lily!" he shouts over the sound of gunfire ringing around my head.

I turn my head, keeping my back glued against the gravestone for protection while I make sure my head is low. Holding the gun in my now sweaty hands, I close my eyes for a flash, taking a deep breath to try to concentrate.

A bullet penetrates the tombstone next to me, the gray

stone shattering into pieces, and I let out a screech, covering my head. In front of me, more Wolfe men are jogging towards us, guns blazing. I let out a sigh of relief while adrenaline keeps me hyped as hell.

"Surrender!" Franklin booms like a raging caveman, his authoritarian voice audible over the mayhem. "Surrender and join the Wolfes, and we will spare your lives."

For a moment, everything goes quiet. I can hear the blood rushing through my head as I wait for what will happen next. The dozen or so Wolfe men around us hold still, their guns cocked and aimed at the SUV where what's left of Cary's men are taking cover. Not sure what the outcome will be, I keep a firm grip on the gun, then glance beside the tombstone.

The last four of Cary's men who are still standing, shuffle from behind the SUV, their hands up in the air, each with wary eyes.

"Drop your guns!" Connor barks.

The men slowly squat down, keeping their arms up until they put their guns on the ground.

"Kick it away." Connor holds his gun, aiming it at the four of them as he cautiously walks away from the tree, Franklin tracking behind him. The men do as they're told, waiting for their next order while Connor walks to Cary who's still bleeding out on the floor, grasping at his neck, squirming on the floor.

When Connor crouches down, Cary tries to grab Connor's arm for support, begging him to help him. Without hesitation, Connor places the barrel of his gun on Cary's head, then pulls the trigger. I flinch at the sight of it, a shriek leaving my lips when Cary's spasming body goes completely still.

Connor's eyes lock with mine, something in his eyes I can't quite decipher.

He stands up, walking towards me with a weird grin on his face. Without waiting any longer, I get up, running towards him, and launching myself into his arms. Wrapping my legs around his waist, I bury my nose in his neck, breathing him in. The familiar scent comforts me, and I finally give my emotions free rein.

"I thought I'd lost you. And then I had Colin, and I was so relieved. But then I realized I can't live without you. And then he had you, and then Franklin … he made that switch, and Killian and I, we were hiding, and I couldn't get a shot, and all I could think about was how you never told me you love me. But Reign says you do, and I want to believe him. And all I could think about was how we didn't have more time. We need more time!" I ramble like a crazy person, my lips twisted into a scowl. "You never told me you love me, asshole!" I slap his shoulder.

His green eyes become amused, a toothy smile on his handsome face.

"I love you."

Not processing his words, my word vomit continues.

"And I know you don't feel like you can love anyone, but actions speak louder than words, and let me tell you—wait, what?" I frown. "You love me?"

He smiles, cupping my cheek while his emerald eyes explore my face.

"I love you."

I still, my heart stampeding as I search his face.

Without another thought, I cover his mouth with mine in a bruising kiss before I press my forehead against his.

"Took you long enough, you tool."

"I'll make it up to you."

Sirens sound in the distance, and Franklin calls out to us.

"Save the PDA for when we get home. We have to go."

Connor lets go of me, grabbing my hand while the other still grips his gun.

"What do we do with them?" he asks his brother.

Franklin looks at the four men. His poised body looks scary as fuck with his intimidating stance and the vicious glare on his face. He brings his gun up, and I gasp.

Bang!

Bang!

Bang!

Three of the four men fall to the floor while the last man standing looks at Franklin in horror, his eyes practically bulging from their sockets.

"Please," he begs.

Franklin takes long strides towards him, putting the gun on his forehead before he reaches into the man's pocket to grab his wallet. He quickly pulls out his ID, reads his name, then throws it down to the ground.

"Spread the word, *Melvin Brown.* If anyone so much as glances at my nephew again, I will burn the city down. You touch a Wolfe, and we tear your head off. Get out of my sight."

Melvin doesn't wait another second before making a run for it.

Franklin doesn't spare him another look before sauntering towards us, his attention focusing on me.

"Are you okay, Lily?" His hand lands on my shoulder, and without a second thought, I slam myself against his body, circling my arms around his waist.

"I'm glad you're okay," I murmur against his chest. I then

look up at him gratefully before twisting my head to Connor. "That you both are."

I let go of Franklin, standing between the two men smiling at me while my eye catches Killian jogging back to us.

"I lost her," Killian pants, hands on his knees.

"Leave her. We'll find her," Franklin replies before his head spins to look at Connor. "Let's get out of here."

39

CONNOR

Not gonna lie...

I'm not happy about the fact that she came back for me, and I'm even more pissed about the fact that Killian let her. That he listened to her. Shit could've gone really, really bad.

But did it? Thank fuck no. So I'm just going to let it slide and give her a little disobedience lesson the moment I get her naked. Tint that luscious ass red with the palm of my hand.

She's snuggling against my chest, my arm wrapped around her shoulder while we watch the city pass by from the back of the SUV with Killian behind the wheel and Franklin in the passenger seat next to him.

"Can we just acknowledge the fact that your girl is a fucking amazing shot?" Killian glances at me through the rearview mirror, pride clear in his voice. My mouth tenses in a scowl, and I narrow my eyes at him.

"Before you go all savage on me," Killian begins, rolling

his eyes, "she saved your life. Without her, you'd either be dead, or Franky would be."

I remain quiet, hearing Franklin snicker.

"So don't give me that bullshit of 'it was too dangerous' or 'you should've taken her home." Lily chuckles at his mocking tone, and I give her a reprimanding squeeze in her side.

"What? He's kinda right."

"He is *kinda* right, Connor," Franklin agrees, smiling at me over his shoulder.

"Fine. But pull that shit ever again, and I swear to fucking God, I will rip your head off before I sew it back on with fishing twine to make sure you can still attend Christmas dinner."

"Yeah, yeah, whatever."

I can feel Lily peering up at me, and when I look down at her, I read astonishment on her face.

"What?" I dip my chin.

"Fishing twine? Attend Christmas dinner? Your mind really is fucked up."

Leaning in, I bite her lip before gifting her with a crushing kiss.

"Don't pretend you don't fucking love my fucked up mind." I move my lips to her ears to make sure my brothers don't hear what is on the tip of my tongue. "I see the look on your face when I torture you with my fingers and the desire in your eyes when I spank you like a little schoolgirl."

When I feel her body shudder, a satisfied grin splits my face, and I shoot her a wink. She lets out an oppressed moan, her eyebrows quirking up as we drive through the gates of the mansion.

The car has hardly come to a stop in front of the steps

before she crawls over me to exit the car. Running up the steps, she disappears into the house. I move to trail behind her until I hear Franklin call out my name.

My eyes raised in question, I twist my body so I'm met by my brother's fatigued eyes.

"She the real deal?" He nudges his head towards the house.

I follow his gaze, then turn my head back to him as I consider his words for a moment.

Killian rounds the hood of the car, giving Franklin a friendly pat on the back.

"Have you seen how much he smiles nowadays? He's almost a copy of Reign. Of course, she's the real deal."

Growing up with my dad beating up my mom on a daily basis didn't really give me a good impression of love or marriage. I guess I didn't even believe in love, other than the unconditional love I felt for my brothers. It's the reason I never wanted to have kids. My own childhood was miserable enough; why the fuck would I put anyone else through that?

But I guess that changed thanks to that one night with Lily.

Even though Colin may have been a surprise or a mistake, whatever you want to call it, he's the best thing that ever happened to me. And, to be honest, I'm not sure he really was a surprise. Because even though that first night with Lily was a one-time thing, the connection I felt with her was one I'd never felt with anyone else. It was a night I recalled many times in my head before I burst through the front door of her apartment like a bulldozer.

Literally.

The last couple of weeks, I thought she occupied my mind because of Colin, because of the living connection that bonded us. She is my baby mama, after all. But when Cary placed that gun to my head, and I saw Killian and Lily run away with Colin safe in her hands, I knew that was just a fraction of what I felt for her.

She isn't just my baby mama.

She's my girl.

She's mine.

"Yeah, she's the real deal."

"Then I'm happy for you." Franklin walks past me, slapping me on the back. "Come on, tool. Let's see how your boy is doing."

40

My feet can't move fast enough as I hurry through the house.

"Reign?! Kendall?!" I barge through the kitchen door, gratitude pouring over me.

Reign is sitting on one of the stools, Kendall right beside him. Colin is in his arms, looking sleepy but clearly awake, as Reign cradles him against his chest. A warm feeling surrounds me, watching how comfortable my boy is, enjoying the touch of his favorite uncle.

"Look, there is Mommy, buddy."

I let out an excited shriek, closing the distance between us. My arms reach out to grab Colin from his arms and hold him in a tight hug while tears stream down my face.

"Thank you," I mouth to Reign, before offering Kendall a grateful smile.

"Hey, baby! I missed you. Are you okay? Do you remember anything?" My fingers trace his cheek, looking for bruises or cuts on his face. Any physical ramifications from this awful day.

"Sleepy, Mommy."

"Are you sleepy? I can imagine, sweetie. Are you hungry? Do you want something to eat?"

He shakes his head, settling his head against my shoulder.

"Not gonna lie … when Colin came home without you, you had me freaking out there for a minute, Lily," Reign scolds, dropping a kiss onto my hair while he gives me a side hug.

"I'm sorry."

"What happened?" I look at Kendall, noticing the stress that's stuck on her face.

"What happened is Lily over here is a fucking sniper," Killian announces as he enters the kitchen. A glint of pride is in his eyes, and I can't say I don't appreciate it.

"What?!" Reign shrills.

"Oh, yeah. She shot Cary straight in the neck. Where the fuck did you learn to shoot like that, anyway?"

"Louisa's Shots," I shrug. "I was nineteen, living in Roxbury with my little brother. I wanted to make sure I could protect us both."

"Oh, that's where Franky taught me how to shoot!" Kendall says enthusiastically.

Footsteps sound behind me, followed by Franklin's deep voice.

"You learned to shoot in *my* shooting range?"

"Wait, that shooting range is yours?" Kendall frowns.

He cocks an eyebrow, ruffling Colin's hair.

"Yeah, of course. Hey, little buddy. Good to see you."

"Unbelievable," Kendall mutters as Franklin moves to stand beside her, giving her a peck on her cheek.

"Told you, I own the city."

Laughing, I turn to Connor who's staring at us as if he's seeing water burn.

"You okay?" I cautiously eye him, not sure what he's thinking. To my relief, the corner of his mouth curls up as he steps closer, bringing both Colin and me into a tight hug.

He kisses Colin's hair before he cups my cheek.

"Never been better, baby."

EPILOGUE

Power.

It's what most men want.

It's what most men live for.

It's what most men crave.

They thrive on controlling other people, bending them to their ways like puppets.

But really, they are dense creatures, unable to look at the bigger picture. They think power is something that is gained by war and brute force. But it's the women who invented the natural way to divide and conquer. You catch more flies with honey than vinegar and all that shit. Men always resort to violence, feeding off the testosterone in their bodies.

The Wolfes may appear to be fair men to the rest of the city, but I know better.

They take what they want, when they want, regardless of the consequences or collateral damage. Franklin took the last thing I had in this life, leaving me like I was dirt to sweep under the rug. I will never forget his face, filled with disdain as he ripped my heart out, barely sparing me a second glance. It was at that moment that I decided I would get it back. I will get my heart back, eliminating every Wolfe one by one until I get what I want. Until I am finally whole again.

When I finally returned to Boston, it wasn't hard to find allies to help me slowly mess with the Wolfes' business, making little dents in their egos. That was just for fun, trying to piss them off before we moved on to the big guns. But Cary and Emerson failed to see what had to happen was done for the greater good.

I gave Emerson everything he needed on a silver platter.

I told Cary we needed to destroy the Wolfes, one by one, making them suffer more with each loss. But instead of sticking to the plan, they felt the need to feed their own ego. Going for the small victory that was standing right in front of them rather than looking at the way to create maximum destruction. What is that other saying? Don't let a man do a woman's job?

It's time to get off the bench.

It's time to get to work.

Game on, Wolfe.

THE END.

BONUS SCENE

Lily

The tiny hairs on the nape of my neck rise, and a smile forms on my face. I can feel his presence standing behind me while I give Colin one last kiss before I tuck him in.

"Goodnight, sweet boy."

We gave him his own room. It's the one next to us that used to be Killian's, but he agreed to take a room on the other side of the mansion, understanding I want Colin close. Colin decided he wanted a car bed, so naturally, Reign and Connor made him a room that looks like a racing car track, including a pit garage and everything. He was ecstatic.

In fact, he didn't want to leave his room when he woke up the next day.

Turning around, I look at Connor's smug grin as he leans against the doorpost with his arms folded in front of him.

"What?" I whisper, sensing that he's up to something.

Reign keeps joking I 'tamed' the beast.

I'm not sure about that, but I have to admit that he hasn't

been as broody as he used to be. He smiles more, laughs more, and even cracks a joke now and then. At least he does with me.

Connor reaches out his hand.

"Come."

"Can I please get a shower first before you jump me like a horny teenager?"

He tilts his head, looking amused, as he tugs me behind him.

"Horny teenager? Really? I just want to show you something."

He guides me down the stairs, my hand in his firm grip, then he leads me into the office.

"Connor, we can't have sex here. Franklin *works* in here."

"I like the way you think, baby. But I wasn't planning on fucking you here. Although, you're giving me ideas." He spins on the spot, his green eyes now filled with a lustful hunger. He charges me, pushing me against the door, and I let out a playful shriek.

"Connor," I reprimand when his lips connect with my neck. My body instantly responds, and I lean my head against the door, giving him better access while a moan escapes me.

"You started it, babe," he says, as he leaves a trail of kisses against my neck, then locks the door. "But that's not the reason why I brought you here."

He takes a step back, and I pout at the lack of contact. He turns, walks over to the desk, and takes a seat.

He's looking smoking hot, sitting behind that desk like a fucking boss, and I can't help licking my lips at the sight.

"Stop ogling me," he chuckles, reaching into one of the drawers. "Come here."

He signals his hand to me, and I follow his request while shrugging my shoulders.

"Can't help it, you look hot behind that desk," I purr.

"Is that so?" He twists the chair so that his legs are facing me before he pulls me onto his lap and his mouth connects with the skin on my neck once more. I grunt at the extremely soft kisses he plants on the crook of my neck, feeling desire growing between my legs as his hands hold my ass tight against his body. "Connor."

"Yeah, babe?" he mumbles before I feel his tongue joining the party.

"You're teasing me."

"I'd never."

"I thought you wanted to show me something," I pant, running a hand through his blond hair. My eyes close, and I give over to the sensation like the obsessed little slut that I am.

I can feel his fingers move in a scorching pace towards the inside of my thighs, and he growls against my neck.

"I know. I got distracted."

He pushes me off his lap, and I gasp as he yanks my jogging shorts down with one pull.

"Take these off," he orders, nudging his chin to the shorts now pooling around my feet.

Like a little schoolgirl, I let out a giggle, doing as he says while he pushes his pants down, kicking them off with a few swift moves. He plants his ass back into the chair, taking off his shirt, and I mimic his move by taking off mine followed by my bra.

"Take off your panties." He narrows his eyes like he's ready to tear me apart, and I lick my lips eagerly. My hands slowly trace the hem of the lace fabric before I push them down as slowly as possible, twisting my body a little so I can show him the swells of my behind. He bites his lip in desire while I stare at him through hooded eyes.

When my panties finally fall to the floor, he crooks his finger, telling me to get closer while I eagerly look at his hard cock, bopping against his stomach in excitement.

He pulls me closer, and I stand between his legs while I patiently wait for his next instruction.

"Do you want me, *little devil?*" I'm momentarily paralyzed by his intense gaze as he pushes his finger through my folds.

My mouth falls open, and I nod.

"Do you want this?" His now slick fingers dip inside of me, my eyes involuntarily shutting before he coats my center with my essence.

"Yes," I huff out, holding still, enjoying how he plays with me.

"Or do you want me to fuck you into oblivion?" My eyes grow wide at his words, and I blink. A devilish smile greets me. "No, you don't want it sweet, do you?"

Without waiting for my response, he directs me onto his lap to straddle him, placing his cock against my center.

"Take it, baby."

I suck in a deep breath, then attach my lips to his lips as I rapidly lower my hips.

"AAH!" I cry out, throwing my head back when he stretches me wide, the tip of his dick slamming into my cervix. My attention snaps back to his, my mouth forming a silent O while my eyes expand at the indescribable sensations he evokes in me. I grab his neck with both hands, holding on as I start to glide my hips over his cock, relishing in the friction of our rapid pace.

He takes my breast in his mouth, softly biting my nipple as I keep going, letting out a torturous moan every time he slides back inside me. It doesn't take long before I feel her walls start to clench, the intensity even greater when my clit drags against his stomach every time I raise my hips.

"Ride me," he whispers against my neck, making me pick up the pace. I close my eyes, moving my hips quicker and quicker, ignoring the pain that forms in my quads, riding his dick as if my life depends on it while my breasts are pressed against his chest.

I can feel my orgasm creeping to the surface, ready to swallow me whole, and I let out a frustrated groan, exhaustedly trying to keep going. Letting out a wail of desperation, Connor connects his thumb with my clit, and I immediately falter as my climax bursts through me like he detonated a bomb by flipping a switch.

"That's it, baby," he pants.

Riding my explosion, fatigue instantly hits me, and my motions slow as my frenzy ebbs, and the pain in my hips becomes more acute.

My forehead falls against Connor's shoulder, panting as I try to recover from my orgasm. With his dick still inside of me, Connor gets up and sets me on the desk.

"Stay still," he barks.

Holding me down with his hand on my stomach, I lay on the cold wood, limp as a wet towel, completely happy to let him have his way with me. He frantically starts to thrust inside of me, slamming his cock into my cunt over and over again. Closing my eyes, I bite my lip, moaning uncontrollably from the typhoon of sensations he's creating in me. When the feeling almost becomes too much, he speeds up his pace as I hold on to the desk.

Pumping inside of me like a madman, his face goes rigid, sweat dripping off his forehead as he plows his way towards his release. A deep grunt comes from the back of his throat when he finally shoots his load inside of me before he drops his body against mine.

"Fucking hell," he mutters.

I can feel his heart race against my chest, and my hand wraps around him, soothingly stroking his back.

"Was that what you wanted to show me?" I joke.

He chuckles, then straightens his back before pulling out of me.

"Actually, there was something else I wanted to show you."

"How good are you with your tongue?" I smile hopefully. I keep my bare ass on the desk, my legs spread, enjoying laying here for him to take me like the little exhibitionist that I am.

"You already know that." I hear him open the drawer again, pulling out a black box with a pink bow around it, tossing it next to my head on the desk. My head twists to look at it.

"What is…? Holy hell!" I screech when I feel his tongue swirl through my folds. I bring my head up, staring into his mesmerizing green eyes. He continues, sucking my inner folds in his mouth, then he darts his tongue inside of me, coating it with his cum.

Fuck me, that's so sexy.

His gaze holds mine as he shows me his sperm laying on his tongue, before he gets up with a sexy grin.

"Open it," he says, nodding towards the box.

"What? Are you kidding me?" I give him an incredulous look. "Keep going!"

"Open the box first."

Annoyed, I growl, then sit up, grabbing the box beside me.

"You're an asshole," I murmur.

Pulling off the ribbon, I place the box on my nude lap before I slowly pull the lid off, giving him another glare.

The box is filled with pink filling, and on top lays something wrapped in a silk sheet. Pushing the silk to the side, I look at what's hidden underneath.

A worn out book appears, and my hand covers my mouth in shock when I read the title.

Peter and Wendy.

My eyes move up. "You didn't. Is this...?"

He nods, and I carefully open the book, looking for the title page.

"You bought me a first edition?" I whisper, feeling tears pool in my eyes.

"Happy birthday, baby."

"Oh, Connor!" I cry. "This is the most thoughtful gift I've ever received. Do you know how special this is?"

He smiles, his hand cupping my neck.

"Honestly, I don't. But it's special to you, and that's good enough for me."

Feeling the book with my fingers, I push out a breath, memories flooding my mind.

"Damien would've loved this. He was smart. He and I shared our love for books."

Connor's hand moves up, stroking my cheek with his fingers.

"I'm sorry, baby."

"Don't be. I love it."

He presses his forehead against mine.

"I love you."

He pulls the box out of my hands, placing it next to me while holding my neck.

"Now lay down again. I'm still hungry."

I chuckle, shaking my head in amusement as I do as he says.

Maybe Reign is right.

Maybe I tamed the beast.

ACKNOWLEDGMENTS

I'm going to try and keep this short and snappy, although I do have a bad track record with that, so you can just roll your eyes when it's taking too long.

First, thank YOU for reading. I hope you enjoyed Connor as much as I did, even though Reign will always be my favorite Wolfe. Connor is a close second.

Secondly, I want to thank Katie Salt. I wrote this book in the middle of Summer while trying to entertain my four-year-old. We went on trips almost every day and I definitely had my freak out moments, but her comforting words, and by comforting I mean 'Shut up, Billie, you know you're going to finish this book before deadline.', pulled me through and I did exactly that. Finished it before the deadline. Hooray! I wouldn't want to crawl through the mud with anyone else.

My beta's, Jordan, Rion, Lea, Sheryn, Rachel, and Mallory, thank you for your time and effort! I always appreciate your feedback and you help me tell the stories I want to!

Kim, thank you again for a great book. You help me polish my writing in any way you can, and I'm happy to put your name on my books.

Lastly, I'm going to give myself a pat on the back, because I wrote this during Summer madness, giving my kid the best summer I could and still sticking to my deadline. Billie, I'm proud of you. Now go sell some books!

Until next time,
 Billie

ABOUT THE AUTHOR

Billie Lustig is a dutch girl who has always had a thing with words: either she couldn't shut up or she was writing an adventure stuck in her head. She's pretty straight forward, can be a pain in the ass & is allergic to bullshit, but most of all, she's a sucker for love.

She is happily married to her own alpha male that
taught her the truest thing about love:
when it's real, you can't walk away.

Check out www.billielustig.com for more info

ALSO BY BILLIE LUSTIG

The Fire Duet:

Chasing Fire

Catching Fire

The Boston Wolfes:

Franklin

Connor

Reign

Killian

Billie Lustig writes mafia romance books filled with suspense, alpha male bad boys, and comes with a trigger warning. But if you also enjoy sexy contemporary romance with a heavy dose of angst and the same level of sass, B. Lustig is your girl.

Check out B.'s books:

8 - It's Only Eight Letters

9 - Nights To Not Fall In Love

Made in the USA
Middletown, DE
24 July 2022

69943251R00191